AFROMYTH

A FANTASY COLLECTION VOL. 1

Afrocentric Books | Mugwump Press
St. Paul, Minnesota

Printed in the United States of America

First printing, December 2017

ISBN 978-1-946595-05-8

Afrocentric Books | Mugwump Press
2515 White Bear Ave A8 Box 227
Maplewood, MN 55109

www.afrocentricbooks.com
www.mugwumppress.com

CONTENTS

Introduction   1

Under the Kolboba Tree   3

Fishing Lake Tanganyika   18

A Drop of Comfort, a Slice of Heart's Desire   43

Sins of the Sister   69

Yemayah   94

Descent   99

The Black Birds of White Oaks   132

Starfall   163

Intangible Evidence   192

The Cradle and the Scribe   215

Death in Nairobi   221

The Eyes of the Goddess Herself   244

Introduction

I COULD BORE you with a long introduction, but Lord knows creative nonfiction is not really my forte. So, I'll just tell you why we've done this anthology. There is a dearth of color in today's (and yesterday's) science fiction and fantasy. In recent years, we've seen more people of color starring in successful movies and television shows, but the literary industry, specifically in the genre of speculative fiction, has been slow to follow. This lack of representation in speculative fiction has been, for me—a person of color—frustrating at best. Afrocentric science fiction and fantasy books have been done, I know. But there are not many, and even fewer anthologies.

Afrocentric Books Presents: AfroMyth is a collection of fantasy stories featuring characters of the African diaspora. It is a platform to showcase promising new and emerging voices. When I selected the stories for this anthology, I did not focus on the author's race, merely the content of the tale. As such, not all of these stories were written by authors of the African diaspora or even authors of color. In compiling the anthology— written by authors of various races—I not only hoped to dispel the all-too-common belief that white authors cannot write characters of color (yes, some of the authors are of European descent), but more importantly, I hoped that this anthology could be part of a movement showing the world that the African diaspora is an integral part of society at every level. I hope, as you journey through the pages of this book, you will see us, hear us, and get to know us.

J.S. Emuakpor
African Diaspora, 2017

DARREL DUCKWORTH

Under the Kolboba Tree

GRANDPA JOBA WAS the oldest man I'd ever known. He was already old when I was a little girl. He was even older when I arrived with my husband and my own little girl to be with him when he died.

He wasn't really *my* grandfather, but everybody in the family called him Grandpa Joba, even my real grandparents. The truth was, no one knew if he was even biologically linked to our family. His skin, although paled some by extreme age, was still darker than anyone in the family. And his features definitely carried more proto-African traits than any of us.

Sorry, that's the geneticist in me talking.

But, biologically linked or not, he felt like Grandpa Joba to me. And to everyone else.

Which was why every member of our far-scattered family traveled from wherever in the world they were to come here when they heard he was dying.

I was the last to arrive, being one of the farthest away.

I crept into the hospital room, eager to see Grandpa Joba again but also afraid of what I might see. Watching Grandma

Connelly, my mom's mother, die of cancer had been painful. I wasn't sure I could watch Grandpa Joba go. But I also couldn't bear the idea of not seeing him one last time.

So here I was.

I held my own little girl tight in my arms, clinging to her like a security blanket. My husband walked in behind me, one hand gently touching my back in support.

Neither one of them had ever met Grandpa Joba, and suddenly, I was aware of how many years it had been since I'd seen him last. Now, I regretted those lost years.

Representatives from four generations of our family had gathered around his bed, pushing the limits for "maximum number of visitors allowed." Mark noticed our entrance and looked up, relieved to see I had arrived. Everyone turned, smiling that we had made it in time, but smiling sadly all the same. The people nearest to us parted like a curtain, and I saw Grandpa Joba lying there, propped up in his hospital bed, wearing one of those silly gowns that was far too small for his massive frame.

He didn't look like a dying man. He looked like Grandpa Joba.

His broad face was smiling, like it always did. His big, bald head was shining in the light from over his bed. His giant shoulders, his tree trunk chest, his gorilla arms . . . they all looked the same. And when he turned and looked at me, his eyes were bright and dancing like they always were.

I expected him to swing his legs out of that bed and sweep me up into his massive arms like he always did.

The fact that he didn't get up was the only sign that the sweet, magical energy we call life was finally leaving his body.

"Judy," he said, his voice as quiet, deep, and calm as it had always been.

And it was like I was five years old again. I wanted to crawl into his lap and cuddle my head against his massive chest like I had as a little girl. Just sit there and listen to his heart beating. So much for the maturity of a thirty-one-year-old geneticist who was supposed to be a rising star in her field.

He raised one massive arm and hand out to me.

Maturity be damned. I stepped beside the bed and laid my head and my daughter down on that tree trunk he called a chest. And there was that sweet thumping sound I had heard so many times, so many years before. I felt his hand rubbing my back, telling me it was going to be all right.

I almost asked him to take me to see the Kolboba tree one last time.

Over the years, Grandpa Joba had taken every child in the family on a trip to the Kolboba tree. Even my grandparents talked about it. It was Grandpa Joba's best magic trick.

Family rumor was that Grandpa Joba had been a traveling magician or illusionist long ago, before he settled down and opened a natural healing store decades ago. But he never told anyone how he did his tricks.

He had taken me to the Kolboba tree so many times when I was a little girl; each and every time I had asked him. Each time, he had smiled happily, scooped me up, and we had made the trip. Again and again, until some time in my twelfth year when I became a too-serious girl who decided that she was "too old for that stuff," not even allowing herself to be curious anymore about how he did "that trick."

Now, I was sad for that little girl, so hungry to be grown-up that she had sacrificed the magic of her childhood.

Grandpa Joba used to say that the journey was necessary for every child in our family. That our family was destined to produce thinkers and artists and other people who shaped the world. So, it was necessary for us to see "the Center of the World," as he used to say, to know where our work fit into the world.

And he always said "the Center of the World" that way . . . with that dramatic tone. You could hear the capital letters on the words.

I guess this was his brand of gentle brainwashing. And it seemed to work because a lot of our family turned out to be writers, artists, entrepreneurs, scientists, special effects people . . . all sorts of creative types.

So, despite the fact that I could spot the mind-conditioning straight out of Psych 101, how could I be angry at a lovable old man with a magic trick who made me believe I could change the world?

Which was the other reason I was so eager to have my little girl here.

I wanted her to meet Grandpa Joba. I wanted her to feel his love, even if only for this short time. To remember him, if she could. She was only just halfway from two to three, a little younger than he usually took children on their first trip. But I wanted her to know him.

So, when I stood back up, I left my little girl lying on his tummy. He took his arm from my back and gently laid his massive hand on her tiny shoulder.

"You must be Amanda," he said, smiling at her.

She nodded and looked at him, unafraid of this man who was a stranger to her. She didn't even look to me for reassurance, the way she normally did when meeting new people.

"I'm Grandpa Joba," he said.

Amanda crawled forward and cuddled against his huge chest. That was all the introduction any child needed to love Grandpa Joba.

He chuckled and cuddled her. He looked up at my husband, standing beside me.

"You must be Brad," he said, extending one hand.

Brad, ever serious and silent, simply took that giant hand, shook it, and nodded.

They let go of each other, and Grandpa Joba went back to cuddling Amanda. He looked up at everybody.

"Could Amanda and I have a few minutes to talk?"

Everyone smiled, nodded, and began filing out, touching my arm as they went. I realized Grandpa Joba had probably been having the same "talk" with other family children. I grew excited for my little girl.

Brad watched them go, his eyes wary.

I tapped his arm and indicated that we should also leave. His eyes darted to Amanda, and it was clear that he wasn't prepared to leave our daughter alone with this stranger, no matter who he was to the family.

"It's all right, Judy," Grandpa Joba said quietly. "You should stay. Might be good for Brad to see this as well."

Suddenly, I was very excited. Grandpa Joba had always been alone with a child when he took him or her to see the Kolboba tree. Now, Brad and I would get to watch him perform his magic trick.

Inside me, the excitement of seeing how he did it competed with the excitement for my little girl, about to go on her first trip.

I remembered how magical my first trip had been.

❉

Twenty-eight years before, Grandpa Joba had sat me on his lap and shown me the old, worn drawing of the Kolboba tree. It was a simple line drawing in some sort of black ink on an animal skin, soft and tan. The picture showed a massive tree with a huge trunk and thousands of branches spreading out above it, forming a giant umbrella. At the base of the trunk was a pair of tiny stick people.

At first, when I had looked at it with my little-girl eyes, the drawing had looked simple, just lines. Then I started seeing things in the branches. Animals. More and more animals. Until I saw all the animals of the world. Then somehow, the branches had leaves. The stick tree had blossomed with leaves and life.

As I had sat in his lap seeing . . . everything . . . with all the wonder of childhood magic, Grandpa Joba had gently stroked my head and told me to close my eyes. I did and felt myself floating somewhere warm and nice until he told me to open them again.

And I found myself standing beside him, underneath the Kolboba tree.

Except it wasn't a drawing anymore. It was a real tree. The biggest tree I had ever seen. We were so tiny next to that massive trunk.

The bark was dark and rich and rough. And filled with squiggly shapes and lines. Some of them were like the maps Mommy had shown me in books. Shapes of places, of the world. But like it was long ago. There were other swirling, intertwining patterns that wouldn't make sense to me until years later in my university classes. And other shapes with lines crossing lines in ways my eyes couldn't understand.

Dizzy from the lines, I blinked and looked up.

Up there, above us, I saw the animals again but real this time. All the animals in the world. Relaxing or playing on the giant branches. Lions and monkeys and birds. Elephants and horses and dogs. Lizards and swarms of insects buzzing. And things that looked like they belonged in water, but they were swimming among the leaves.

On other branches, I saw animals from fairy tales and things I didn't recognize at all. Farther away, deeper in the branches, there were more that I could feel but couldn't see.

It all felt wonderful, not at all strange to my child's eyes. As though it were perfectly normal for horses to rest on tree branches a few feet from unicorns and for fish to swim among leaves way up in the air.

We stood in the cool shade of the tree's huge, leafy umbrella. Far beyond that soft shadow, harsh light beat down on a landscape that I would later come to think of as the Serengeti, the way they showed it on those nature shows. Other things moved out there in the blinding light, but I couldn't see what they were.

And still other things crept around in the deeper shadows surrounding the roots under the tree, just out of sight. But I wasn't afraid of them the way I was afraid of the things in the dark in my bedroom.

Here, by the Kolboba tree, we all belonged.

And it all seemed as real to me as the things in my own house.

I heard the breeze in the leaves and animal noises above us. I smelled the tree beside me and the earth under my feet. I felt the rough bark and the roots as we sat down with our backs against the tree. I felt the cool of the shade and the heat of the sun beyond it.

All my child's senses told me that it was real as I sat there with Grandpa Joba, cuddling close to him, feeling his massive arm around my tiny body, listening to him tell the stories of the Earth.

And it felt just as real every visit after that. I nagged him to take me again and again, to tell me the stories over and over. And he always did. Happily.

Until I foolishly decided that I was too old for magic tricks.

We never realize what we sacrifice to pride until it's too late.

*

Today, in the hospital, he showed me another magic trick: to my amazement, he pulled out a rolled-up animal skin from under the hospital blankets.

"I thought it was destroyed in the house fire years ago," I said, stunned.

He chuckled. "A little, old fire can't destroy this."

He unrolled it and showed it to Amanda.

Amanda pointed excitedly to the simple drawing of the Kolboba tree.

"Horsy!"

"Ahh," Grandpa Joba said. "You see them already."

Amanda nodded and pointed at more spots, naming animals. Every second, she apparently saw more and more things among the stick lines of the crude drawing.

He chuckled. "You got good eyes, Amanda. You see a lot. This here is the Kolboba tree. It's a special tree at the Center of the World. Would you like to go see it?"

Amanda nodded eagerly and pointed at something else she had just spotted.

Brad craned his neck, trying to see what she was pointing at. Like me, all he was seeing was the crude, stick drawing.

Grandpa Joba stroked her hair. "Well, then. Why don't you and I go see it? Just close your eyes for a few seconds. That's a girl."

He looked up at Brad and me.

"We'll be back soon," he said, smiling.

And they disappeared.

My heart stopped.

The beige blanket settled slowly down onto the mattress, dropping through the empty space where his body had been.

Cold fear stabbed into my stomach.

Amanda!

My baby! He took my baby!

It was the worst fear I had ever felt.

Brad dove forward, slapping the mattress and pillow where Grandpa Joba and Amanda had been lying. He spun around and stared at me. In his eyes, I saw the same panic I was feeling.

A little-girl voice spoke inside my head. *It's Grandpa Joba. He won't hurt her. He's just taken her to the Kolboba tree.*

It's a goddammed magic trick! the grown-up inside me shouted back, panicking. *There is no tree! It's just a goddammed trick!*

She'll be back, the little-girl voice said. *He always brought you back.*

Brad started to shout for a nurse, but I grabbed him. My hand was shaking.

"He'll be back," I told him, staring at the empty bed.

Maybe, I was saying it to myself.

"He'll be back. He always comes back."

Brad stared at me like I'd lost my mind. He spun half round and pointed at the bed.

"Back? Where the hell did he—"

And Grandpa Joba was suddenly there, lying on top of the blanket that had fluttered down in his absence. Amanda was curled on his chest, smiling.

I dove forward and snatched her up, hugging her close while doing that mother thing of checking her all over to make sure she wasn't hurt, making sure she was really there. I clung to her, keeping her from disappearing again.

"Mommy!" she cried out happily. "I saw big tree. And horsies. And monkeys. And—"

Her voice was muffled as Brad and I crushed her between us, Brad glaring down at Grandpa Joba.

Grandpa Joba lay there in the ridiculous hospital gown that barely covered his modesty. He smiled at me.

"What were you worried about, Judy?" he asked. "You knew where we go."

I stared at him stunned. "I didn't think it was . . ."

"Real?" he finished for me.

I nodded.

"You used to know it was real. Afore you got grown up inside."

He smiled and rolled up the animal skin drawing. He extended his arm and handed the animal skin to Amanda who clutched it in her tiny hand.

"Now you can go there any time you want, Amanda. Maybe you can take Mommy there sometime."

He breathed heavily, like he'd finally finished some long task.

"Now, I got to rest a bits. Would you excuse me for a while?"

Shaken, we nodded. I leaned down, still holding Amanda tight in my arms, and hugged him again. He hugged us both, and we left him to his rest.

As we exited his room, we saw a nurse approaching with a tray of meds. She entered the room across the hall from Grandpa Joba.

"Judy?" Brad said, his eyes still wide. "What the hell was that? How did he . . . just disappear?"

I wanted to say that Grandpa Joba used to be a magician. That it was just an illusion trick . . . of some kind. But I couldn't make my mouth say the words. I just stood there, shaking my head slowly. Amanda tried to unroll the animal skin in her tiny hands.

"I saw big tree, Mommy," she said, managing to open the picture and pointing to it. "I saw big tree."

I gently took the picture away from her. It was irrational, but I was afraid she'd disappear into it.

The nurse walked across the hall with her tray of meds, into Grandpa Joba's room.

Brad continued to stare at me, waiting for an answer I didn't have.

From inside Grandpa Joba's room, the nurse shrieked.

We started to rush back in, but she was already running out. She ran headlong into Brad who grabbed her.

"He disappeared!" she shouted. "I was handing him his meds . . . and he smiled . . . and . . . and he just disappeared!"

And that was it. Despite a doctor trying to calm her down and despite all attempts at logic, she stuck to the same story. Grandpa Joba had just faded away right in front of her eyes.

In the room, lying on the bed, were his gown and the plastic hospital bracelet. The plastic bracelet that couldn't have slipped over his massive hand was uncut.

✻

The funeral and the family gathering after it were a peculiar mixture of sad and hopeful. Somehow, it didn't feel like Grandpa Joba was really gone. Not like if we had seen him breathe his last and close his eyes forever. But he also wasn't there with us, smiling at us, like he'd always been. For as long as anyone could remember, he'd been with us, smiling.

And, wherever he was now, he wasn't *here* anymore.

Four generations of family tried to help each other say goodbye to an old man none of us had completely known but all of us loved.

I flew home with Brad and Amanda but without answers or "closure."

We got home late, and I took Amanda straight to her room while Brad struggled with the suitcases.

"Mommy?" Amanda asked sleepily as I tugged her out of her clothes.

"Yes, honey?"

"Can we go Gran'pa Joa 'gain?"

I felt the sadness again. How do you explain death and "gone forever" to a two-and-a-half-year-old?

Then again, how do you explain "disappeared into thin air in the middle of a crowded modern hospital?"

"Grandpa Joba had to go away, sweetie," I said.

She looked at me, sleepy and confused . . . and upset, like I was telling her she wasn't allowed to see him.

"Grandpa Joba had to go away to a place where we can't visit him," I said, pulling her nightgown over her head. "We're all going to miss him, honey. But you can dream about him if you want."

I swung her legs under her covers and laid her head down.

"But Mommy," she said. "We can go Gran'pa Joa."

And she held up the animal skin drawing in her tiny hand.

How had she gotten ahold of that again? I had it stowed in my carry-on.

Gently, I took it from her. She got that "don't take it away" pleading look in her eyes so, I laid it on the table next to her bed.

"Yes, honey, of course we can." I tucked her in. "But, for tonight, why don't we just dream nice dreams about Grandpa Joba? We can go see him tomorrow. Okay?"

Reluctantly, sleepily, she nodded.

I tucked Mr. Wuggles under her arm and kissed her good-night. Exhausted as she was, she was breathing softly, already asleep before I stood up straight. I picked up the animal skin drawing from the table and took it with me. The rational scientist in me told me I was being foolish. The mother in me wasn't taking any chances.

I stopped near the door to turn on her night-light before turning off her bedroom light. And curiosity got to me. Standing in the half-light, I unrolled the animal skin and looked at the stick drawing.

Seeing it again made me smile, remembering the first time I had seen it. I could almost see the animals in the stick drawing of the tree again. A panther lounging here. Some horses there. And the hot, dry Serengeti wind blowing in from the blazing sunlight beyond the shade of the tree. I could feel it. Smell it. See it. As if I'd just been there today, not twenty years ago.

A gentle hand touched my shoulder. I turned, expecting to see Brad.

And there was Grandpa Joba.

Only he wasn't standing with me in Amanda's room. We were standing under the Kolboba tree. I turned slowly, feeling the heat and cool, smelling the rich earth beneath us, seeing the blinding light and dark shadows, hearing the breeze in the leaves and the animals above us. I stood there, too stunned to remember that I didn't believe in this anymore.

"'Bout time, girl," Grandpa Joba said.

I turned back to face him, and he was smiling.

"I knew you'd come 'ventually. I knew you'd be the one, from way back when you were a little girl, always asking to come here and hear more stories."

I reached out and touched his chest. He was warm and solid.

He laughed.

"Yeh. It's me. I always been here."

He waved a hand at the tree.

"Always."

He stroked my hair with his massive hand.

"And you can come here anytime you want. Like your little girl said. Her too. After all, that's why people have children. To remind them of where they come from."

He waved a hand at it all again.

"The Center of the World."

And he gently wrapped his arms around me and pulled me softly against that massive chest. I closed my eyes and listened to his heartbeat. Deep and solid.

Like always.

After a career in high tech, **Darrel Duckworth** returned to his first love, writing. He now spends more time on other worlds, occasionally returning to Earth to refill his coffee mug. His stories can be found in magazines such as *LORE*, *Bards and Sages*, and *Plasma Frequency* and in anthologies such as *Coven* and *Wild Things*.

CLIVE TERN

Fishing Lake Tanganyika

DZONZI NBELOU WATCHED the line for the mid-week lottery and decided against joining it, despite the packet of money in his pocket.

"Hey, Dzonzi, you coming for a farewell beer?"

"Not today, Namu. I need to get back. Liseli isn't well and . . ." Dzonzi shrugged and waved in the direction of home where Shawa, his wife, would be preparing their evening meal and corralling their four children—the youngest of whom was ill, a cough that was keeping them up at night. The sleep loss wouldn't be such an issue now that his job was gone.

A light breeze blew from Lake Tanganyika. It carried the smell of the fishery he'd worked at until an hour ago. The odor of dead fish clung to him even after changing out of his work overalls for the final time. He walked along, head up as if seeing the trees and bushes, hearing the cormorants calling as another fishing boat headed to shore. But really he was miles away, his mind on the last visit home.

The village was in Zambia or the Angola, depending on who was drawing the map. A couple of hours drive from the town of Kalabo, it was a gathering of small adobe houses in the scrub, which no one cared about but the small tribe of his family. The few hundred kwacha he sent home each month had lifted the village from bare subsistence to previously unconsidered levels of comfort. A new well had been dug, deeper than the old one and with a proper protective cover.

The last visit had seen Dzonzi bring a solar panel, a television, and a satellite phone. While his cousins, father, uncle, and younger siblings had fought over setting things up and his mother had interrogated Shawa over the health of the children and how thin her son was looking, his grandmother had beckoned him to her hut.

"Mama, how are you?" Dzonzi asked.

"Come and sit with me." She pounded cassava in a deep wooden bowl. "Tell me, how is Mpulungu?"

"It is a small town with little happening. But the fishery gives me work, and Shawa makes clothes, and we have a nice house with neighbors who are friendly."

"And you bring gifts home to the village." She kept pounding but turned to look him in the eye. "You must keep more money for the children and your wife. We've lived without these white man's gadgets until now, but it's a stupid man who keeps a poor wife."

"We have more than enough. And now that there's a phone, the children can speak to their great-mother."

She stopped the pounding and smiled. "Yes, I'll like that." She shouted for one of the younger children to come and take the cassava. When it was gone, she said, "So, Dzonzi, you were always the one with dreams bigger than the village, bigger than the sky. Why have you stopped dreaming?"

Dzonzi looked at the deep lines of his grandmother's face and tried to remember if they'd always been there, if they'd existed when he had sat on her knee and listened to stories about great beasts, real and imagined.

"You need to dream again, Dzonzi. Without dreams, your family will wither and die."

"What do you mean, Mama?"

"When I first came here, as your grandfather's second wife, Zambia didn't exist. Not as a nation—we were the white man's property, all of us. They say they abolished slavery, but that didn't make us free. Still, we dreamed of freedom, of being our own people. I dreamed of having a big, big family." She chuckled and waved a hand slowly around the village. "Everyone here is my family, and Zambia is a free country." Tapping Dzonzi on the chest she asked, "What do you dream of here?"

He hadn't known what to say and was quiet. A cheer went up as the television turned on. A young child came running over. "Mama, Uncle Dzonzi, there is a film about someone with a house bigger than our village, and his pond is so clear he swims in it because he can see there are no crocodiles in it." The child ran off, breathless and in awe of the world's wonders.

"Mpulungu has made you rich, but it's stealing your soul as easily as if you'd stayed here and gone nowhere. You're not a man to live a humdrum life. You'd have been a fine Bantu explorer; there is the questing spirit in you."

"I made my quest, Mama. And now I have work, a fine wife, and lovely children. Now I strive for them and for my great family."

His grandmother had frowned, grinned, and patted his knee. He wondered what she'd say to him now. He wondered what Shawa would say.

✳

After three months with no work, Dzonzi came to a conclusion. "We must return to my village," he said one evening after putting the children to bed.

"No!" Shawa said. "We live here, in Mpulungu. Our friends are here; our home is here; our life is here."

"Our poverty will also be here. We are two payments away from having no money for rent, no money for electric, no money for food. Having friends is fine. But will they still be our friends when we are living in the car?"

"Please, Dzonzi. Just a little longer. You'll find work; I know it. You look so hard. Like a hero on a quest. Don't give up." She took his hand, pulling him toward her. "Please?"

Her scent filled his nostrils, the subtle smell of soap, perfume, and the indefinable Shawa-ness that was his wife. He closed his eyes and inhaled, holding her close. The tension and panic, which wound in him like a steel hawser on net-winding gear, didn't disappear, but it did relax.

He thought of the words she used, of his quest for a job, and how they chimed with those of his Mama. It didn't feel like a quest but a slog, hard graft against unrelenting opposition. He had the skills for the jobs he applied for but rarely got as far as an interview. He'd even been back to the fishery, seeing if there was even a low-paid job available. The foreman had shrugged and said, "There's hardly enough work for who's left, Dzonzi.

There's just not enough fish. Maybe you should find out where the fish have gone."

Dzonzi could guess where the fish had gone. Instead of small open boats of two men working with handwoven nets, trawlers with ice holds had been shipped across land and deposited into the lake. They stayed out for days, filling the hold with more fish than ten normal boats could catch in one.

Fish had been scoured from the lake with the grim, ruthless efficiency only humans applied to a task. No thought of what was needed or what should remain, only what could be taken, what could be profited from.

Now, though, birds were coming home to roost. It had happened in other places. The Aral Sea was now a tiny lake created by Kazakhstan building a dam. Lake Tanganyika was as deep as ever, but the fish had gone the way of those in the Aral. This wasn't the first time there'd been a collapse. Older fishermen said it was the same thirty years before. The fish came back, slowly, and not to the same extent.

※

The fishery shut down a week later, and youths ignored such trivialities as locks and doors to claim the site as a playground. The whole of Mpulungu felt the effect of the crisis. An air of despair settled over the town, as if it was giving up on the whole idea of being somewhere humans lived together.

Still Dzonzi searched for work, caving to Shawa's entreaties to stay just a little longer. Now, instead of him sending money back to the village, small parcels of food came the other way, maize and cassava.

"I'm going to try fishing," Dzonzi said one morning.

Shawa stopped pounding maize, wiped hair from her brow, and looked at him. "How? There's no fish."

"There's no fish for a factory, but there's always something. And Namu's taken his family back to Kasama to work for his brother-in-law. He said I can have his boat and net."

"Do you know how to fish?"

"Throw net in water, pull up, repeat."

"That sounds easy. Why doesn't everyone do it? Why is Namu not doing it?"

"Namu bought a huge house and filled it with many, many children. I think numerous people will be looking for Namu and the money he owes them. He used the boat on the weekends with his children."

"We should go and say goodbye."

"I did. And they've already gone. Last night."

"Oh. So, when will you start fishing?"

"Namu said to use a lantern and go out in the dark. The fish swim toward the light and are easier to catch."

Daylight still held the sky when Dzonzi made his way to the shoreline. Namu had hidden the boat among ones that were abandoned and left to rot away. Dzonzi pushed it into the water, climbed in, and pulled the starter cord on the outboard motor. It coughed to life, pumping a small waft of dark, oily smoke into the air that the light breeze soon dissipated.

Sitting with his hand on the tiller, Dzonzi tried to affect the calm assurance of other fishermen, a pretense that this was nothing new or strange to him. His cautious speed and uncertain course gave the lie. Others sped past him, their wakes rocking his boat, making him fear capsizing. Some grinned as they went past, others called greetings he struggled to hear over the rush of blood in his ears.

Darkness fell with its customary swiftness, and stars glittered down. Looking back, there was no sign of Mpulungu, already too far away. Over to the right, a small group of lights shone on the shore, he wondered what village it was. Scattered around were other lights, the lanterns of fishermen already at work. Dzonzi pushed on, wanting the anonymity of complete solitude, where his inexpert efforts would not be accidentally overseen.

When, at last, he could see no light but that of faraway suns, Dzonzi turned the outboard off and let the boat drift. He turned the lantern on, momentarily blinding himself, and clipped it to a pole suspended over the side of the boat to shine on the dark water.

Namu's hurried instructions rolled through his head. *"When you have set the light, relax. The fish will take time to come up. Eat, have a beer. Throw some bait in. Fishing is about lots of patience and a short period of fast but furious work."* There was nothing to eat. Only the children had eaten today. Maybe tomorrow, if he caught something, they could all eat together.

The silence of the lake was a quiet he wasn't used to. The wind that had blown earlier was gone, leaving wavelets slapping the boat as the only sound. At home, there was always sound, dogs barking, people shouting, cars. Back in the bush, it was never silent, scurrying, calls—or cries—caught the ear. Here he strained for sound as if he could discern where the fish were, could parse their position by listening to the water.

When the Pleiades had moved from just on the horizon to a hand's width above it, he took the net, stood, and threw. The boat rocked, and he sat, almost collapsing to the floor. Water splashed over the boat's edge, and for a long moment, he thought this would be it. A capsized boat and him drowned, or found clinging to the upturned hull miles from land. He was thankful he'd remembered to secure the net with a line.

When his heart had calmed, the iron taste of nausea retreated from his mouth, he sat straight, took hold of the line, and pulled. Hand over hand he drew the net in, heavy and wet. Eventually the net broke surface, and he leaned over to grasp the mesh, hoping to see the fruits of his tentative and inexpert labor.

There were fish, *buka-buka* and *kapenta*.

Relief and exultation swept Dzonzi. He could do this. He would feed his family; he would catch more than his family needed, and Shawa would sell it at market.

He emptied the net into the boat and stood again. This time he threw with only his arms, keeping his body as still as possible. The boat still rocked, but only a little. He sat down.

There was a splash in the lake. Dzonzi turned to the noise. The light of the lantern showed a circle of ripples moving across the flow of water but no sign of what made it. A fish jumping? A crocodile? He didn't know if crocodiles swam this far out, if even there were any near this part of the lake. There were none near Mpulungu, but the Nsumbu National Park bordered the lake and hunting the creatures was illegal there.

Taking the lantern from its hook, he looked around, seeking other disturbances in the water. There were none. He began pulling the net in, dragging the line across the gunwale, keeping his hands inside the boat just in case there was a crocodile about.

The wet nylon line felt heavier in his hands; hoping that meant a bigger catch, he pulled faster, urging his haul to the surface. His next handhold slipped; the line was wet but also slimy. He recoiled from the unexpected feeling, and the line began sliding back into the lake.

He hauled it in, slower this time, waiting for the change in texture. Slime was visible on the nylon. It clung thick and shiny. A faint smell of ammonia wafted up. Prepared this time, he continued pulling until the edge of the net caught the side of the boat.

Dzonzi wondered what creature produced such an excrescence. Nothing seen at the fishery produced anything like it. He hooked the net and pulled. It was heavier and entirely covered in the slime. The smell was stronger now, thick and pervasive. He wished he had gloves and was worried what might be in the glop and what it could do to his skin.

The net slopped into the boat, splashing slime and bits of fish all over—and they *were* bits of fish. Something had chewed the catch. It couldn't drag them through the mesh of the net, but had teeth and jaw big enough to pierce and tear the catch.

Dzonzi's skin contracted, goose bumps rose on his arms. The instinct was to run, to get to safe ground. He peered into the darkness, scanning the water for any sign of the croc that had done this. He powered up the outboard, checked his compass, and turned the tiller until it pointed back to Mpulungu.

❋

Dawn was still an hour away when he reached home. Before pulling the boat up to the shore, he stood waist deep in the water and rinsed the fish and nets, gutted and cleaned the catch.

The realization that he'd nothing to carry the catch home in struck while looking to put the fish somewhere to clean the boat out. He kept them in the net

Back home, the children were all asleep. Shawa was awake, sitting by the window and watching the street. She opened the door for him.

"You're safe," she said, hugging him.

"Yes. Tomorrow I must take something to carry the fish home in."

"Right now you need to go wash. You stink worse than when you were in the fishery."

"Yes. Something in the lake smells bad."

"Something here smells bad, you."

They laughed together.

"You going to cook some fish while I shower?" Dzonzi asked.

"Are they gutted?"

"Yes."

✳

Later, when the children had gone to school, Dzonzi and Shawa lay in bed.

"Why were some of the fish half eaten?" Shawa asked.

"Something attacked the net."

Shawa propped herself up and looked at Dzonzi. "A crocodile? I didn't think they went out deep, or did you go in too close to land?"

"No, I stayed far out. And I don't think it was a crocodile. Crocs don't produce stinky slime like this thing did."

"So, what was it?"

"I'll ask someone tonight. Now, I need to sleep."

"Right now?" Shawa asked, scraping her nails across his chest.

❋

The children helped Dzonzi carry nets and bags down to the lake. They chattered excitedly, asking if they could come with him. Maybe during the holidays, he promised.

After stowing his things in the boat and checking it over, he strolled along the shore to two other fishermen. He recognized them from around town but didn't know their names. A short way behind them, others looked up but carried on with their own preparations.

"Hey," he called, waving an arm.

"Hey. How was your first night?" one of them asked.

"Was it that obvious?"

"Namu said he was giving his boat to a friend. I'm Habanji. He's Gomani."

"I'm Dzonzi."

"You catch much last night?" Habanji asked.

"Enough for today. Can I ask you something? Something had a go at my second catch. Bit right through the fish, but couldn't break the nylon."

"Sounds like you were too close to shore and a croc came," Gomani said. "They love an easy catch. Lucky it didn't have a go at the boat."

"I thought it was a croc at first. But I'd stayed out in the lake, and crocs don't leave slime all over the place, really stinking glop."

Habanji sucked his teeth. "Slime?"

Dzonzi nodded.

"Sounds like you found Chipekwe. What do you think Gomani?"

"Yeah, sounds like it," Gomani said. "Nasty critter. Lives deep in the lake. Nasty."

"Bite a boat in half if the fancy takes it," Habanji said

"Chipekwe?" Dzonzi asked, conscious of grins and suppressed laughter.

"Yes, the Lake Tanganyika monster," Habanji said.

The laughter came freely, huge guffaws that rippled along the shore.

Dzonzi allowed himself to be the new boy who falls for the old jokes. "Well, maybe I'll catch it tonight. We'll all eat well tomorrow." He grinned, showing he shared the humor.

The laughter was renewed.

They stood and shared more talk. Appreciating his willingness to be made fun of, the men suggested places to avoid, dead zones where there were never any fish and places where the take was always small, though none of them guided him to places of plenty.

Dzonzi headed onto the lake earlier than the previous evening. He used his phone's GPS to guide him back to the same location, arriving before darkness had fully fallen. He was far enough out that the shore wasn't visible, as he'd thought last night. The breeze was stronger today, pushing from the east.

Thoughts of the beast below filled his mind. The others may have laughed, but something had eaten his fish and left the slime. He knew of Chipekwe, the mythical horned beast legend said lived around the shores of the lake. Mama had included tales of epic battles between it and matriarchal elephants protecting their family herd.

Nothing like it existed, of course. No tracks, no carcasses, no bones. The odd victim laid at Chipekwe's feet was probably killed by crocs or hippos; both had the power, and neither feared humans. People had lived on these shores for thousands of years; if Chipekwe was real, someone would have its bones as a trophy by now. Even if it had been found already dead, a mighty tale of hunting the beast would have been spun.

Dzonzi cast his net before the sun was down, hoping to catch fish feeding on the plankton lurking at the warmer surface. It brought in a decent haul. Cheered, he tipped them into the bottom of the boat and sorted out the smallest, throwing them back into the lake. One of the perch was a female thick with eggs; he threw that back as well.

Night fell, the sky cloudy and the moon yet to rise. Tonight, he could see a couple of other lights out on the lake, other fishermen. It cheered him. Last night, he'd needed solitude, but that one night, and the successful first cast, had given him confidence—and it was nice to know others were close while it was so black on the water and a strange beast lurked below. He cast again, flowing his hips and arms so that the net flew out and the boat hardly moved.

Hauling the net up, he heard a cry and looked up. One of the lights was wobbling; he grinned. Someone else had overbalanced while casting. He resumed pulling, and the net broached the surface. It was thick with fish, and he struggled to pull it over the side. The floor of the boat was soon thick with fish too, more than he could carry in the bags he'd brought. He set about throwing the smallest back into the water and checking for any pregnant females.

An outboard motor chugged toward him, and he looked up.

"Hey," called a voice he recognized from earlier.

"Hey, is that Habanji?"

"Yes. Who's that?"

"It's Dzonzi. We met earlier."

"Ah, yes. Listen, did you hear Gomani call out?"

"I heard someone. Is he in the other boat?"

"No. He should be, but he's not."

"Can he swim?"

"Of course. But I can't find him."

They searched, spreading out from Gomani's boat, calling for him across the dark water. Their calls became desperate, beseeching, as if urgency and intensity would reach the missing man's ears more readily.

They met up at the empty boat. The net had been cast, but not retrieved. Gomani's meal packet lay unopened, though a can of beer had been broached.

"What do we do?" Dzonzi asked.

"We haul his catch in, take his boat home, and I tell his wife she's a widow."

"I'll help."

"Hold my boat while I climb over." Habanji slid from one boat to the other and began pulling the net in. Suddenly he recoiled, rubbing the fingers of his hands against the palms, as if trying to remove something. A strong odor hit Dzonzi, and he knew what it was. He took a pair of latex gloves from his back pocket.

"Here, put these on. I came prepared tonight."

Habanji looked at Dzonzi. "What is this thing? What's it done with Gomani?" His voice was high, pinched.

"I don't know. That's what I asked you earlier this evening."

When the net came over the side, it was like Dzonzi's the night before, covered in slime and full of half-chomped fish. Habanji looked around fearfully as if expecting the creature to attack the boat.

※

They motored back to Mpulungu, Gomani's boat tied behind Habanji's.

Dzonzi offered to go with him to tell Gomani's wife.

"No. I'll take my wife. They're cousins." Habanji looked at Dzonzi. "What have you brought to us?"

"Me?"

"There was no slimy, man-eating monster in the lake before. You found it. You deal with it."

Dzonzi watched him walk up the beach, disappearing into the darkness of nighttime Mpulungu. He was left with those words. How could he be responsible? This was only the second time he'd ever been on the lake. Gutting and rinsing the fish gave him more time to think things through. Yesterday's research had yielded nothing to indicate what the creature could be. Even mythical creatures, like Chipekwe, failed to match what he'd experienced.

Maybe it was something else. At the bottom of the lake was old water, eons old, without oxygen to sustain fish. What if something lived down there? Maybe its slime was oxygenated in fresh water, and the creature drew from that while down in the stale depths. Like whales or dolphins that breathed air while living in the sea.

He decided to research more later in the afternoon.

※

The following evening, he came to the lakeshore and found a hole in the bottom of his boat, the ragged edges suggested something large and heavy had been dropped in it. A group of fishermen stood down the shore, arms folded, watching. Staring at them, he wondered who'd done it or if they'd all had a hand, sharing the task of driving out the bad luck bringer.

Explaining to Shawa would require telling her about last night. The fisherman's disappearance hadn't made the regional news, and he hadn't told her, not wanting to cause worry.

He kicked the side of the boat and glared at the watchers, daring them to say something. One by one they turned away, heading to their boats.

Dzonzi returned home. He said nothing about the men, just that there was a hole in the boat. Between them, they blamed out of control youths.

"It'll be nice to have you in bed tonight," Shawa said. "Though I've enjoyed having more space." She grinned, alluding to his habit of sleeping with arms and legs spread out.

Their son came through from the other room. "No fishing tonight, Dad?"

"No, son. I need to fix the boat. Will you help me tomorrow?"

"Instead of school? Sure!"

Dzonzi laughed. "It won't be that when I make you finish school and start working, and you have to be up early every day. And no, not instead of school, before school."

"Before? And then school after? It's okay, Dad. I have homework I can do instead."

"Then you should be doing it now!"

"I was, but I heard your voice."

"Good boy. Go on, finish up and get to sleep."

※

Shawa did sleep well, curling into Dzonzi and breathing deeply. The night was noisier than he remembered. Out on the lake, there was silence, a calm rhythm to the breeze and slap of water. Now he heard the birds, the barking of dogs, the mewling of cats. A neighbor shouted, her voice high and angry. A man answered with equal ferocity. It was a short argument followed by the crash of a slamming door.

While he concentrated on the minutia of sounds, another part of his mind worried over what had happened to Gomani, of the creature that left slime and stench and must have eaten his fish and Gomani's. For want of a name, he thought of it as Chipekwe.

Maybe it was Chipekwe, as Mama's stories told.

In the darkness, he thought about her words to him the last time he had seen her. He'd given up on his dreams, but there was no regret. How many men plan to be an astronaut, or a train driver, or president when they are nine or ten, and find that a loving wife and happy children are more fulfilling than they could have ever imagined? Maybe he could have done different things with life, but his childhood dreams of discovering new worlds weren't being achieved in the way he'd hoped. Sifting through screeds of data to infer a planet's existence wasn't the same as flying through the universe in a spaceship, stepping boldly onto fresh worlds, and discovering how life was different there.

But he needed something right now. No work, and what money they had dwindling rapidly, left an uncomfortable feeling. There'd need to be another discussion about leaving. Unless he caught Chipekwe.

The thought came in the hazy fog of pre-sleep and snapped him awake. Catch the creature and things changed. It wouldn't give him back a job that no longer existed, but snaring a creature no one knew about must have some rewards.

※

Fixing the boat and making plans and preparations took three days. He waited until the fishermen were back from their night's work and finished before they arrived to start anew. Taking a net, he threaded it with sharp hooks, jagged shards of metal that would be baited with fresh fish. He gathered empty plastic barrels, long lines of nylon twine that he secured together to make even longer lengths, long poles of wood and metal that he sharpened at one end and drilled a hole through the other to allow for the twine to pass through and be tied. He secured one end of twine to a spear and another to the barrels, creating a float that even the strongest creature would struggle to take below the surface.

Working in daylight, with the hot sun pouring heat into him, made Dzonzi wonder on the sensibleness of what he was doing. Each time he did, the memory of the empty boat trailing behind Habanji, of the slime and stench, returned.

After finishing preparations, he watched the rest of the sunset. More clouds had formed, and now the sky shone in purples and pinks, and the lake shimmered with reflections. Dzonzi faced his doubts, his fears. Not just of the creature, but for his family, for their life.

Mpulungu had been a good home these past seven years, the only home his children had known, but unless something changed, they would be leaving. Shawa did not want to go back to the village, his village. She enjoyed being independent, not subsumed into a larger whole that was alien to her. Neither did she want to return to the stifling and overbearing parents she'd left behind, who had disowned her for marrying a bush dweller.

Mpulungu had been their compromise. Now there might need to be another one, from him. The thought of city living made him shudder. The noise, the constant proximity of strangers, light that turned the night sky into a pale imitation of its own glory. But he could find a job.

Maybe.

And *maybe* kept him going. It wasn't definite. Nothing was, not even hopes and dreams. He'd compromised on his because he treasured the warmth of his wife and children over the cold happiness success might bring. But he would never give them up.

Daylight was gone now. A velvet sky sparkled with diamonds, and wind whispered on the water like Shawa's breath on his skin when they made love.

He stood, stance assured, and tossed the net into the water. The splashes were the loudest thing around, then they disappeared into the darkness. Twine unspooled, sinking through the inky water with a swishing noise as it slid against the wooden side of the boat. He held the twine and swithered between desire for it to be taken and hope that it wasn't.

The rope jumped in his hand. A small leap as if the net had caught on something. This was the moment. How would it react? What would any creature do when its mouth filled with sharp metal that sliced through cheek and tongue? The line went slack.

Dzonzi took up one of the sharpened poles he'd prepared, gripped it in his hand, and waited for the creature. He drew breath deeply, like a free diver preparing to descend in pursuit of the exquisite peace of deep water. Fear fled, anticipation remained, the knowledge that now there would come the fulfillment of whatever this dream was, whatever hope this could be.

The lake erupted, and Dzonzi stabbed down at the heart of the disturbance. His arm shook with the impact, a solid jolt as the makeshift spear struck home. A cry of unearthly anguish echoed over the water. As quick as the first spear left his hand, Dzonzi had reached down and scooped up another. He stabbed down once more, a scream of effort erupting from him. Again, there was a solid connection, the weapon striking home, slicing into the creature. Dzonzi yelled once more, reached for another spear, and stabbed again. This time he struck water, almost overbalanced. He jerked back, the boat rocked, and he danced on his heels and toes, juggling his body in an attempt to remain upright.

The twine slipped down once more, a barrel bobbed past, then another. The creature must be dead or badly wounded because the barrels didn't move away; they hung in the water, bouncing up and down on small waves.

Adrenaline sang in Dzonzi's system, a choir that screamed in his head, arms, heart. He turned to the rear of the boat and yanked the starter. The motor grumbled to life.

He sat down and grasped the tiller, turning it in a long shallow loop until he was headed back to Mpulungu. The boat set off smooth then jerked, as if hitting something. He turned to look, fearful. Forward progress continued; the barrels bobbed behind the boat.

Heading home again, with the creature—whatever it was—Dzonzi felt good. He smiled, imagining Shawa greeting him, the fishermen watching him be lauded by state media, maybe even international. What would *National Geographic* give to have his story? He chuckled. Surely enough to let him and Shawa decide where they would settle next, what job to pursue.

He chugged down the lake. Lights shone in the darkness, the lamps of men casting their nets and hoping to catch enough to sustain them through another day. This was the fate he'd been bound to, the one he'd been banished from, the one he was escaping. Already he saw Shawa's proud smile through the darkness, heard the excited chatter of his children as Daddy came home triumphant. He'd keep the creature underwater, out of sight, until the fishermen were returning in the morning. Then, in the glare of their disapproval, he'd drag it ashore and ask them what it was, knowing they'd have even less idea than he did.

The boat jumped as something slammed into it, a solid thunk that made the remaining spear bounce and rattle. Dzonzi looked around, his mouth suddenly dry, a knot forming in his gut. Another bang, this time from the side. A long metal pole pierced the side of boat, it had twine tied through a hole drilled near the top. The pole shifted side to side, then slid back leaving the boat rocking. Water slopped through; the lake's small waves lapped up it.

Dzonzi picked up the last spear and crouched in the bottom of the boat. The creature had been wounded, not killed. Now it would be angry. It had attacked a man who had done nothing to it. Dzonzi could only guess the primitive rage that would be flowing through it now, the pain it must be in. He peered at the water, turning his head from side to side, wishing the lamp was brighter or that it was daylight.

He turned to a faint swish of water and the boat was struck hard, almost capsizing. Dzonzi was flung into the lake. Cool water enveloped him, faint light reflected at odd angles. Orientation was lost, up and down became foreign terms as bubbles of air exploded from his clothes. Something brushed against him. It slid, but was hard. The creature. He waved the spear, the water slowing his movements to that of a child getting to grips with self-motion. The creature bumped him again, on the other side. Dzonzi jackknifed his legs, seeking the surface. He dropped the spear and reached up, pulling himself through the water. A jaw clamped his elbow. Needles sliced through his sleeve and into his skin. He wanted to scream. The creature yanked sideways, turning him in the water.

It had been only seconds since falling from the boat, but Dzonzi's lungs burned. Terror of drowning, of losing not his life but his family, flooded through him. Ignoring the pull on his arm, he kicked once more for the surface and broached it. He gasped in air, just in time. The creature dragged him down and spun him around. It let go of his arm, and Dzonzi felt the twine he'd used to snare the creature being wrapped around his legs, restricting his movement.

Clarity swept through Dzonzi—the creature was suited for this dark battle; it didn't need light. He closed his eyes and pulled his knife from the leather scabbard on his belt. Its long, sharp blade filleted with ease. Maybe it would finish the job the spear had started.

Turbulence came on Dzonzi's left. He turned into it, holding his arm tight, the knife facing where the motion came from. It struck home, a solid blow that jarred his wrist and shuddered through his shoulder. A massive flood of air erupted through the water before him. All motion by design stopped. He was floating in the water as was the creature, but it no longer moved. More than that, they were sinking.

Dzonzi tried to swim up but was wrapped up with the creature, bound together by twine. Pressure built in his lungs as they drifted down. He wrestled the knife from the dead creature and reached down to saw at the nylon, cursing the tough material. Finally one loop gave way, then another, then a third, and he was free and striving for the surface again.

The water pressure lessened, but the desire to breath increased. He dribbled air from his mouth, trying to eke the process out, to trick his body into thinking it was fine. His limbs burned, and his lungs felt like plastic bottles that had been collapsed, the air forced from them so they were distorted approximations of their original form.

Finally the surface came. The silence of the water collapsed as splashes sounded around him, as his gulp of breath echoed over the lake.

A lamp offered dim illumination a small way off, and Dzonzi struck toward it, assuming it was his boat as no one had called out.

He almost capsized twice clambering aboard, and when finally in the boat he lay on the bottom dragging in huge breaths. Above him, stars shone with what felt like unusual intensity. Sparkling jewels more glorious than any ever hewn from a De Beers mine.

Deep throbbing built in his muscles as the adrenaline leached away and the effort of survival claimed recognition. Parts of his body felt like he'd been punched. A couple were places the creature had banged against him. A sharper pain enveloped his elbow. The teeth had bit deep, which the creature then pulled, making the wounds wider. He eased himself up and looked. Even in the lamplight, his arm was a mess of red. He didn't want to roll the sleeve up and inspect the damage. Shawa would help with that.

Dzonzi started the outboard, wincing with effort. His phone, with its compass, was gone, so he looked at the stars and guessed his way south. The breeze had blown from the east all night, and he hoped it hadn't switched while he'd been fighting the creature.

As the boat chugged through the blackness, he thought about what to do now. The creature was gone, sunk back to the dead depths from which it had risen. With it went any hope

Dzonzi had of using it. He hadn't even seen it, nor felt its full form.

He thought of the creature. He was more convinced than ever that it had never been cataloged. With its hard carapace and slimy coating, it was like nothing ever encountered. And it was smart. It had attacked the boat, had wound itself around Dzonzi, wrapping him with the twine it could not escape from. Only chance had saved Dzonzi. That last blow had struck some kind of dive bladder, rupturing the creature's internals fatally.

Where there was one such beast there must be more. Whether it was an ancient and undiscovered thing or some newer offshoot of something more common, there must be more than one.

Hope flared in Dzonzi's chest. Here was his new quest. His mama had told him to find his heart again. He had.

They would stay in Mpulungu.

Clive Tern is a writer of short fiction and poetry from South-West England. Apart from writing he enjoys open water swimming, cooking, and a well made martini.

www.clivetern.com

SARAH L. BYRNE

A Drop of Comfort, a Slice of Heart's Desire

ANGELINE TOOK up her newly sharpened knife and, with painstaking care, cut off the rough-baked outside edge of her creation. The blade slid easily through the soft substance, and the crust fell away, revealing a perfectly even layer of delicate air bubbles trapped in the structure of the cake as though caught in time.

She straightened up with a sigh of satisfaction. Her new ingredient, the product of many long months of experimentation, had done its job perfectly. No one in London, or in England—or in any other land she knew of—made a sponge cake as light, as airy, as sublime as this. Whatever else Angeline D'Emico—confectioner to London's elegant society from the gentry to the regent—might be, she was good at her trade.

Miss Catherine Fairley watched with fascination from where she sat on the other side of Angeline's kitchen table.

"It is quite like magic," she exclaimed.

Angeline glanced up from her work. "A kind of alchemy, perhaps."

"I understand. A secret, of course." Miss Fairley's eyes were wide with imagined intrigue. "I am certain Lady Milne will be delighted. How astonished her guests will be when it is served. I assure you I will not breathe a word of it before then, Angeline."

As though I would allow you even a glimpse of a true secret, Angeline thought, *with your silly head as full of bubbles as this cake.* The new raising agent was a valuable formulation indeed, but it was the least of her mysteries.

"And quite like a sponge itself, as though it had grown that way, all alive," Miss Fairley chattered on excitedly. "I always thought it diverting to hear it called sponge cake, for what a thing to compare, but now I see why."

"I believe it was Miss Austen who first called it so," Angeline said. "An astute observation." She bent to attend to the other side of the cake, carving with the same care she'd applied to the first.

"I am fond of Miss Austen's novels," Miss Fairley remarked.

"As am I."

"Papa does not quite like us to read novels," Miss Fairley went on. "But he says these are entirely suitable for young ladies."

"Miss Austen's writings are an interesting thing," Angeline said. "Something more than they seem, each reader finds what she wishes to see." A kind of magic, that, indeed. Angeline sometimes wished she had met Miss Austen while that lady lived, though there was no telling what the Sussex clergyman's daughter would have made of a tradeswoman with the look of one from across the wide sea and a coronet of braids as elaborately decorated as one of her sugar confections.

"Are your cakes more than they seem?" Miss Fairley asked suddenly. Angeline looked up sharply. The young woman held her eyes with an unaccustomed boldness, a flush rising in those pale English cheeks, so transparent. She'd been some time building up to that question, behind all her nervous babble.

"Well, that would be telling," Angeline replied, curving her mouth in one of her enigmatic smiles. No transparency here, implacable. She did that well. Miss Fairley looked a little disappointed. "You may assure your papa, though," Angeline said. "My cakes are entirely suitable for young ladies."

Miss Fairley leaned forward eagerly.

"So you will do it? You will make the cake for my ball, for my betrothal? With pink and white sugar-craft, for I tell you I am quite set on that."

"If your mama agrees to it," Angeline said mildly.

Because I am not cheap, nor altogether respectable.

"Oh, she will!" Miss Fairley exclaimed.

But I am the best.

A silence fell. Angeline took up a smaller knife, continued to sculpt the cake in careful, precise cuts.

"Lord Aston is rather . . . advanced in years," Miss Fairley began after a moment. She paused, looked down. Her hands twisted together. "They do say . . . about older men . . ."

Angeline glanced up, raised an eyebrow.

"They say many things about older men."

That they didn't always long survive a new young bride, for example, though their name and fortune lived on, and a wealthy young widow had her life ahead of her? Or that they could be an unsatisfying prospect in the marital bed?

Is she asking me for poison or an aphrodisiac? Angeline studied the girl's face carefully, the awkward tension of her body. *I do not believe she knows herself.*

"I must go," Miss Fairley broke off suddenly, her eyes darting toward the door. "Mrs. Shaw will be waiting for me."

Angeline acknowledged this with a little bow of her head.

"Think carefully what you would ask of me. Pink and white sugar-craft covers a great many possibilities."

Miss Fairley stumbled awkwardly out of her chair and fled to where her chaperone waited in the carriage outside. Lips surely pursed in disapproval and nose wrinkled at the pungent odors of everyday living in this inelegant street, mixed with the glorious smells of baking rising from the mysterious basement below.

❋

As evening fell, Angeline strode the streets alone, hatless, hair braided tall, red velvet hem sweeping the pavement. The curious stares from ladies in carriages, gentlemen on horseback, and children begging in the gutter alike slid off her like rain off a waxy leaf.

The cake was completed, ready to be collected by Lady Milne's cook tomorrow morning. The sponge was as light as air, the sugar-craft as intricate and fine as any the people of this town had seen. Lady Milne would be delighted indeed. Her party would be a great success. Her guests would remember it as the finest evening of their lives, one that left them with a warm glow and a sense of awe they craved to repeat, even if they could never afterward quite remember why. And Angeline would have another faithful customer for life.

But that was for tomorrow. Now, a quick glance over her shoulder assured Angeline that none of Lady Milne's set was passing, none to see as she turned aside into a darker, narrower street where fetid liquids puddled stagnant in the cracked and broken paving. There were a great many streets like these. Behind the clean but functional trade districts like the one where Angeline lived above her bakery, behind the elegant curving terraces and carriage walks favored by the fashionable set for their London seasons, there were streets so many that a soul might lose themselves in the warren-like entanglement. Not Angeline, though. She drew up her hem in one hand to keep it clean as she walked, but that was a habit of her latter years.

She'd come from here. Not from whatever overseas land of spices and silks her more fanciful customers chose to imagine. Only from here.

But there were deeper places still than these streets with their rickety facades leaning so precipitously over the pavements. Angeline walked on toward the river, her memory guiding her feet, the green, pungent smell of it calling to her. The smell of home. Of childhood.

The tide was far out when she reached the riverbank, and the mud glistened silver gray in the low afternoon sun. Angeline made her way down the green, tide-marked steps, the embankment walls rising forbidding above her, the sewer tunnel entrances dark and silent as they spewed their contents toward the low water.

Small figures dotted the gray mudflats, combing the shores with bent heads and methodical steps. A girl looked up sharply, froze momentarily at the sight of Angeline, then slogged across the mud toward her. She stood without speaking, eyeing Angeline's fine gown with suspicion and clutching her basket, her hands and ragged dress encrusted with gray mud.

I was like you once. But Angeline didn't speak the thought aloud.

Instead, she reached into her reticule and took out a little sugar-craft figurine, carefully wrapped in parchment. Nella took it suspiciously, undid the paper with her muddy fingers. Despite herself, her eyes rounded at the sight of the tiny, perfectly formed white horse. She wrapped it hastily again and shoved it into her apron.

"How does Auntie do, Nella?" Angeline asked at last.

"She don't do well," the girl muttered. She stared up at Angeline, accusing eyes under the dirty, tousled hair. "She's been asking for you, Miss Angeline. Asking day and night."

Angeline's face was too well schooled these days to show the inner twinge of shame she felt. Nella was right: it had been too long since she'd remembered her duty here. And in truth, she'd only come now to ask for what she needed.

"Take me to her, then," was all she said.

Her eyes took longer now to adjust to the darkness of the underground tunnels than they once had. Every visit, they took a little longer, or so it seemed. Angeline kept her eyes on the dim flicker of the oil lamp Nella carried, following the sooty smell trailing from the flame. She kept her footing well enough, stepping carefully on the ledges that hugged the tunnel walls, never flinching at the rats that shot in and out of the water below.

There were some things you did not forget, however many years might pass. Only the bravest of the children ventured this far, up into the labyrinth of winding tunnels that crisscrossed for scores of miles beneath the city. Tales abounded of wanderers lost in the darkness, never to find their way out, only the skeleton ever found, bones gnawed clean by the rats. Tales of strange creatures encountered.

There was truth in those tales. But Auntie's children—the most desperate, the most homeless, friendless, with nowhere to go in the world but into this underground lair in search of survival—they had nothing to fear.

"Angel." The voice echoed out of the shadows, the presence there lurking, familiar, yet a scent that wasn't quite right, quite as she remembered. But still . . .

"*Tante*," Angeline said, and she heard her own voice soften, her accent sliding back into its old shapes even as the large gelatinous form emerged from the darkness and arranged itself into a maternal shape.

"Run on now, Nella," the creature said. "You've work to finish before the tide turns. Good girl."

Angeline never knew how Auntie spoke like that, how the cephalopodan gills and tentacles could form a woman's voice. Sometimes she wondered whether Auntie even spoke at all, whether the words slid into her consciousness through some other means. It didn't matter. She knew that voice, and she loved it. The closest thing to a mother's voice she remembered.

Nella disappeared back up the tunnel, taking her lantern with her. There was only the iridescent greenish glow that emanated from Auntie's shimmering body to light the darkness.

"So long, my Angel, since you came to me."

"I . . ." Angeline hesitated. How to explain it, why she'd stayed away so long this time. "My work keeps me occupied; I have many new customers."

"You do well in the world, then. Better every year. I never doubted you would."

"I do well enough," Angeline admitted.

"And how do those fine folks take you, my Angel? Do they treat you well, as one of their own?"

Hardly, Angeline thought. Though how would Auntie understand such a thing?

"They think me some exotic creature, from a faraway land," she said dryly, tracing a fingertip down her own cheek, flicking it at the tight-braided coils of her hair. Auntie laughed at that, the wobbly laugh they all loved, but it bubbled and caught in her mouth sacs and she had to pause to suck in a wheezing breath.

She does not look well, Angeline thought, her eyes adjusting to the dark, remembering Nella's words. Not well at all. Her body bloated and distorted, the tentacles sagging weakly as though she didn't have the breath to inflate them fully.

"I am dying, my Angel," Auntie said gently, in answer to Angeline's look.

She knew it; she'd known it from the moment she walked in here today.

"No," Angeline said. "No, that cannot be. We'll have you well, whatever must be done—"

"Enough, now." Auntie's gentle murmur broke through her thoughts. "Let me give you what you need. What you came for."

There was no use denying it. Angeline took the vial from the hidden pocket inside her dress, held it in her hand still warm from her body. She hesitated.

"But you should not . . . surely you do not have the strength . . ."

"Give it to me, Angel. For you, I always have the strength."

But you will not, always.

The unspoken words hung between them in the dark as Auntie reached for the bottle, the tip of a tentacle brushing against Angeline's hand. That touch, how she'd craved it, how she always would.

"I thank you," Angeline said softly as Auntie brought the bottle close against the membranous skin of her torso, pressed it there until a clear vesicle formed, swelled, and opened, the magical essence oozing slowly into the bottle. So slowly, this time. So little magic left to give, Auntie's last gift.

"There now, a drop of comfort for my Angel, making her way in the hard world out there." Auntie held the filled vial out to her, tentacles trembling with weakness. Angeline reached to take it, but Auntie's tentacle tip curled around it a moment longer. "It troubles me, though, Angel," she went on. "Who is to comfort the children, when I am gone?"

As well it might trouble her. What would become of the tribe of children she'd been an aunt to all these years, who'd come to her for comfort. For a mother's voice, a gentle touch, a hiding place from those that would harm them, true. But also for a drop, a sip, of that liquid she made within herself—absorbed from the filthy waters in which she lived, her gelatinous body submerged, from waste and stench—somehow distilled down into something pure, clear, the essence of comfort itself.

"Surely some kind person . . . the orphanages, workhouses . . . ?"

But they both knew the truth. The children would drift like the flotsam they gathered. Angeline's fingers tightened around the little vial she held, the precious liquid that had made her reputation—the finest baker in London with her cakes that were more than they seemed. She felt the familiar pang of guilt at the thought—if Auntie knew what she used it for. It wasn't for that.

It was for the children. The orphans, the penniless, the abused who found their way down here to escape a life of backbreaking work, sickness, danger. Auntie couldn't take that away, couldn't change the world. But she could offer them a drop of *comfort* to ease their short lives. Most were glad to take it.

Angeline closed her eyes a moment, remembered how that drop had tasted, the first time she'd found her way down here— barefoot, bruised—feeling her way through the tunnels by touch and smell as much as sight. She'd closed her eyes then, terrified at the sight and sounds of Auntie, closed her eyes and taken the drop on her tongue straight from a tentacle, felt it diffuse through her body. It had been comfort, certainly; it had taken away the pain of the beatings, of fingers worked to blistering, of an empty, gnawing stomach. She'd seen it do the same for the others around her.

She'd watched, and slowly she'd begun to understand what it truly was—not comfort, but heart's desire. How else would it be, all the hopes and dreams of a city's people refined and purified? It was just that the only desire some hearts were able to muster was for a little comfort, a little relief. A little oblivion.

Oh yes, Angeline had watched what it did to the others around her and decided she didn't want that for herself.

Instead, she'd started to save it, spat into her palm, secreted into little bottles and vials she found on the riverbank and washed clean with precious drinking water. Taken it tucked into the pocket of her pinafore to her kitchen job where, as in all kitchens, enough sickness and accidents befell the maids and cooks that some days all hands were needed—even the brown, calloused little hands of a scullery brat. The kitchen of the grand house where slowly, over time, no one could deny that the cakes this girl mixed, baked, decorated with increasingly intricate carvings of sugar as her skills grew with every inch her height increased—that those cakes were the ones that brought the most glowing praise and generosity down from those above. And so Angeline D'Emico, master confectioner, was born.

"I'm sorry," Angeline told Auntie, taking the vial firmly. "Sorry for the children, truly. But I cannot be you."

"Can you not, my Angel?" The disappointment was soft in Auntie's voice.

"I cannot," Angeline repeated. "I have my life now, my own life. I do well. I am happy. Is that not what you wanted for me?"

A sudden surge of anger rose up in her. She'd climbed out of here, by her own strength of will, her own ambition. She'd learned her trade, starting by sweeping scraps from bakery kitchens and scrubbing pots until her hands bled. Now Auntie would draw her back into this dark, sad world, tentacles of kindness closing around her, relentless as the tide. She wouldn't—couldn't—let it happen.

Auntie just watched her, sadly.

"It was all I ever wanted."

✳

Angeline stalked the streets, the river behind her. The smell of it still drifted in the air on the evening breeze, still clung to her boots and hem. *The gown would have to be laundered,* she mused. Still, the bill she was about to present to Lady Milne would more than pay for that, not to mention whatever she might be able to charge for Miss Fairley's ridiculous pink sugar-craft confection.

She walked faster, as though she could leave the smell behind her, as though she didn't carry it with her. As though her world was not shifting under her feet like the river mud, the surging tide of grief dammed up tight and waiting to flood through her. Auntie, dying. She'd never thought the day would come, had never even considered the possibility—whatever creature Auntie was, she had always been there, had she not? Would always be there, it was inconceivable that she could not be.

She pushed the thoughts down, but they welled up: more than grief, terror. The life she'd built for herself was falling apart before her eyes. Losing her business, her income, her home. Scrabbling for work again so she could have a place to lay her head, to eat, even if that meant back to the scullery again, scrubbing pans and hauling water—no, surely not, with her skills? But there were head cooks in some houses who would rejoice to see Angeline D'Emico brought low. Growing old, with no husband, no children, no family to fall upon for charity. No Auntie to run to for a mother's comfort.

For a moment, her hand twitched with a sudden craving for the vial in her pocket, with the need for it. *Just a little, just this once.*

No.

She would never go back to that. That was as dead an end as any sewer tunnel. Her mind spun over the possibilities. There had to be something she could do. She'd always found a way, with hard work and determination. There had to be a way. The raising agent had been a difficult task, but she'd perfected it, hadn't she, after many long days and nights of experimentation? Distilling, grinding, measuring, adjusting the minute quantities until the result was just so. And then there was the *comfort* itself—hadn't she watched and noted its effects closely enough, long enough, to deduce its true nature. She would solve this problem like all the others.

"Miss Angeline!" She stopped, turned sharply at the voice.

"Nella." The girl stood on the far side of the road, trailed by three of the smaller children. The littlest one, young enough to still be in breechcloths, clung to her skirt with tiny fists. Likely to be motherless then, or as good as.

"You stay here," Nella told the small children. She pried the smallest one off her skirt, pushed it toward the oldest one. "Watch him for me."

"I know what you do with it." She gestured at Angeline's reticule as if she could see clear through the leather to the little vial hidden there. "I followed you the last time. I know what you're using it for, and it's not right, Miss Angeline. It's not right and you know it."

"That's hardly your concern," Angeline replied, drawing herself up to her full height and looking down at the girl disdainfully. She'd learned that trick from some of the ladies she'd baked for, just like she'd learned the accent, the way of speaking that came out of her mouth now without her even thinking about it, and for a moment, she hated herself as she saw the flash of resentment in Nella's eyes.

"It ain't right," Nella repeated. "If you don't need it no more, you shouldn't be taking it away, not when she don't have much left. It's for the children."

"For you, you mean to say?" Angeline asked. That was unedifying, and she knew it. But Nella held her gaze steadily.

"No. I don't touch it."

"You gave it up?" Angeline let the surprise show in her voice before she could catch it. She didn't know of anyone but herself who'd done that. To this day, she woke sometimes in the dark, frantic with the need for it for a short moment, before she remembered where she was, who she was now.

"Same as you did, miss," Nella confirmed.

"Does she know?"

"No." Nella looked away at that, and Angeline drew closer, almost forgetting her concern for appearances.

"Why?" she asked, barely above a whisper. "What do you do with it, with what she gives you?"

"I give it to them," Nella snapped back, no hesitation this time. She jerked her head toward the little gaggle of children peering at her from across the road. "Or I take it home, sometimes, for my ma. For those that need it more than me."

"You think it helps them? Truly helps them? Or does it just keep them from bettering themselves?" She'd asked herself the same question many times, chasing it around in circles as she tried to justify to herself what she did, what she'd say to Auntie if she ever found out. She'd never found a satisfactory answer. Nella had no such doubts, it seemed.

"It's easy to say so with your silk gowns and your money purse and mixing with the toffs and all. Easy for you to say they shouldn't have a drop of comfort. We can't all be like you, Miss Angeline."

"I worked for what I have." Angeline caught the words on the tip of her tongue, hearing them ring false before she'd even spoken them. Oh, it was true that she'd worked hard, in the kitchens all those years. That she'd taught herself to read and add up figures from discarded bills and recipes, by the light of old candle ends. But she'd had strength and health on her side, in mind and body, and she'd had luck. And most of all, she'd had the *comfort*. The magic that hadn't been hers to take, to dispose of as she wished, to use to build her own wealth and reputation. "And now I have work to attend to."

And I won't be seen bandying words with a pauper girl in the street like this.

She turned away, hearing a carriage approaching.

"Too good for the likes of us now, are you?" Nella shouted after her, as though she'd heard the unspoken thought. Angeline kept her back to the girl, began to walk back up the side street that would take her back toward her shop. Angry that she'd been drawn into the argument, at the betrayal in the girl's accusing eyes.

She never knew why the smallest child ran into the road. Whether he ran after her, seeing her stride away and hoping for some sugary treat from her pockets. Whether he ran to latch onto Nella's skirts again. Only the clatter of the horses' hooves, the rattle of the carriage wheels on the cobbled street. The little feet, running.

And then Nella's scream.

Angeline turned, froze where she stood. Nella, on her knees in the road, hands held out helplessly toward the small, broken body. The coach, coming to a stop, half swerved across the road, too late. The driver cracking his whip toward the weeping girl.

"Get out of the road, you dirty brat. Don't you know who this is?"

Nella did not know, that much was clear from her face. But Angeline did. Knew the crest on that fine, gilded carriage, knew the plump ringlet-framed face peering from the window with mild curiosity at the scene, then turning carelessly away—she had seen that face in enough newspapers and fashion plates, resplendent in royal wedding finery, the face of the most coveted of all possible customers—and for another moment, she could not move, or speak, or breathe.

Then the driver turned his whip back to the shaken horses; the wheels began to turn again, and the carriage was gone. And Angeline could move once more. She ran to Nella's side, pushing the girl back from the horror of her broken, bloody . . . sibling? Fosterling?

"Child, I will stay with him, you must run for assistance . . . I know a doctor on Leadenhall Street, let me tell you . . . "

"It's too late, miss," Nella sobbed. "Can't you see it's too late?"

Angeline knew the truth of it.

There was only one thing to be done. She took out the little vial, held it to the dying child's lips. Just a drop, just one tiny drop for such a tiny creature, a drop of comfort.

A drop was enough. She saw the pain ease, the fear and confusion. Saw the life fade from the child's eyes—nothing could have stopped that—but it went gently, painlessly.

Slowly, she looked up again to meet Nella's tear-filled eyes. The girl rubbed a hand defiantly across her face, spoke in a flat, emotionless voice.

"He wouldn't've had much of a life anyway."

How can she say such a thing? Angeline wondered. But the girl spoke the harsh truth again, she knew that.

"Not your brother?" Angeline asked gently.

"No. Just a boy. His ma died from drink, so he got to following me all over." She was staring in the direction the carriage had gone, toward the leafy squares and townhouses—the palaces— to the west. "They never even looked. At what they done. Never even got out of their fancy coach."

She really did have no idea who that had been. *And how would she?* Angeline asked herself. How would a girl from the sewers know the Crown Princess?"

❋

Hunched over her bench in the workshop behind her kitchen, Angeline stared at failure in a miniature glass flask. She'd decanted a small amount of the precious liquid into the flask, attached it to her still, heated it over a flame. Watched as the water collected drop by drop in the reservoir at the other end of the still, and all that was left in the flask was nothing.

Nothing. Just nothing. It wasn't possible, yet there it was: nothing.

She'd tried over and over, trying to refine it down further. Always nothing. The liquid had no residue, no scent, no flavor— she knew that well enough. Perhaps this was not something like the raising agent, something that could be analyzed, formulated. Perhaps Auntie's magic was not that manner of thing.

Angeline got up and paced, pressing her hands into the aching small of her back. She'd worked all night—again—trying over and over, thinking, studying her books, while cakes sat unfinished, ovens grew cold, raps at her door went unanswered. It was bad business to turn away customers, to fail to fulfill orders on time; it was contrary to every rule she'd set for herself, once upon a time. But now, it did not seem to matter. Now, she was not certain she could face the gentlest of her customers without that rage surging up, the rage she'd seen behind the tears in Nella's eyes as she stared after the royal coach, because how were any of them different? How many of them would have stopped to help instead of rushing on to whatever ball or society supper they were late for? How many would understand—could ever understand—what the comfort was truly for, why it was needed? Why it wasn't for them, for their frivolous wishes and inane hearts' desires.

She wouldn't do it anymore. Wouldn't give them another drop of her precious comfort. She'd find a way to carry on Auntie's work, whatever it cost her.

But she'd reached the end of her ingenuity, tried everything she could think to do. All for nothing. Angeline could not, *would* not, admit defeat—it was not in her nature to do so—but she could not create out of nothing.

The dawn light was starting to slant in through the windows at street level above, the occasional carriage already rattling by, and Angeline flinched a little at the clatter above her head. How much had the child known of what had happened? How much pain had there been before she'd administered the comfort? Her hand shaking slightly, Angeline extinguished the flame under her still, caught up her cape, and made her way up the stairs, out into the street.

She walked.

The city was coming to life around her, delivery boys hauling crates, housemaids emptying last night's ashes, the first smoke of new fires and smells of cooking rising from kitchens. Despite the noisy bustle, the streets were like the lingering shadows of a dream upon waking. Sleepless, hopeless, she walked.

The cry of a newspaper seller broke through the fog of her thoughts.

"The beloved princess," the voice was calling. "The princess to be confined by summer. A royal child for the beloved princess!"

Angeline stopped, stared, not caring who saw her unguarded.

"Is it true?" she asked the man. "It is certain?"

"Aye, it's true, Her Highness is expecting again. They say there's every reason the child may come to birth this time, and the physicians have high hopes for a boy."

Angeline walked on, her mind churning the news, mixing it with fury, helplessness, despair at a world in which such things happened. A royal heir for the woman who was to be queen, a child for her happy marriage, her prince. A child to be king after her, perhaps. The city now ruled by a regent who cared more for his own pleasure than the proper governance of his capital, to be succeeded by a queen who cared no more for a child dead in the street beneath the wheels of her coach than she might an insect ground under her heel, to be followed by whatever child a mother like that might produce.

And the woman didn't even wish to be queen. That was the irony of it, if the newspapers and the society gossip were to be believed. The succession was forced upon her by her parents' inconvenient separation, by her father's inconsiderate failure to produce a male heir to supersede her. The princess had no interest in ruling, in government. She was fond of exotic Russian-blue gowns, they said, of dancing, of eating and drinking. And of her prince, a love match, they said, a rare indulgence for a girl of her standing. She'd wanted nothing but to marry her prince, to live the rest of her days with him in comfort, and to never be queen.

Her heart's desire.

Angeline stopped dead in the street.

She knew what she had to do. And where she must go first.

❊

Angeline's feet took her to the sewers despite her distracted mind. She could have made the journey with her eyes closed, she realized, guided by smell, by memory, by a need she barely knew how to acknowledge even to herself.

She stood before Auntie, afraid, ashamed. But the monster's voice was gentle as ever, loving.

"So soon, my Angel? I am glad. I feared . . . you might not come soon enough, that I might not see you again."

Angeline was silent. How could she ask for more, have Auntie think she came back only for that. Even if it was the truth . . . because it was not the whole truth. The need almost overwhelmed her then, the need to spill out the truth, to kneel before Auntie and tell her everything that had happened, everything that she had done. All that she planned to do. To beg her help, her forgiveness—her blessing. But she could not. *Auntie would forgive*, she thought, *but never approve*. Never give her the last of the comfort she needed to do this thing. Would never understand why it had to be done—not personal revenge only, but to change the city, the kingdom. To keep that woman from the throne, and then the one who would come in her place, some half-sibling or cousin not yet born, to guide that one to make all different . . .

"Do not talk so" was all she said.

"Not talking will not make it otherwise. It comes quickly, Angeline. Another day, perhaps. I am glad you have come."

"Another day?" *Surely not so soon.* "No . . . there must surely be something. I might go to your people; I have the means to travel now, only tell me where—"

"My people?" The tentacles curved again, then unfolded to encompass the sewer world. "Little Angeline, my people are here. All of you."

"No, but I mean . . . your people, your kin, where you come from."

And where had that been? How had it been that she'd never asked, that she hadn't wanted to dissolve the images in her head, Auntie swimming the seas from some far-off place because it pleased her to imagine that, just as she once liked to imagine she might have come from such a bright and sun-drenched land herself.

"We all come from here. Every one of us, Angeline."

From here. This gray city, this fetid water that lay beneath, all the mysteries, everything of home, all perfectly here. She'd always known that, deep down in the sewer tunnels of her mind, hadn't she?

Angeline felt the long-forgotten sting of tears spring to her eyes, and she put her hand up to her face in dismay. How long had it been since she'd wept? Not since her hands and apron were as grubby as little Nella's, her tattered skirts tucked up over spindly brown legs, mud splattered. Not since that other life.

"No tears," Auntie said gently. "It comes to all of us. Death is nothing to fear, as long as others live on to continue our work."

"I cannot," Angeline whispered. "I tried . . . I have tried so hard to understand the comfort, to make it myself . . ." She took a breath. *The truth.* "I have lied to you, Auntie, stolen from you. I do not need the comfort for myself, have not for many years. I use it to . . . for my cakes . . . "

"Child"—Auntie's tentacle reached out, touched her hand gently—"did you think I did not know?"

"There is more, I must tell you, what I planned to do—"

"No." Auntie stopped her, the tip of a tentacle brushing her lip. "You need tell me nothing. It is your time now."

"You must tell me, then," Angeline pleaded. "Tell me how it is made, what manner of a thing it is, the comfort. Tell me so I can do what I must."

"Did you not say, the last time, that you cannot be me?" Auntie reminded her.

"Who can live down here, without the sun, for a lifetime?" she asked. "Who is there alive who can be what you are?"

"Oh, little Angel. Do you think I have always been this way?"

Angeline stared at her, shimmering in the phosphorescent light. She followed the direction of Auntie's gaze, looked down at her own hand, her own dark skin glimmering in that strange blue-tinted glow.

"I . . . I cannot . . ." she faltered, her voice suddenly like a little girl's again. "*Tante*, it is not possible . . ."

"I said the same, when my time came to change."

"I am afraid . . ."

"Every woman changes, when the years catch her up," Auntie said with a gentle chuckle. "You have grown old enough to find that out in few enough years, little Angel. How the time goes by." She held her tentacles wide, a mother's embrace. "Some of us change more than most, no more than that."

Angeline came forward, knelt. Put her lips to the softness of Auntie's body, of her oozing surface that was not skin. It flowed into her, the flesh that was not flesh, the comfort that was not comfort, that would never be or make comfort—that was Auntie's work, borne out of her kindness, and that work was done—but becoming something more than comfort, something *Angeline*.

She drank deep.

❄

Miss Fairley's cake was everything its amiable owner could have wished for. Tiered like a ball gown, blushing rose pink, and veiled like a bride in lacy cascades of spun sugar. Standing in Angeline's kitchen again, the young lady herself gazed at it in transports of delight, her hands clasped, wordless for a moment with astonishment at its loveliness.

Beside it, and almost completed, was a less-towering creation, but one astonishing in its delicate beauty. A circlet, formed from a dozen miniature cakes carved into fluted peaks. Decorated with sugar flowers of violet with petals so thin one could almost see the light through them, with leaves of gold, with tiny teardrop jewels like pearls fit for a princess.

"A gift for Her Royal Highness," Angeline explained, in answer to her fair customer's questioning look. "To congratulate her on the happy event. A small offering, to be sure, a little thing to amuse her. But if it pleases her, it will please me to send more."

"Oh, I am certain it will delight her exceedingly," Miss Fairley exclaimed.

And I share your certainty, Angeline thought, but she contented herself with silence.

"I do hope," Miss Fairley chattered on, "that the princess will not indulge too heavily. They say the doctors have warned her against increasing too greatly, for fear she may not be able to birth the child, should it grow too large."

"That," Angeline replied, "will be a choice entirely hers."

The young lady left, all smiles, her creation carried before her by two servants like some church procession, and Angeline turned to her silent companion.

Nella was mixing cake ingredients in a huge ceramic bowl, sleeves rolled up, a determined grip on the wooden spoon. Her arms must have ached from the stirring—Angeline remembered how her own arms had been as thin as that once, how they'd hurt those first long days of labor in the kitchens. But she hadn't complained, any more than Angeline herself ever had in those days. Nella's hands and face were still a little reddened from the scrubbing they'd needed to get the deeply ingrained dirt out of them, her yellow hair still straw-like from the harsh soap and her own fiercely determined efforts to tug out the knots.

Miss Fairley had stared openly at her when she first entered the kitchen, and Nella had stiffened at the scrutiny. *Giving away too much.*

"My new apprentice," Angeline had said smoothly. "She is here to learn my craft."

Nella had quickly adjusted her expression, catching the tone beneath the words.

"Good," Angeline said with a wry smile. The girl learned quickly. She would do well, go far.

Or perhaps not so far at all, Angeline thought. *Perhaps she would stay right here.* Angeline crossed to the window, silk skirts whispering over the floor, pushed up the sash to let the evening air in.

Nella blinked at her in surprise.

"You'll let all the heat out, Miss Angeline," she said with reproach in her voice,

"There's warmth enough, with the ovens burning, I should say. Are you cold?"

"No, miss, not a bit of it. I never was anywhere so warm, I'm glad not to be shivering at night. I'd have thought you'd feel the chill more than me, mind. Coming from the hot lands over the sea and all."

Angeline didn't turn away from the window. Instead, she leaned her cheek against the wooden sash. The smell of baking drifted out into the quiet evening street, and the smells of London drifted in: smoky, cool, the yeasty fog of the breweries and meat roasting in the chop houses. And through it all, the distant scent of the river.

Were her senses becoming sharper, the essence of Auntie changing her already, little by little? How would she change, as the years passed? Would her skin grow translucent, her limbs morph into tentacles? Or would it go differently for her? Only time would tell.

"I come from here, Nella," she said softly. "Only from here, the same as you."

The same as Auntie before her, and all the long line of guardians stretching into the past, into the future.

This was her city, her home. As it always had been.

As it always would be.

Sarah L. Byrne is a writer and editor in London, UK. Her short speculative fiction has appeared in various publications, including *Daily Science Fiction*, *Nature Futures*, and *Best of British Science Fiction 2016*.

www.sarahbyrne.org

N.D. JONES

Sins of the Sister

PÁNIN HURRIED past the main lobby of the Mirage Hotel, eyes cast down, and away from Melea Cross—the front desk clerk and hotel owner. At the thought of the other woman, she snorted—low and with malice. Melea would get what was coming to her, the same as everyone else. Once Pánin was free, and she would be free, blood and death would be her reward to them all.

Before turning the corner, she chanced a glance in Melea's direction. Soulless, dusky eyes stared back at her, no pupils, just twin holes of inky blackness that seemed even darker the longer her warden held her bold gaze. Wanting nothing more than to dig a sharp blade into Melea's sockets, gouging and cutting and making the bitch scream her agony, she turned away. It wasn't yet time. And Melea, at six feet and with a dangerously high magic level she didn't bother to conceal, was far too powerful right now. But Pánin was a patient woman. Besides, this piece-of-shit hotel couldn't hold her forever. Soon there would be a vacancy at the Mirage Hotel.

With purposeful strides, she walked away from the clerk, who'd already begun speaking to herself. She did this all the time, whispering, laughing, and even arguing on occasion. But there'd never been another person on the other end of Melea's odd ramblings. Just as no one else worked at the Mirage Hotel.

No matter the day or time, Melea was always there. In the main lobby and at the front desk. The scents of cinnamon, hickory, apple, and hibiscus hovered about Melea, a distasteful shroud of smells that clung to the woman's toffee-soft skin, shoulder-length braids, and days-old tunic dress.

Sighing, Pánin made her way down the drab and piss-scented hallway, passing the rooms of other inmates. The wind howled, a daily screech that splintered already cracked windows. But they wouldn't break, no matter how wickedly the wind bellowed or how hard fists and head banged against the panes.

Her lithe form glided on stale winds of pain and anger. A few steps to her room and it would begin. Once inside, she gathered a weathered book from an antique desk that had long since lost its luster. Shoved haphazardly against the peeling painted wall, the mahogany desk, like the four-poster bed, chaise lounge, and marble bathroom with claw-foot tub, teased at what the Mirage Hotel could have been or perhaps once had been before it was left to rot and turn on itself and its inhabitants. It was all a brutal form of mockery that cut deep for a woman made to rule and to subjugate.

She sat cross-legged on the threadbare Oriental rug. Opening the book, she read. This was the thousandth recitation. Tonight was the third full moon that fell between the autumn equinox and the winter solstice. The blue moon that appeared once

every ten years would seal her revenge and return to her all that
had been stolen.

Pánin's power, unlike Melea's, was undetectable. She'd made
sure of it. Gathering the ether around her, she kept her returning magic hidden under layers of false obedience and submissive
manipulation.

Melea enjoyed her power play. Relished the control she had
over the punished souls at the Mirage Hotel. She never aged.
Was as beautiful and as mysterious as she'd been when Pánin
had awakened in this hotel.

In this room.

She'd screamed then. Cursed. Cried.

How long had she been here? She wished she knew.

The one thing she did know was that she was morbidly,
depressingly alone. Well, not quite. She had her grandmother's
grimoire. It had materialized the first time she'd deigned to leave
her room. The book tempted her compliance with the red glow
of familial power and whispered promises of vengeance.

Her red-rimmed eyes ran over the well-worn pages, her mind
having memorized the passages long ago. But still, she read with
the enthusiasm of a Cuco gobbling up a fat newborn with its
razor-sharp teeth, a delectable treat to savor.

"'Queen of the demons is Lilith. She was the first wife of
Adam. Before Adam, however, was Samuel, whom she had
wed and abandoned. From the illicit union of Lilith and Adam,
demons or shedim came forth, bringing illness and plagues to
the land.

"'It is said, the quarrels between Adam and Lilith were worse
than the shrill cries of banshees on the hunt. Lilith refused to
submit to any man. In time, she left Adam, as she had done

Samuel. When three angels, sent by God, ordered her to return to Adam, she declined with a haughtiness that angered Gusion, an archangel with a penchant for bloody retribution. Even with the threat to kill a hundred of her offspring a day, Lilith still did not return to Adam. Gusion cursed her as a "she-demon" and vowed to have his revenge against Lilith and her children. He would see them all dead.'"

With reverence, she closed the book. "Your loyal servant calls you, Lilith. Adam lives again, and he has grown fat with wealth and pride. He cares nothing for others. Except one. My betrayer. I can kill him for you. In return, I want only one wish. For you to kill my betrayer. The portal to this world awaits you, dear Lilith."

The old radio crackled behind her, the reception barely audible. But Pánin, a once mighty sorceress, heard it, the solemn percussion like a lion's claws digging into her chest and shredding her icy heart.

The station and its message were meant for her ears only. This hotel of torture and torment fed off the ravaged souls of the inmates. It denied life, freedom, but gave them grotesque slivers of hope that fueled their rage and bitterness.

"In a month's time, the King and Queen of Ashanti will welcome their little prince and princess. Let us rejoice and pray for a healthy delivery. The citizens of Ashanti are—"

The radio crashed to the hardwood floor. The sorceress stood over the bits of metal and plastic, her eyes glowing a violent shade of venomous red. It was time to open the portal. Time to make Osei Tutu and Ataá Kúmaa pay.

❁

"Osei Kofi Tutu I led the largest alliance of Ashanti against the Denkyira in a great and fierce battle. Magic and the scent of blood thickened the humid night air, turning men into beasts and the battlefield into a wasteland. Warriors clashed, blood spurted, and men savaged. And the Sorceress of Jukwaa looked on, relishing her destruction. But in the toxic vapors of the war zone waited Osei Tutu's best and most lethal weapon. When the sorceress thought the battle won, thought her victory assured, she emerged from the ether of magic shrouding her. And it was then—"

"Are you trying to scare them so they'll never want to come out?" Kúmaa looked down the line of her body at her husband. Admittedly, it was a bit difficult to see him past her ever-increasing stomach. And the fact that Osei lay on his own stomach, facing her, head between her raised legs didn't help.

Osei raised himself onto his elbows, rubbed and kissed her belly, and then sat up. "I was just about to get to the good part."

Only a descendant of Osei Tutu I, the Ashantehene, King of all Ashanti, would define what happened next as "the good part." Death was never good, no matter its seeming necessity.

Kúmaa closed her eyes and settled deeper into the plush gold and white bed linens. Her mind traveled, as it often did, to the past.

"Kúmaa, I will kill them all. They deserve to die. Every male."

"You can't. You mustn't."

"But I will, and you will be by my side. It's our way, sister."

"A bloody bond. That's no way to live, Pánin. Not anymore. Can't you see? Do you have no love in your heart?"

"Only for you. Only ever for you. Now come, let us slaughter these beasts and make jewelry from their hides."

"Why the tears?"

Kúmaa opened her eyes, and Osei was now beside her, his deep-set brown eyes shimmering with concern. She had no idea how long she'd drifted to a time her mind kept replaying but her heart would rather forget.

His large, gentle hand wiped at the stray tears, then cupped her cheek. "Hormones?" His voice was so soft and tender, his worry over her health and pending birth obvious. She hated to lie to him, but the truth would be too hard and painful to explain.

She nodded.

He relaxed, then smiled. "Well, it won't be much longer. Just a couple of weeks more and then . . ." Osei's wide, infectious grin split his handsome face. "Then the fun part begins." He rubbed his hands together as if he were plotting a diabolical plan. "I can't wait. Twins!"

A sigh slipped from her. To the nation, to her husband, twins were a "blessing from God."

She disagreed.

Kúmaa sank further into the pillows and covered her face with swollen fingers.

Strong arms hoisted her to a seated position. As large as she'd gotten over the course of her pregnancy, Osei was still much bigger. He lifted her as if her added weight was of no significance and deposited her with care onto his lap.

"Do you want to talk about what's bothering you?"

He knew her well, but not as well as he thought he did. She couldn't give him what he wanted. Couldn't peel back the rancid layers of lies that brought her equal parts pleasure and pain.

Leaning her forehead against Osei's thick neck, Kúmaa inhaled his fresh, masculine scent. "I'm just tired and a little hormonal. Nothing more. I'm sure it will pass."

Lifting her chin with a single finger, Osei planted a sweet kiss on her lips.

She smiled into the kiss before opening her mouth and inviting her husband inside, though he never needed much of an invitation. He swooped in, claiming all she offered, all she willingly gave.

He tasted divine—like innocence and youth. But unrealized wisdom was there, in the roaming hands and tongue, in the pounding heart. The longer they kissed, the more magic sparked between them. The magic of a demon witch and her soul-bonded human.

Pulling out of the kiss, Osei appeared both sheepish and aroused. "It's too late in your pregnancy for what I want to do to you." He glanced from the noticeable erection in his boxers to her belly full with their children. "Doctor's orders. Bed rest and no sex."

Yes, Kúmaa remembered. She frowned.

Laughing, Osei kissed the tip of her nose, then settled her under the covers. Taking his usual spot, he fitted himself against her back, one hand tucked under her pillow, the other splayed across her belly.

She loved this male. Loved him more than anything or anyone else. And wasn't that a sin? It had to be, for she'd sacrificed all for him. A sister's trust. A twin's freedom.

Please forgive me, Ataá Pánin.

※

As Pánin stared out of the window of her prison room and up to the glowing blue moon, she sent her demon spirit outward and to the Daka River, a perfect ley line of magic the sorceress could tap into on this rare night. Pánin's spirit knelt on the rocky sand at the shore of the river, her dingy black cloak concealing her head and her intentions. A small smile creased her lovely face. The smile felt odd, the muscles out of practice.

Her smile grew. After tonight, she'd have much for which to smile.

"'Wildcats shall meet with hyenas, goat-demons shall call to each other. There too Lilith shall repose, and find a place to rest.'"

Her betrayer wouldn't live long enough to bring her bastard children into the world. Lilith would rise, no longer in repose. The strange, brooding reflection in Isaiah 34:14, on the tragedy of a woman left cursed and broken, but never completely forgotten, was a myth to many. But not to her, not to one who understood the mystical arts, the wickedness of God's curse and his allegiance with man over woman. Women weren't meant to be subservient to men. The idea of Eve coming from Adam's rib as a symbol of the submissive role of women was absurd and demeaning.

Pánin raised light-brown eyes to the rare blue moon, and the wicked show of teeth broadened, slicing through the grim shadows like a lethal scythe. Her hands gripped the muddy, wet sand, and the water from the shore lapped against her knees, dousing her cloak in its cool moisture.

She'd waited for this night, prayed for the return of the power-granting blue moon. The massive ball of blue magic seemed to sparkle even brighter for her, lifting her ragged spirit and purging her scorched soul with a light of optimism.

"Lilith, I call on thee. Oh great she-demon of myth, she-demon of vengeance, hear my call, heed my plea. Come forth and help me take revenge against those who've trespassed against us. Come forth and free your child, your faithful servant. Kúmaa awaits her judgment. Judge her now, Lilith. Judge her now."

She closed her eyes and sank her hands deeper into the sand. Head falling to her knees, Pánin recited the prayer again and again.

After the fifth recitation, she stood, drenched in the sopping heat of her magical workings. Opening her eyes, the sorceress raised her outstretched hands.

"I open this watery portal for you, dear Lilith. I welcome you to the modern world of man, the world of Adam, the world of Ashanti. I open this watery portal for you, dear Lilith. I welcome you to the world of greed. I open this watery portal for you, dear Lilith. I welcome you to fill your cup, to take our revenge."

A volcanic gush of water exploded from the depths of the Daka River. A whirling tornado of red and gold liquid nectar gleamed in the night sky, reaching out to the blue moon in its fervor to be free.

"I open this portal for you, my savior," the sorceress said, dropping to her knees as the tornado of water erupted from the confines of the river and onto the sandy shore where Pánin knelt.

From the red and gold specks of rotating water, she could discern a head, legs, and arms. Not yet fully formed but well on their way.

"I have pledged myself to you and you to me, dear Lilith. By coming through my portal, you have accepted my call, my plea. You know what I seek."

Almost imperceptibly, the vague head in the spiraling water nodded.

"Go forth and do my bidding. But understand, she is yours, but he is mine."

The red and gold specks exploded, and water cascaded down on her in a heavy shower of satisfied acceptance. Then Lilith was gone, a stream of water vapor slithering to the north, toward Kumasi, the capital of Ashanti and home of her enemies.

❈

Dull gray surrounded Kúmaa, like a fog rolling off a toxic lake and onto a deserted pier. The vaguest glimmer of light glowed in the far-off distance, but not so far that Kúmaa's dark-brown eyes couldn't make out its beauty.

And it was beautiful, the tiny sliver of light daring to breach the dreary cold of the morbid fog. Kúmaa lifted her hand and reached for the light, drawing back when she met bitterness instead of warmth. Sadness and anger suddenly permeated the fog, the smell of the malevolent brew rancid and ancient.

"Who are you?" Kúmaa asked, taking a blind step forward.

"Who are you?" echoed back, a distorted version of Kúmaa's voice.

Another blind step. And another. She walked along an invisible path. The feeling of sand squished below her bare feet, the tiny granules sticking to toes. As she walked toward the beacon of light, Kúmaa repeated the same question. "Who are you?"

After long minutes and with no response, she added, "What do you want?" She repeated the questions, ignoring the reverberation of her voice—the only reply.

Then there was another sound, another voice in the fog.

Crying. A baby?

Kúmaa stopped walking, turned in the direction of the faint sound and listened carefully. Not a baby. A whimpering woman.

She moved as swiftly as she could, her twins making her slow and cautious. Hands outstretched in front of her, she inched closer toward the sound.

Kúmaa halted when sand gave way to rough ground and sharp rocks that cut into her exposed feet.

The sound came again, but Kúmaa dared not move. But she saw the source of the weeping—a female figure on the other side of the ravine. Kúmaa's eyes dropped to the huge chasm that separated her from the crying woman—its depth forbidding.

The woman's long onyx hair was wrapped around her body like a heavy shawl, hiding portions of her nude form. Bronze and beautiful, the woman sat at the edge of the ravine, her tears the source of the water Kúmaa had seen at the bottom.

Out her eyes.

Down her cheeks.

Into the ravine. No splash. Just a ripple of grief and hatred.

"Who are you?" Kúmaa asked again.

No answer, but the woman's tears had filled the ravine.

Kúmaa stepped back from the river's edge, the rocks cutting even deeper into her feet. The weeping woman raised her face and looked directly at Kúmaa. She saw them, the woman's eyes.

Blood seeped from the corners of her eyes, and the beauty Kúmaa thought she had seen was marred by a face contorted in unbelievable agony, undeniable pain.

Kúmaa continued to retreat but refused to turn and run. She had the woman's attention now, but damn if she really wanted it. Not like this, not when the woman, *the thing*, was looking like death incarnate.

"Who are you? Why are you here?" Kúmaa asked again, now fearing the answer.

The woman's head twisted, glaring at Kúmaa with heart-clinching curiosity. A black python appeared. It slithered from the bloody froth of the river and found the woman's leg. Slowly, very slowly, it inched its way from her ankle, up her thigh, and to her shoulder, where it managed to glide its way between her shoulder blades and her impossibly long hair.

There it rested, its body curled around the woman's, its head falling to her midsection, stopping right above her pubic area, looking like the scariest fig leaf Kúmaa had ever seen.

With blinding realization, an image popped into her mind. A scene she'd seen many times in books, museums, and paintings.

"Eve?"

The woman's eyes came to life, the black giving way to fire red. Blood blazed from them. Streaks of red slithered and stained her face, her body, her snake.

A waterfall of crimson.

"Not Eve," the woman growled, her voice a thunderous cloud of magic and menace.

She placed one foot in the river, then the other, and Kúmaa gasped. The river held her weight, her toes and heels as firm on the flowing liquid as a tree on the sturdiest of soils.

Kúmaa couldn't move. She tried, screamed at herself to take a step backward for each one the bloodied woman took toward her. Nothing. Was she paralyzed with fear? Or simply paralyzed?

Move dammit, move. A silent yell inside her head.

Nothing.

And the woman came nearer.

She was so close Kúmaa could smell her breath—volcanic ash and death.

The blood that ran from the woman now washed over Kúmaa, bringing with it the scales of the python.

The snake's forked tongue slipped into her ear. The smell of brimstone assailed her nostrils, burning them and creating a liquid mix of tears and blood.

The snake spoke to her, but it was the woman's voice she heard. "Do you know me now?"

God in Heaven, she did.

"You protected him when you should've cast your fealty with your sister."

The forked tongue withdrew and so did the scaly beast.

Kúmaa didn't watch it glide down the demon's body and into the river of churning blood. She was too focused on the eyes she hadn't seen in centuries.

Eyes that haunted her dreams.

Eyes that saw her for the betrayer she'd been. The betrayer she still was.

"You are no innocent to pain, to heartache, my child. I felt it as soon as I saw you. I wanted to bask in the glorious rays of your anguish, the grief and guilt you know so well."

Arctic lips dripping with blood pressed to Kúmaa's forehead, bringing back more memories of old. "Say my name, daughter. Claim me, as you once did. As your sister still does."

She didn't want to say the cursed name. Didn't want to be there, across from this monster whose blood ran through Kúmaa's veins. Whose blood of her human and demon children stained her hands but not her selfish soul.

She felt her little ones move within. And though she was still paralyzed, Kúmaa gave an inward smile. They were with her, safe inside and hers to protect.

The way her so-called mother should've protected her children. As Adam should've protected his wife. As God should have protected them all.

An inhumanly strong hand came to Kúmaa's throat. Nails pierced sweaty skin, and blood droplets formed and fell.

"I said say my name, daughter, or I'll slit your throat before cutting my children from your womb."

Defiant tears bubbled, and with a strength that surprised her, Kúmaa fought through the paralyzing magic enough to raise a hand to her belly. It wasn't much, but she would fight for her children. Kill for them. But first, she needed to survive this most unwelcome of family reunions.

"Lilith." She spat the name on a spray of blood.

But the demon didn't care. Her lips lifted into a satisfied sneer. Then she licked the blood from them, smacking and smiling at Kúmaa with a childlike devilment that sent chills down Kúmaa's spine.

"You think you aren't like me," Lilith said, "but you are. All my daughters are. In time, you'll see that no man can be trusted. They will turn on you, just as Adam turned on me."

Her twin had thought the same. For too many years, so had Kúmaa. But when she'd been captured by the Ashanti, it had been Osei Kofi Tutu I who'd spared her life. He'd told his warriors, "Men of honor do not slaughter innocent women for fear they will stab them in the back when they sleep. We take care of them. And they will take care of us. When we slumber, our sleep will be peaceful because we have earned each other's trust and love."

She did not tell Lilith this. Self-preservation kept her silent.

"He defiled you when you were captured."

He hadn't.

Kúmaa's virginity had been a gift she'd pleasured in giving to Osei Kofi Tutu.

Lilith flicked her eyes down to Kúmaa's stomach and the hand that rested protectively across it. "And he's defiled you once more." Dark eyes lifted. "He broke our Trinity. And you allowed him to trick you into betraying your sister."

Lilith had been wrong then. She knew no more all these centuries later—neither about Kúmaa's heart nor about good men like Osei.

The Mother of Demons' eyes fell, once more, to Kúmaa's pregnant stomach. The scent of sulfur rose from the river of blood, and the blinding fog returned.

And something else. Something wet and scaly.

Lilith's python was back. And it wasn't alone. Five. Ten. Twenty. Kúmaa could not tell. God, they struck out at her, biting into her with vicious, vengeful fangs. They sent her crashing to the rocky ground. On her back and without her magic, Kúmaa could do nothing when they attacked her stomach.

Tearing their way inside, the snakes feasted.

Kúmaa screamed in agony, in terror that she could not protect her children. She bled, cried, and heard Lilith whisper, "You have been judged."

※

On this night of the sacred blue moon, Pánin's demon spirit would have her revenge. And there he was, Osei Tutu, the man who'd ripped her world apart. Tall of frame, broad of shoulders, and arrogant of heart, the unsuspecting male took in the blue and green nursery. The room disgusted Pánin, even more evidence of how fully her sister had betrayed her. And Kúmaa would willingly birth this male's children?

Blasphemy.

The door's hinges creaked when it slammed shut behind him. Osei spun around, raising his hands, prepared to use magic to defend himself. But it wouldn't come, not on this night of Lilith's emancipation and the rise of her demon child of retribution. Not when the sorceress's spirit drew from the Daka River's ley line of magic, encasing this room and Osei Tutu within an impenetrable wall of mythos and menace.

He scanned the room, a fiber-optic light the only illumination. Not that it mattered, he couldn't see her, but she made sure the oppressor of women knew he was in the presence of a she-demon. Her sulfurous scent was cloying and unmistakable.

Osei whirled to the right, then left, searching for the demon he now knew shared the space with him in a nursery that would never hold the sleeping forms of his wretched offspring.

A blast of red energy sent him flying against the back wall. He lessened the impact the best he could, using his arms and legs to break his fall. But the sizzling handprint on his chest had him staggering to his feet.

"You will not survive this night. But you are free to try. Defend yourself, male, if you can."

Osei Tutu backed up against the closest wall, a window to his left. He raised his elbow, and she smiled, knowing, even if she allowed him to break it, only the mystical elements of the Daka River waited on the other side. No freedom, just a sorceress's well-planned revenge.

An energy blast rocked him against the two cribs. This time, he didn't have time to break his fall.

Crash. Down he went, breaking furniture and hitting his head on the hardwood floor. Osei's left shoulder and side had taken the brunt of the attack. Flesh hissed down his arm and dripped onto the floor.

Pushing to his feet, Osei squinted into the darkness. "Who are you? What do you want?"

"Death. Revenge."

Her contempt for the male reverberated through the room.

Holding his dangling arm, Osei slid along the walls until he found the door. Reaching behind him, he wiggled the knob. The foolish man. How could her sister ever give her heart and body to such a worthless creature?

"She was supposed to lure you to her bed, weaken you with her body and her magic." Her brittle laugh was full of resentment. "She did both. Males are disgustingly weak of flesh. You thought you saved her from your warriors. Thought yourself the mighty Ashantehene who'd protected a weak damsel of a witch."

Another laugh, laced with so much loathing, the sulfur in the room thickened.

"Tell me how I've aggrieved you."

"How you've aggrieved me? You took everything I loved, everything I held dear. She betrayed me because of you. Me! The Sorceress of Jukwaa."

"Sorceress of Jukwaa? No, no, that makes no sense. That she-demon was killed by my ancestor Osei Kofi Tutu's—"

Brutal laughter slashed across his face, jolting him forward and down to the floor. Two more slashes landed against his side, breaking ribs. Smartly, the male rolled out of the way, just as Pánin sent another blast of red energy toward him, grazing his forehead and leaving a trail of blood fire.

Laboring to breathe, Osei stood. He coughed and choked from the sulfuric fumes, her demon scent disorienting and poisonous.

"For what you've done, no amends are possible. You have taken from me, and now I will take from you. Everything. Everything you love. Everything you cherish. Your every dream and desire. And when you die, when you truly, finally die, she won't be able to reincarnate you. This will be your last life."

Pánin was upon him, invisible hands clutching his neck, lifting Osei as if he weighed no more than a sprite. He struck out, and strong, vicious blows connected. But she didn't let go. Osei twisted and kicked and fought with all his might.

"Stop it!" She held Osei close, encircling him in her acidic vapors and burning through skin, flesh, and bone. "You will not deny me."

He gagged on the blood bubbling past his lips as he whispered his undying love for a wife and children who no longer existed. Just as he would soon be dead.

Sweet revenge.

Pánin laughed.

❄

Melea was bored . . . and thirsty. She'd seen this scene all before—one century bleeding into the next. But Gusion, a fallen angel who had a long memory and a ravenous appetite for vengeance and torture, smiled.

Wickedly handsome and dark, Gusion's thickly corded dreadlocks hung down his wide, muscular back, covering the permanent scars of his fall from grace. His lack of wings, however, didn't make him any less powerful. If anything, the ugly, jagged reminders of his banishment gave him a sexy, roguish appeal. So appealing that Melea Cross had given her soul and her hotel to him. And he'd turned it into one of his many hellacious playhouses.

Melea stood inside room 169, next to Gusion.

He smiled, and she knew he was pleased. The twins always pleased him.

They slept on a queen-sized bed, naked as the day they were birthed but no closer to reconciling their hearts despite the bonded souls of sisterhood.

Creeping closer, Melea cast her eyes over the pair, waiting for them to awaken. So innocent did they appear in tortured slumber.

So beautiful.

So damned.

"How much longer?" When the fallen angel remained silent, Melea didn't bother repeating the question. Instead, she said, "Show me again."

A draft of thrilled magic eased over Melea, curling about her tall frame until she stood enveloped in the cool mists of Gusion's devilment. She breathed it in with sensual pleasure.

Her eyes closed, and she drifted back. When she opened them, men were everywhere—bloodying, fighting, and dying. Burning torches of magic lit the blackened sky, casting wild, wide eyes into hellish relief.

Unflinching warriors screamed their battle cries and met their enemies with daggers, spears, and shields.

Broken and bloodied, the men fought. Through exhaustion. Through pain. But they were mere pawns of the one who hid in the shadows, her demonic powers fueling their anger and strength.

Melea knew what came next. She'd been there before, on this ancient field of battle, in this forest of love and loss, encased by the sweet smell of sin.

The Sorceress of Jukwaa stepped from the ether that concealed her presence. Wavy, black hair spilled onto bare shoulders and over naked breasts. Her single item of clothing, a red and black wrap, fell to her knees.

Raising her hands, aglow with red energy that matched her glowing eyes, the sorceress joined the battle. But she took no sides, massacring the men of Denkyira, who she'd manipulated into waging war against Osei Kofi Tutu as mercilessly as she slaughtered the Ashanti warriors.

Hacking one after another with her slicing magic, the sorceress cackled as decapitated heads fell, severed limbs spurted, and men's screams filled the carnivorous night air.

A matching bolt of red demon energy slammed into the sorceress. Spinning, eyes and hands searching for the one who dared to attack her, she met none other than the echoing form of her twin sister.

"Kúmaa? What do you think you're—"

"You must stop. This isn't right."

The sorceress's glowing red eyes searched the tall, wide trees behind her sister. When she spotted her next victim, her full lips lifted into a vicious sneer before she turned four already dead warriors into Asanbosams.

The corpses grew, stretching and twisting, pulling and contorting until they were hideous fifteen-foot ogres with burnt umber skin, iron teeth that protruded from wide, salivating mouths, and iron-hooked feet that turned to where the sorceress pointed.

"Get the Ashantehene and bring him to me," she ordered.

With a wild gait that shook the forest floor, the four ogres bounded after their prey.

"No!" Kúmaa screamed, her magic flaring up and outward. The beams of red demon energy hit two of the ogres in their backs, disintegrating them on contact. The other two crashed into a formidable force field.

"You can't protect him."

"Stop this, Pánin, before more people die." With barely a twitch of her hand, two more beams of demon energy raced from Kúmaa to the ogres banging against the force field. Unlike the noise of carnage surrounding the she-demons, the ogres made no sound when their bodies exploded and turned to dust.

"Look around, Kúmaa, there's an entire forest of men I could use to kill your little plaything. But I shouldn't have to. It was your job to get close to the Ashantehene." Pánin stepped toward her sister. "You permitted yourself to be captured for that very purpose." A glowing hand came up and slapped Kúmaa across her face. "Now you ally yourself with that male over your own flesh and blood." Another brutal slap.

Kúmaa stood her ground, accepting her sister's fury with loving yet unwavering eyes.

When the sorceress made to level yet another blow, Kúmaa caught her by the wrist.

The air around the twins quieted, no screams of pain, no death cries or agonal gasps, no clanging of shields. Just Gusion's magic and Melea's enraptured eyes taking in the moment that had both damned and freed the twins.

"Please stop." A soft, desperate plea from Kúmaa.

"I won't stop. They must all die. Lilith said they must all—"

Kúmaa yanked her sister forward. Wrapping magic and arms around the woman, Kúmaa held Pánin in a fierce embrace, her tear-streaked face buried in her sister's thick, wavy hair.

"We are the last of Lilith's children, Pánin, and it is our time. We can no longer run from our fate. I'm tired, so very tired. And if I can't have Osei, then I'll have my judgment."

The sorceress pushed against her sister, but to no effect.

"Let me go! Curse you, Kúmaa. Release me at once."

"I'm sorry. Please forgive me."

The bloodstained ground below the women cracked and opened. They fell.

Osei Kofi Tutu ran toward the swiftly closing chasm, Kúmaa's name on his tongue. He dropped to his hands and knees, searching the ground that had swallowed his beloved.

Melea shook her head at the vision of a fool. He'd fallen in love with one of Lilith's cursed children. And Kúmaa had selfishly bound his soul to hers when she'd lain with him. They would never have a happily-ever-after. Only love and loss.

"It's time," Gusion said. Melea opened her eyes. Tendrils of Gusion's magic ebbed as she regained her bearings.

With a long, dark finger, Gusion touched Kúmaa's forehead.

As always, she awoke with tears in her eyes. She'd died countless times at the hands of her sister and Lilith. Yet she'd also tasted moments of love and bliss with her Osei, Gusion's timeless gift.

But it came at a high price. Kúmaa's penance was not enough to absolve her of her past sins.

A trembling hand rose to a flat, childless stomach, and Kúmaa wept even more. A life and family with Osei had been Kúmaa's greatest desire in the end as she plummeted from life into death and straight to the Mirage Hotel.

Gusion, the fallen angel who could discern the past, present, and future, had granted Kúmaa her final wish. In his own way, of course.

And he'd granted Pánin hers.

The sorceress had created her own hell, wanting nothing more than to punish her sister and kill the man responsible for turning Kúmaa against her. Getting her heart's desire every night wasn't her punishment.

Pánin sprang from the bed, eyes searching the room, then cursing and screeching when she realized she was still in room 169, and it had all been a cruel dream.

That was the Sorceress of Jukwaa's hell—to taste victory, to have her glorious revenge, and to then awaken in this hotel out of time and place, tricked by her mind and Gusion's vindictive cunning.

One twin cried, while the other screamed bloody murder. But neither knew the other was there, sharing the same room and feeding off of one another's deepest emotions.

Tomorrow it would begin again with Kúmaa dreaming of Osei Kofi Tutu. She'd bring him back to life as one of his descendants. They'd meet and fall in love as Kúmaa remembered the first Osei and their soul bond.

Kúmaa's happy dream would trigger Pánin's vengeful one. It was an endless cycle of pleasure, pain, and sisterhood.

Melea quirked her lips.

He may have been cast out of Heaven after losing his perspective and his wings in pursuit of Lilith and her demon offspring, but he'd won in the end. They all belonged to Gusion, perpetual tenants at the Mirage Hotel.

Gusion smiled, then disappeared.

Melea closed the door to room 169. There was a tasty cup of spiced apple cider rooibos tea waiting for her at the front desk.

N. D. Jones lives in Maryland with her husband and two children. She is a dedicated educator, committed to equitable and excellent education for all students. N.D. has served in the role as teacher, department chair, and professional development teacher specialist, supporting the learning of students and the professional growth of teachers. She writes what she sees as a dearth in the romance genre — African/African American love with a paranormal twist. She spends a lot of time developing the mythology of her novels, as well as the execution of the paranormal element. When she writes a book with witches and shapeshifters, for example, she thinks it's important to show what it means to be a witch and shapeshifter. That's one thing a reader of books by N.D. can look forward to. The paranormal is not a sidebar in her novels. It's center stage and critical to the plot.

www.ndjonesparanormalpleasure.com

JAMES PYNE

Yemayah

YEMAYAH SLOWLY SPUN through space without an
Extravehicular Mobility Unit; her lungs breathed the thin air
molecules just fine. Her proud, regal face still showed through
the damage done by an intense heat blast: one eye puffed shut,
with long deep gouges down one side of her face, the rest of
her dark skin scorched here and there. Her sword twirled around
her, mocking her, out of her reach; death was better than this
fate. Much of her armor was melted and tattered; her once
crimson wings were now singed around the edges and looked
moth-eaten in places. She was a massive wreck from the last
and final war of her kind. It seemed she was the only survivor
within this tormenting darkness, with every other living thing
and every planet and every sun, everything, obliterated by a
technology that many had warned a stubborn few to abandon.
Or had the starburst of a thousand planets exploding somehow
pushed her into this empty dimension? She'd run through a million scenarios with no way of confirming any of them.

   Like every living species, she emitted a microbial cloud;
it included dust from her world, emissions from her dented

armor and her humanoid skin, along with wiggly bacteria. The glow of the microbes moving from and about her body was the only light source in this void; some drifted or swam away into the darkness like sperm cells. Not long ago, focusing on such tiny things was hardly worth the strain, but now, all alone in mostly blackness, watching germs swirl about was the only entertainment left besides her memories. Recollections that had once made her smile now tormented her, made her yearn for the company of family and friends and even enemies.

There was regret, of course, as there always was with the life of a defender; the biggest regret was never mothering any younglings, though she had treated many as her own, adopting them into her family, helping them on the path of enlightenment. She had chosen the glorious path of being the champion and liberator of the oppressed. A mother figure to them all.

But she'd gladly turn in her sword, all her medals and victories, all those times her enemies had bowed to her for mercy, she would turn all of that in to breathe in the old forest scent of home one last time. To see the loving smile of her mother, to taste a home-cooked meal of *ugali*, to feel the unconditional love of her father, Obatala, even when she didn't deserve it, to experience the taunting of her older brother, Aganyu, to see the look on her brother's face when she rescued him from bullies after so many years of him protecting her. To witness the burst of the sunrise stretching across the sky like flaming wings. She would never see that again. She'd never again be awestruck at the sight of her planet's two moons turning everything and everybody into shades of rust, a sight that never tired her imagination; now the memory of it depressed her. She longed for the feel of branches scratching her face and burdocks sticking to her clothes and hair as she frantically searched for friends who were hiding in the woods, determined not to be found and tagged "it" because then it would be her turn to run and hide, and no one wanted that because no one ever found her. She missed her youth, when things were simpler. She missed it, the good and bad.

I want those simpler days back, she wanted to shout, but her vocal cords were shot. *I'll do anything,* she shouted in her head. *I'll do whatever it takes. Please.* But this dark place didn't answer back. She kept slowly spinning, slowly dying, as if this place prolonged her death. Would it even let her die? Was this her fate, spinning forever in this emptiness, forever alive? *I don't deserve this. I defended the weak. I mortified bullies into shameful submission. I should be rewarded. Not punished. Damn you. Hear me! Answer me. Rescue me from this hellish abyss.* She felt the darkness staring at her, as if studying her, as if deciding whether to swallow her or let her go mad. *Then kill me. Swallow me up. Punish me for the millions I've slain by my sword. Surely some were innocents. All those orphans my sword gave birth to, that alone surely has earned me a swift end? Or is the darkness afraid of me too?* She laughed, loud, in her head at such a thought. *That's it, then. The darkness is spineless in the presence of Yemayah.*

She'd kill herself with her sword if she could. Such an act was an honorable thing amongst her clan. With her kind dead, there was no point in her existence. Her living on was just a mockery of a once great race that had tamed the universe but couldn't tame its own ambitions. *You mock me by allowing me to live on. Like a beast trapped in a cage, the last of its species for you to point and laugh at it.* A finger moved; it was all she could will. If only she could close all digits but one and give the darkness the middle finger.

Hear my thoughts. I want to experience the jarring cold of the ocean, the gritty sand of Skeleton Beach between my toes as I explore the wreckage along it, feel the sun tan my skin, the scent of lilies at a wedding, lilacs in the spring, that ozone smell after a heavy rainfall. Let me experience it all one more time. Just once more. Why is it so much to ask for? You've got to be out there. We existed. So, you surely must. Her kind believed in a greater power. It had been the cause of many of their wars early on in their evolution, with everyone fighting over whose version was the closest to whatever the Supreme Being was. *I know you're listening. Answer me, dammit.* She sometimes imagined the universe was actually inside this Supreme Being's head, and somehow, they had blown it apart with technology they weren't ready for, and she was all that remained while the Supreme Being was immortally comatose. Silly notions of someone going insane. Madness in such a hopeless situation was the only way one could cope.

The microbes abandoned her like escape pods from a mother ship, not that she blamed them; she was doomed, a sinking ship, now blending in with the darkness. What was odd was the speed with which they were ditching her. They rushed toward each other and embraced, with some suddenly spiriting off into comets. The sudden rapid breakdown of her spiraling sword, the fast deterioration of her armor and flaking skin, all of it joined with the microbes, forming new rocks, some misshapen. One lit up like a sun and showed a new solar system to her as she swirled away from it.

She was dying, then. Slowly. Pain became more prevalent, as if her endorphins couldn't keep up with the sudden velocity of her breaking apart. Pieces of her charred skin broke off, forming black holes. Microscopic pieces scattered from her whirling body; they were like giant objects in this new universe. She fell apart quicker with the pain getting louder, making her mad in the head . . . she wondered if life would form on those new planets, and would those inhabitants follow the same doomed path of her kind or blaze their own trail?

I accept the pain, she shouted in her head. She smiled inside. *Like a mother feels pain giving birth. Look at me. The Life Bringer. I'm a goddess now.*

She slowly broke apart, becoming the universe, her good and bad memories its foundation.

James Pyne was born in New Glasgow, Nova Scotia. His writing has recently appeared in *Grey Matter Monsters, Clockwork Wonderland, Renegades of Prose, X5, Death and Decorations, Only the Light We Make,* and is forthcoming in many others. Feel free to add him on Facebook.

www.facebook.com/jjamespyne

J.S. EMUAKPOR

Descent

I WALKED across the vast emptiness of sun-hardened and cracked red earth, steadily approaching the figure that stood in the center of that desolate landscape. Arms folded, he regarded me with an expression that I could neither decipher nor be bothered to ponder. One thousand years of exile had wearied me. I could not care less what thoughts percolated in the mind of the god of the Crossroads.

"Thus, the prodigal son returns." A slow grin spread across Nakada's face. "I knew you would come."

"You knew I had no choice," I said dryly.

"We all have a choice, Brother."

"I am not your brother."

"That is a mere technicality."

Upon reaching him, I stood, hand on the pommel of my sword, regarding him down the length of my nose. Having spent the last thousand years masquerading as a mortal and failing woefully in that endeavor, I realized how much more human than me Nakada appeared. His height, not quite a head shorter than mine, would be far less intimidating amongst men, though he stood a good five inches taller than most. Nakada, likely the most deceptive of us all, would have been welcomed where I had been greeted with loathing and mistrust. Even his skin, with its coppery hue, implied a warmth of character he did not possess; whereas my skin was the cold, impenetrable dark of a starless night.

"Why are you so sour, Dafaru?" He uncrossed his arms. "You are home, filled with the divine. You should be ecstatic and doing what Dafaru has always done best."

Ignoring his now outstretched arms, I slid the longsword from its scabbard and rested its tip on his chest. "I am the god of war. Do you want me to show you what I do best?"

"Ah." He glanced down at the sword, the smile never leaving his face. "And I once thought you were the god of drink."

"Just show me the way, trickster."

The god of the Crossroads rolled his eyes. "Great Father God Almighty, you have grown dull." He turned and strode into the vastness, calling over his shoulder, "And insufferably heroic."

I followed, my longer stride bringing me quickly to his side. As we walked, the landscape transformed around us. From the desolation of a sand sea, over the blinding white of a snow-capped mountain, and through the void of a blackness so complete that it seemed I had fallen into Nakada's eyes. His eyes—two gateways to infinity—were the only things about him that could not pass as human. None of our eyes could. Even when I had lost my divinity, my eyes had not been quite *normal*.

We traveled through the changing landscapes for what may have been seconds, hours, weeks, or years. My long association with the mortals had made me sensitive to the passage of time;

I now measured it in much smaller increments. But in Nakada's demesne, time did not progress in a linear fashion.

He came to a halt and I stopped beside him. We had been traveling between two mountain ridges and now stood in a narrow crag, sandstone peaks rising high above us into the pale and cloudless sky. Raising a hand, Nakada brushed his fingers along the stone. A crack appeared in the stone's face. It spread outward, horizontally, from Nakada's fingers and then angled downward at each end to outline a doorway. Silently, the outlined piece of rock slid backward, revealing the darkness within.

Nakada faced me. No grin, no mischief. "You tread a dangerous path, Dafaru. If your Father—"

"My Father contemplates loftier matters."

He inhaled and let out a loud sigh. "Once you enter, you will be powerless."

I shrugged. I had been powerless for a thousand years; I could survive one trip through the underworld. Still, I found myself adjusting the leather arm bracers that channeled my powers. Ducking my head to keep from hitting the low doorway, I entered the dark passage.

"Remember," Nakada said. "If you are still there when the sun sets upon the sea, you will be lost."

"Noted." I kept walking and resisted the temptation to glance back, lest he assume a lack of resolve on my part. My commitment to this task was unwavering. Either I succeeded, or I gave myself over to the Demon Lord.

The sound of stone scraping against stone came from behind me. The door, which had quietly opened, was now sliding noisily back into place. I should have brought a torch. Without my power, the dark shroud descending upon the passageway would be, in fact, *dark*. To my surprise, however, it was not. As the seams around the door disappeared, taking with them the orange tint of the outside world, the walls came to life.

Hundreds of pairs of eyes. Human eyes—or perhaps what had once been human eyes—blinked open on the walls. Each pair glowed soft green to coat the passage a ghastly shade. *These* humans, at least, were useful.

I followed the passage. There were no forks, thus no other routes to contemplate. The farther I went, the danker the air. Time passed, though I could tell neither how much nor how little, and a dull light marked the approaching end of the tunnel. I quickened my pace as the sound of water lapping against a shore reached my ears.

Near the end, other tunnels spilled into mine. I peered into each as I passed and saw no other beings—human or demon. Grey-yellow light soon met me at the tunnel's mouth, which opened onto a vast sea with tiny waves splashing murky water into the tunnel. I moved to the opening and leaned out. The sea was at my feet. The cliff wall spread to my right, left, and high above me until it disappeared into the misty gloom. Tens of thousands of tunnels terminated all over the cliff face, and at each arched opening, a small canoe either awaited, was arriving, was loading a dead soul, or had undocked to ferry its cargo across the water.

This was the Sea of Oblivion, much as Nakada had described it, and this, he said, was as far as he had ever come. His demon refugees claimed the oarless canoes were attuned only to the dead and to the soulless. As I was neither, no boat awaited me. I would have to find some other way across.

Sea and mist came together far in the distance. It was impossible to see where that distance lay or even what might be found on the other side. In any other realm and with my powers intact, I might have attempted the swim, irrespective of how far and in spite of the agonized, twisted dead faces silently screaming beneath the water's surface. However, if the demons were to be trusted—and Nakada seemed to inspire their loyalty—the water was an extension of Maciji's own being. Were I to swim across, the Demon Lord would become aware of my presence here. The last thing I needed was for him to find me before I found *her*.

I turned back and took one of the offshoot passages, as there was no point in going the way I had come. This tunnel was identical to the other in size, shape, and illumination—nothing distinguished the two. The eyes followed my movements as I passed, and it occurred to me that there might be minds behind those glowing green orbs.

A shadow moved in my peripheral vision. I turned toward it, but it was gone. Aside from the souls in the boats, this was the first time I had come across anyone—any*thing*—else. In the domain of the dead, many objects could occupy the same space at the same time and never know it. Whatever I had seen, it would reappear or it would not. Even as that thought manifested in my mind, the shadow darted across my field of vision. I went after it.

The thing was fast. It surged down the corridor, and I could not tell if it was of mortal derivation or demon. At a fork in the passage, it veered right. I ran after it and entered the right-side tunnel, which quickly widened into a cavern. A few more paces in, the shadow unfurled from the ground. I halted and pulled back, watching as the blackness dissolved to reveal an old man.

He was famine thin, which coupled with the green glow emanating from the walls to give him an ephemeral yet grizzled appearance. "All paths lead to oblivion." His voice was as feeble as he looked and belied his surefooted speed.

"I do not seek oblivion, old man."

"I do," he said. "I have wandered these passages for so long that I can't remember who I am. Who I *was*. In life."

"Who you were is of no relevance to me."

"Spoken like one who reeks of life," he said with a sneer. Sharp eyes scanned me from head to toe. "Only the dead may cross the Sea of Oblivion. Or a demon. Are you a demon?"

He did not wait for a response, but sniffed and said, "No. The odor of the netherhells is only faint upon you. Not like a demon." He crumpled to a heap in front of me. "Only the dead may cross the Sea of Oblivion."

"What lies beyond the sea?"

The man shrugged. "I will never know. That is my punishment."

My brows rose heavenward, if indeed heaven was above me. *Humans.* Even dead they were irritating. But this man would not distract me from my purpose.

"Unless you can get me across the sea and to Maciji, I suggest you remove yourself from my path."

The old man raised his head at the mention of Maciji. "Who are you? No one seeks out the Demon Lord."

"Clearly, I am no one."

His eyes narrowed. "Maciji resides at the heart of this realm. You must cross the Sea of Oblivion to reach him." He looked at me from head to toe. "Only the dead may cross, and I will never find it."

"Yet you say all paths lead to oblivion."

"All paths but mine."

"Where does yours lead?"

"Here." A low strangled noise sounded in his throat. "Always here. No matter how far I wander, I always end up here."

"You are bound by magic?"

I considered the man and considered the sword on my back. A sword forged by the god of war did not easily relinquish its magic. I had made this one to sever any bonds Maciji may have placed on Salima, for he must have known I would eventually come for her. Though my own divine powers were smothered, the sword drew upon base magic. And base magic thrived everywhere.

The old man's laughter deteriorated into a paroxysm of coughing. Upon catching his breath, he said, "Not magic. Nothing so elaborate for me. Only demons."

My brow furrowed.

"They will soon be here to drive me away. They do not let me rest. Tortures. Endless torment. I run from one tunnel to the next and always end up here. I have never seen the Sea of Oblivion. They herd me like cattle. First one direction then another. But always away from oblivion. That's my punishment." He shrank farther into himself, choking back a sob, as he whispered, "That is my punishment."

"If I were to rid you of these demons?"

The man looked up. Something flashed briefly in his eyes—hope, perhaps—and was quickly gone. "Who are you?" he asked again.

"I told you, I am no one. But you will get me across the Sea of Oblivion."

The man opened his mouth to speak and stiffened. His face fell, eyes widening in obvious terror. "They're coming." He scrambled to his feet, looking this way and that. "They're coming!" He flattened himself against the wall, his breath harsh, stuttering gasps.

A whip split the air and chains clanked on stone—both accompanied by guttural laughter. Two demons sauntered into view at the far end of the passage. Back the way we had come, two more appeared. These were smaller than the first two, though not by much. And all four were taller than me. One of the big ones—the one with a sharp-fanged underbite—held a chained mace, which he dragged along the ground. The other, who looked utterly human aside from the overly long arms that reached well past his knees, cracked a whip that had multiple spiked tails.

"Brought a friend, did you?" one of the smaller demons said.

These two were identical, from the fiery scales covering their bodies like suits of armor to the long tails writhing behind them like angry snakes. I could not tell whether they were male or female. They carried no weapons, and when they spread their hands, I could see why. Each finger—four on each hand— terminated in a sharp blade.

"Let's play," said the demon with the whip.

Before Whip even finished speaking, Underbite swung his mace. It slammed into the wall beside the old man, who let out a low whimper. Blood spurted from burst eyeballs and ran down the dented wall when the weapon fell away. The other three attacked. The old man slid to the ground. His arms covered his head, and he curled into himself.

A faint smile touched the corner of my lips. It had been too long since I had fought a well-matched opponent.

"Indeed." I drew my sword from its scabbard. "Let us play."

Sword in hand, I spun around, slicing the head from one of the twins. The other roared. Its tail shot out, catching me around the ankle. It yanked, and I stumbled forward but did not fall. Underbite and Whip paid no attention to me, their singular focus on the old man. The mace swung around the demon's head as he made to let it fly.

The tail yanked me forward. Again, I did not fall, but my momentum pulled me into the remaining twin. I crashed into it. It let out a loud breath as it toppled, pulling me down.

Now I had the attention of the other two. The mace ceased spinning in mid-swing while the whip lashed out in my direction but was still too far to reach me. Pushing against the downed demon, I got to my feet. As I rose, I drove the sword into the tail still tight around my ankle. Howling, the demon released my leg in time for me to jump away from the incoming mace. The mace drew back for another attempt. I raised my sword to block it. The two clashed with a shudder that shook the tiny cavern.

The demon twin at my back was on its feet. I heard it rush toward me. The mace flew again. As the twin reached me, I pivoted to the side. A quick shove propelled the twin into the mace. Its jaw found metal with a loud crack. The twin's head jerked backward, and the demon fell, spread-eagled onto the ground.

A snap of the whip and it wrapped around my neck, its many spikes boring into my flesh. The underbite with the mace howled, teeth bared, spittle shooting from his mouth. My hand rose to the whip. I pulled hard, drawing the demon forward, and rammed my head into his face. The demon bellowed—a sound cut short when my sword entered his belly.

And then there was one.

All of these demons were fast, but no one would ever call me slow. The mace hurtled toward my head, and I spun away, sending my sword in an upward arc. The demon stepped adroitly back and brought his mace to bear once again. It swung downward. I sidestepped, and the mace buried itself in the ground. My sword arm shot out. The demon grunted and fell to his knees. His head lolled to the side, then tumbled off his shoulders.

I straightened, breathing heavily. The old man still whimpered on the ground. I looked down at him and frowned. The skirmish had taken more exertion than I had anticipated.

"On your feet," I said, exhaling.

Slowly, the man unclamped his arms from around his head and raised his eyes to mine.

"You seek oblivion, no?" I bent to slice a piece of cloth from the rags the man wore as clothing.

He cowered.

"For the love of sanity, get up." Grabbing his arm, I drew him to his feet, then used the torn rag to wipe black, tarry demon-stuff off my blade.

The old man looked around at the now smoldering bodies of demons. "What are you?"

"At the moment, I am a man." I gestured down the passageway. "Can we go?"

✳

As the old man had said, all paths led to oblivion. Our tunnel terminated at the sea, but at one of the higher tiers of the cliff face. Odd that I had not felt the ascent. This time, a boat was waiting. I got in, followed by the old man, and we stood. Around us, the dead climbed into their canoes, which immediately began floating away from their docks. Our canoe did nothing. It simply sat still on the air, as though clamped into place by invisible arms.

"Only the dead may cross," the old man said. He stared wistfully into the water.

I understood then that, when he said he was seeking oblivion, he meant to drown himself. "There is no oblivion beyond death," I said. "Look closely."

The man peered into the water and saw what I already knew: the souls of the dead were trapped beneath, their torment unending. He drew back, breath hitching.

"You must cross," I said.

He looked at me and nodded, his face blank. Silence descended as I contemplated. The vessel had responded to the old man's soul and come to ferry him across the water. However, it seemed my presence had moored it. No doubt, if I stepped back into the tunnel mouth, the boat would carry the dead man to the opposite shore. Me disembarking, however, was *not* an option.

The man spoke. "I think, if you are to cross with me, we must cross as one."

My brows drew together, but before I could ask what cryptic nonsense he was spewing, the old man changed. In one moment, his solid essence faded into something far more spectral. And then he was in my head.

I pressed two fingers against my temple to quell a rising ache. A frequent occurrence during my millennium on the mortal plane, the rate at which the headaches manifested had declined since my return to divinity. But they still occurred and, at times, with great intensity.

Memories unfolded—not mine. The old man. Ancient times. Long before my thousand-year exile. He had been a practitioner of the old magicks. A good man until death had taken his child. Grief had driven him to seek out the darker spirits, and he had inadvertently summoned the four heaps of ashes scattered in the cavern behind us.

His past was now mine, and it appeared mine would be his. Memories rose, unbidden and unwelcome, to the surface of my mind.

Exiled by my Father, who had stripped me of my identity and divinity but not my immortality, I had woken in the mortal realm, filled with rage and no memory of who I was. No memory of the spirit world. My talents, however, had remained. I was strong, a skilled warrior, and had a way with metal. Though they had regarded me warily, my skill as a blacksmith had kept me in favor among the ruling tribes.

I had believed I was mortal. I had taken pleasure in what gave mortals pleasure and feared what was frightening to them. Until they—and I—realized that I did not age. And then *I* became what they feared most. They had hunted me like an animal, and it had quickly become evident that I also could not die. But I could bleed and feel pain. Any who took pity on me had felt it too. Even now, the screams of village children burning alive rang through my ears. I shuddered—or perhaps that was the old man—as the wooden canoe began to move.

We drifted in silence, memories racing through our collective mind. As on the other side, the boat docked at our own private landing. I all but leapt from the canoe. The old man—Tolu—may not have known who he was before we climbed into the boat, but he certainly knew now. His diaphanous form separated from me. My thoughts were my own again, and I exhaled in relief. In my divine aspect, I could enter the minds of mortals; the reverse was unpleasant.

The shapeless form solidified before me, and the man fell to his knees. "Forgive me," he exclaimed, his forehead touching my feet. "I didn't know it would happen like that. I didn't know who you were. I merely thought it, and it happened, and I was sharing your memories. Had I known . . . Forgive me, my lord."

I briefly considered tossing the man into the sea. Having shared my thoughts, he seemed to now fathom them. He glanced nervously at the water, but nerves were not enough to still his tongue.

He said, "Salima wasn't your doing. Mankind has always been cruel to the best of us."

Mankind is a pox, I thought. Except, it was not mankind who had trapped Salima here. I turned away from the old man, before he made any more useless declarations, and walked through the dark tunnel.

Grey-yellow mist behind me, I followed the tunnel a few paces and stepped into a brightly lit, cavernous chamber. Dead souls swarmed from wall to wall, their noise a buzzing irritant in my ears. I shoved my way through the crowd. Confused or angry looks met my gaze, though none confronted me. Vaguely,

I wondered whether I might meet some of the people who had once hunted me on the mortal plane, but none of that was important now. None of them mattered. All that mattered was that I reach Salima and free her from this eternal prison.

The chamber had thirteen wide exits through which the dead slowly filed. The central doorway was the largest, and without seeing what lay beyond, one *knew*. Serenity radiated from the other side.

Most of the dead scrambled to reach this exit, but this was the point in their journeys where they each began drifting toward their eternities. And they drifted not of their own volition. Pulled by an unseen force, they moved to their destinations. Only a few—very few—went through the central doorway. The rest, many screaming in terror, went through one of the other twelve exits, the smallest from which emanated the darkest despair. I took that one.

The beleaguered souls floated at a frustratingly slow pace with me among them. At least I did not have to contend with their verminous odor. Without the flesh of their bodies, humans had no scent. I followed the herd for a time, pebbles crunching beneath my feet. The trail wound downward, so I knew it was the correct path. As we made our descent, little by little, souls turned from the main route and onto smaller tributaries. The tunnel passage led to an open trail, with solid rock on one side and a long drop on the other. By the time I stood on the smooth obsidian floor of the lowest level, only a handful of dead souls remained.

A soft thrumming reached my ears—the steady beat of a million hearts. Like the eyeballs of the uppermost level, these hearts were embedded into the rock. Blood seeping down the walls glowed crimson in the darkness and revealed rows of prison cells that stretched deep into the shadows of the dungeon.

The souls looked around with anxious, wide eyes. No one spoke, for they knew the fate awaiting them. These were the worst that mankind had to offer, human putrefaction. They were murderers all, but not all murders were equal. Salima did not belong here, and Maciji knew it. In the mortal realm, she had killed a man in self-defense and then tried to sever my enemies' hold on me by taking her own life. I had survived another two hundred years with the mortals, her death heavy upon me, before regaining my mind and my divinity. After all that Salima had suffered for me in life—the destruction of her home, her family, herself—to learn that she also suffered in death had plagued me. As the old man had said, she was the best of their kind. I could not leave her to the mercy of Maciji.

Loud, heavy grating signified the cell doors opening. As boulders rolled away from the wall, the unseen force dragged the pleading souls to their prisons. The boulders rolled over the openings, locking the prisoners away in darkness. Salima was here. She had to be. I would search every cell until I found her.

Without my full power, moving the boulders that served as cell doors was a difficult task—I rested after the first dozen. By the time I completed the second dozen, however, the method to Maciji's madness was clear. The damned were housed in accordance with the times of their death—the most recently dead imprisoned in the nearest cells. It did not take much longer to find her.

She lay crumpled on the floor, her body twisted to expose her torso, though her legs were folded tightly to her. She was covered in filth, cuts, and bruises. An arm across her eyes half hid a battered face with swollen lips. Streaks of blood coated her chin and neck, matted her grey hair. If not for the birthmark, which looked like a firebrand upon her breast, I would not have believed it was her.

"Salima." I knelt beside her.

A soft whining escaped her cracked lips.

My heart clenched. "Salima, I am here." I tried to gently remove her arm from her face, so she could look at me. The whining rose in pitch. "It is me. Dafaru. I have come for you."

A ragged breath shuddered out of her. "Dafaru?" The word was scarcely audible.

Her arm fell away from her face. Swollen lids parted to reveal the glassy emptiness of the stare beneath. She coughed, and rage bubbled like hot lava in my chest.

"Dafaru," she said again.

"I am here." We needed no further words. I lifted her into my arms and carried her from the cell.

I moved quickly down the column of locked cells. Salima's head bobbed against my chest. Were she not already dead, I would at this point have raised her to my face to feel for breath. I stepped onto the gravel to begin our ascent. A voice behind me spoke.

"Did you truly believe you could enter my dominion and I would not know it?"

Silent curses spilled from my lips as I turned to face my Father's most ancient adversary. Even in the crimson gloom of this chamber, Maciji was a void from which no light escaped.

"I believe you have my property." He strode forward. With each step, his essence—a black nothingness—trailed behind him. "I want her back."

"What you want is of no consequence."

"Your arrogance is ill placed." He shook his head, shrugged, and his body rippled. It bubbled and cracked, the molten core beneath breaking through its hardened, black shell. As each bubble swelled, it took shape—something vaguely human or animal or a melding of the two—and each demon dropped fully formed from Maciji's rippling flesh.

I set Salima on her feet and stepped in front of her, drawing my sword.

Maciji scoffed. "Do you think they will not cut through you to reach her?"

"They can try." I brandished the sword before me, and his minions attacked.

I fought them off, exerting exponentially more energy on these seven than I had on the four in the tunnels above. Maciji was toying with me, and I had no choice but to play the game he dictated. Were I not who I was and newly reanointed, this is when doubt would have begun chewing at my confidence. But drenched in blood—both mine and theirs—I raised the sword, ready to dispatch anything else the Demon Lord tossed my way. No new demons emerged. Instead, he turned his silver tongue on Salima.

"Have you not suffered enough in his name?" he asked.

"Do not listen!" I glanced at her, but he had claimed her attention.

"He tires," Maciji said. "He cannot keep this up much longer."

"Nor can you," I taunted.

"Is that what you think?"

The next two demons that spun from his flesh had the bodies of trolls and the faces of pigs. Even as I watched, oversized boar tusks sprouted from one's lower jaws while the other grew a rhinoceros horn. I ran forward to gut them and be done with it. However, these two were not like the others. They were faster, and as I learned when Boar Tusks knocked me across the floor, they were stronger.

"You can stop this, Salima." Maciji continued to croon.

"No!" I rolled to my feet. "He lies!"

"I will kill him."

"He cannot kill a god!"

Laughter radiated from him like heat. "Perhaps not, godling. But I will take what is mine, and then I will make you suffer. Both of you."

His voice took on a harder edge, and he spoke to Salima. "I *will* destroy him, and I will punish you for all eternity. There will be no escape for you. Unless you return to your cell."

Again, I glanced at Salima. Fear clouded her features. She raised both hands to her face and gnawed at her knuckles.

"Do not listen to him, Salima. Do n—" Wind rushed from my chest, halting the rest of my words, as Boar Tusks slammed his head into mine.

I grunted and stumbled backward to meet Rhinoceros. Clawed fingers clamped down on my ribs, ripped through my skin and into flesh. I swung the sword, but he moved too fast and I sliced through air. A blow to my back sent me skidding into the wall, crimson hearts squelching.

"The choice is yours, woman," Maciji said. "Return to your cell, and I will release him. And you? You will be free once you have repented your transgression against me."

I turned, and as if they had one brain, the two attacked. Boar Tusks sank his tusks into my chest as Rhinoceros drove his horn into my abdomen. Groaning from the pain, I dropped to one knee. They fell upon me, driving me to the ground and wrenching the sword from my grasp. Sinking under a sea of fur and gnarled flesh, I sought out Salima.

"No more," she said.

Had I not been looking at her, I would not have known she had spoken, so quiet were the words.

"No," I shouted.

But it was too late. She was already at Maciji's side. A cold grin split his face. I struggled against the demons, tried to get to him, to tear away his self-satisfied expression. The demons pinned me beneath their collective weight, my sword kicked out of reach.

Past the heaving mass, I saw Maciji's mouth move as he spoke to Salima. She came toward me, her gait unsteady. Walking past, she picked up the sword. It was more than half her height, though not as heavy as its size would have suggested. Holding the grip with both hands, she dragged it over to the Demon Lord.

"There you have it, godling." His tone was infuriatingly smug. He glanced at Salima. "She stays."

At his side, Salima said nothing. The sword she had taken from me clattered noisily to the obsidian floor. She stood, eyes lowered, shoulders slumped.

I was not angry with her. How could I be? For me, she had given her life, her soul. Once again, for me, she had sacrificed everything. And I could do nothing. She had weighed her soul against mine and found hers to be insignificant. She would be imprisoned for eternity—or until her spirit joined the lost souls in Oblivion. What she did not know was that Maciji was the ultimate liar. He would keep her, and he would not fulfill his end of the bargain. He would keep me as well.

A thousand years of suffering at the hands of mortals was a minor thing compared to the fresh tortures Maciji would plan for me.

"Remove her." The Demon Lord came toward me, gesturing at the two demons, who released me and ambled over to where Salima stood, a broken thing.

No longer fettered by their combined strength, I started to rise, but Maciji pressed a taloned foot to my neck, shoving my face onto the fire-molded floor.

"Forgive me," I said loudly, trying to get the words out despite my face being pressed to the ground.

"What is this?" Maciji laughed. "You beg my forgiveness?"

"Not you, you self-aggrandizing ass."

I struggled to turn my head, to glimpse Salima once more before he removed her from the room. Boar Tusks held her by the neck, his thick fingers digging into her flesh. The other fumbled with a set of metal collars meant for me and for her. Salima's tear-filled eyes rose from the floor to meet mine for only a moment.

"Forgive me," I muttered, but her gaze had already dropped.

"Wait," Maciji bellowed. "Release her. I want her to watch this."

Boar Tusks let her go. She did not move, her head still lowered.

"I said watch!"

She slowly raised her head.

"See?" he said to me. "She is mine. And so are you."

Her hoarse voice cracked. "But you said . . ."

"I changed my mind. Collar!"

Rhinoceros rushed over with the collar.

Salima had believed the lies that the Demon Lord had dropped like honey down her throat. Now confusion turned to fear and then anguish on her face.

Rage burned inside me, and I fought to free myself. The pressure on my neck lightened as Maciji raised his foot. Again, I started to rise, and his foot came down on my face. Grunting, I fell back onto the floor. He kicked me again, the force of it throwing my body to the side. I groaned, rolled onto my back, and gagged, as his foot slammed onto my throat. I grabbed his ankle, but the collar clamped around my neck, binding me to his will. I fell back, impotent.

"I cannot kill you." His foot eased off my neck, pulled away entirely, then crashed down on my chest. "But your time here will not pass quickly. It is a fitting outcome." Again, he stomped on my chest. "And most fitting?" This time, it was a foot to the face. "It is your Father's own covenant which makes this possible."

Father's covenants. I wanted to laugh but was having difficulty expanding my ribcage.

Maciji had no such constraint. He continued, "You are mine, Dafaru. And you will pay for every insult your Father has heaped upon me. You will suffer for every injury He has caused me."

He raised his foot again and brought it down on my face, his talons slicing into my cheek. "For every slight, every dismissal." His foot went up. "Every—"

The foot came down but not on me. Maciji teetered and stared at me, eyes wide. I stared as well, though I was staring at the tip of my sword protruding from his belly. The sword had sliced through him with the ease for which I had forged it. Salima stood on the other end, a small spark of life in her eyes. She looked at me, and I tugged at the collar. Anger flared on Maciji's face. He would soon heal, but Salima was awake and present. She scurried to my side and jammed the sword tip into the collar's hinge. The collar fell away.

The two demons, slow to react, now sprang into action. I was on my feet with the sword in my hand before they reached us. Ushering Salima behind me, I faced them. Maciji let out a feral howl. The demons charged, but with their focus torn between me and their healing master, their efforts were no longer so coordinated. They were still quick and still strong, but they no longer used their strength as one. I made swift work of them, but new demons were materializing from Maciji's flesh.

I guided Salima onto the gravel path and attacked Maciji head-on.

The sword slashed through one of the embryonic demons, cleaving it from its maker. The demon floundered on the ground like a fish on land. Maciji screamed his rage and extended his claws, raking his arm across my chest. He lunged. As I spun away from him, I severed the other emerging demon. Maciji roared anew. He was still healing, and this would be my only opportunity to truly slow him down.

I plunged the sword into his chest. He lurched forward, heedless of the wound. I pushed, but still he came. I wrenched the sword half a turn. The pained grimace that swept across his features was my only reward. He continued to advance. With both hands on the grip, I jerked the sword, slicing upward. He staggered back and back until we reached the far wall. Then I drove the sword into the rock. When the sword caught, I took a backward step and rammed my foot onto the pommel, pinning the Demon Lord. It would not hold him long. I turned and ran after Salima, scooping her into my arms as I sprinted up the path.

We had not gone far when I heard them coming. I tried to quicken my pace, but my wounds hampered my speed. If Maciji's new creatures were as fast as Boar Tusks and Rhinoceros, they would soon catch us.

They were. And they did. A host of snarling demons skittered into view, led by a centipede that rose six feet tall on its hind limbs.

I set Salima on the ground for the second time. "Continue upward, until you reach the sea. Take the boat across. Nakada will find you."

"But—"

"Now!"

She backed away, turned, and scurried up the path. Unarmed, I faced the demon horde. At least Salima would have the time she needed to escape this place.

The horde advanced. The sheer drop on one side made the path too narrow for them to rush forward as one. Or so I thought, but I was wrong. The centipede scuttled up the wall, followed by another many-limbed demon. Their clamor drowned out my loud sigh of frustration. I braced myself for the onslaught.

They poured over me as a single howling, hissing mass, choking me in a cloud of fetid breath. I raised an arm over my head as the wall climbers dropped down and teeth closed on my bracer. Without knowing what had clamped onto me, I swung my arm. The creature crashed into its neighbor, their armored bodies clanging like metal, and it released me. The face of another demon filled my vision. I rammed my head into it. Sparks exploded behind my eyes; this creature's skull was not ordinary flesh and bone. My head spun, and I struggled to keep my feet planted.

Feet and hands clawed at my face, torso, and legs. I tore them off me and sent two of the demons tumbling off the side. Still there were too many. And they were overpowering me.

One of the demons, reminiscent of Boar Tusks, roared. He rose to his full height, which rivaled my own, and swept his misshapen arm across the writhing mass of demons. Scythe-like talons pierced a smaller counterpart, and Boar Tusks Number Two tossed the other into the void. The centipede had wrapped itself around my body and was poised to bite. Boar Tusks Two grabbed it with two massive hands and yanked. The centipede tore in half, black ichor spraying in my face, and I shook myself free.

Another demon leapt from the wall. Boar Tusks Two caught it before it reached me. Lips pulled back to expose a set of sharp teeth in what I took to be a grin, he snatched the thing's head from its body.

Still grinning, he looked at me. "It seems gods are not the only ones I can possess." The demon spoke with a familiar voice.

"Tolu? Old man, is that you?"

The disconcerting grin widened. "I lost you in the sorting room, but you weren't too difficult to find." He threw his burden over the side. "I saw your friend; she's not doing well."

I nodded briskly and ran up the path.

❋

Salima had not made it far. Again, I swept her into my arms and resumed the ascent, with the old man in demon form at my side. Several times, we were confronted by Maciji's minions, but the old man quickly put them out of commission. We reached the upper levels and burst into the sorting room. Salima would not find salvation here because she did not believe she deserved it. I did not stop but plunged into a random tunnel, certain it would lead to the Sea of Oblivion. A loud bellowing echoed behind me. Maciji. He had worked himself loose and was in pursuit.

As expected, this tunnel terminated at a private landing. There was no boat. Of course, there was no boat. I spat out a string of loud curses. I had not anticipated this, nor had Nakada warned me of it. But there had to be a way across. The demon refugees who begged asylum at the Crossroads obviously made it to the other side.

"What is inside that demon's head?" I asked the old man.

"Nothing, my lord. I believe I'm alone in this shell."

Maciji's yells continued to echo through the labyrinthine tunnels. I needed to think. But the Demon Lord's roaring drew ever closer and rendered it impossible to form a fully coherent thought. The old man wearing demon skin looked from me to the doorway and back again. The grey-yellow illumination in the mist had already faded to twilight purple. The sun would soon set on the sea. I lowered Salima down and she sank to her knees.

"Get her across." I started back toward the sorting room.

"No," Salima said feebly.

I turned and helped her to her feet. "We do not have much time." My hands rose to cradle her face, and I touched my lips gently to hers. "I will see you soon."

Her arms slipped around my waist, and she laid her head on my chest. "Dafaru, don't" was all she said. A request with which I could not comply.

"The demons can cross," I said to the old man. "Find a way." With that, I released her and headed back down the tunnel.

I had barely stepped foot in the sorting room when a flash of brilliant flame incinerated my clothing. Shrouded in fire, my arms flew up to shield my body, which tensed against a pain that did not come. As I lowered my arms in relieved confusion, the entire room burst into a white conflagration.

Twice during my exile with the humans, they had burned me alive. Each time, bathed in flames, my flesh had boiled and melted away. The pain had been excruciating. With my divinity returned in the spirit world, fire did not touch me—as the goddess of flames could attest. But demon fire had properties unlike the flames of the mortal and spirit worlds. And in the underworld, I was powerless. Why then, was I still intact?

As the fire began to subside, I looked at my gauntlets. The implements of power, though quiescent in this domain, remained invulnerable. Perhaps that invulnerability extended to me? I dismissed the thought before it was finished. As my many injuries showed, I was not invulnerable here. Here, I bled.

Only . . . I pressed a hand to the gore wound in my belly and the one in my chest.

Steam filled the chamber. The flames had burned so hot that the room was melting. Molten rock dripped like heavy rain from the ceiling. It ran in slow rivulets down the walls and pooled at my feet. But it did not cling to me. Maciji stood in the haze, arms still upraised.

"Inna." He spoke my mother's name with the deepest disdain. "The Earth Mother schemes with great intricacy." A stream of fire sprayed from his fingertips and hit me in the chest before I could contemplate his words. The force of the blast threw me into the melted, misshapen wall. Shrouded in flame, the wall began bubbling around me, though I remained unscathed. "She stole from me." Another blast of fire. "She stole my essence." Another.

Each fiery assault pushed me back until I staggered into the passageway. Each assault also healed my wounds. Every time fire engulfed me, I felt the wounds come together. After the flames died, energy surged through me. It radiated through my veins. It flowed into my hands and tingled at my fingertips. I raised my fingers and contemplated them, contemplated the smooth skin healed on my abdomen and between my ribs. As Maciji came into view, I turned my palm toward him and forced the energy out.

Liquid fire poured from my hand. It hit him in the face and he reeled back, but quickly righted himself. His inhalation sucked the flames into his body. The stream died on my fingers as abruptly as it had emerged. He exhaled, smoke wafting from his nostrils.

"She gave it to *you*. My essence. Pulled from my offspring and planted in her unborn child." Perhaps he had exhausted his anger, because his demeanor was now calm, unhurried, as he strode slowly toward me. "The netherhells burn in your veins, godling."

This was the Demon Lord, Lord of Lies, and he could not be trusted. The idea that my mother would take the essence of a demon and weave it into my being was absurd. Yet something within me knew it to be so. From the way my body used this demon fire, I knew Maciji spoke the truth. A truth that my mother had hidden from me. Perhaps it was *she* who could not be trusted. The rage that Maciji had abandoned began to seethe in my gut. I stifled the boil and steadied my own voice before responding.

"Save your lies, Demon. I have no use for them."

"I tell no lies and well you know it." A cold chuckle echoed down the tunnel. "There is irony here."

His utterances were neither ironic nor amusing. I looked behind me at the tunnel mouth, which again opened onto the sea.

"The sun is setting," he said. "You cannot cross. I need only wait and your will is mine." His grin revealed a set of teeth that shone shockingly bright, like stars, in his mouth. "I shall tear every last bit of my essence from your being. You will not enjoy it." He said the last with a nasty chuckle.

Across multiple realms, myriad worlds, and a thousand years of mortal endurance, I had feared very little. But for the second time in what amounted to a single day in the underworld, I feared I would be the Demon Lord's prisoner and that I had failed Salima. I retreated to the end of the tunnel and looked over the side, scrutinizing the thickening mist. Above me, below, and all around, I searched for Salima or the old man in demon form. I stared intently down at the mist-shrouded sea and attempted to listen for her thoughts. In spite of my brief trick with the fire, my divinity remained muted. My mind did not hear hers.

"The water is a quagmire from which even the likes of you cannot escape," Maciji said, fathoming the idea that had fleetingly traversed my thoughts.

The idea inched back into focus, and I asked, "Even though your essence clings to my very soul?"

For the briefest moment, the confidence drained from Maciji's eyes. It was answer enough. I dove into the mist.

My body plummeted to the sea below. Icy water met my arms. It closed over my head and torso and drew my body beneath. I came up treading water that was not water, but the stuff of souls. The sea was a gelatinous cloudy mass of people who once were. At first, they seemed wary of me and floated away as I swam forward without impedance. Then they began to wail.

Shrieking cries rose around me. Whatever part of Maciji I possessed was not enough to ward off the clawing dead. High-pitched keening and loud moans obscured the words behind them, and the souls fought one another to reach me. They slowed my movements and dragged me under. I could neither hear nor see him but imagined Maciji's laughter above.

Though perhaps I was not imagining it. Gleeful laughter, complete with offensive snorts sank after me into the depths of forgotten souls. A hand clamped onto my shoulder and the clamoring souls scattered. My head rose above the surface, a silver wisp still clinging to my face. I snatched it off and looked into the eyes of the trickster.

"I see you lost your clothing." He reached out a hand to me.

I gladly accepted, and he pulled me onto a column of mist, which rose into the darkening clouds above.

"Salima?" I asked as silver threads continued to reach for me from the water's surface.

"She is safe. In the company of a souled demon." He regarded me inquisitively. "Your woman is pretty, but I still do not see why you risked so much for her."

Evidently, he had not deigned to look into her mind, else he might have known that Salima was many things to me, and I to her, but lovers was not one of them. Now that she was out of danger, the tightness in my brow relaxed a fraction. "You said you could not cross."

He shrugged. "I lied."

"Bastard."

"Unfortunately not."

I followed his gaze, knowing what I would see even before my eyes found Maciji looming large and walking above the mist.

Nakada inhaled loudly and exhaled. "My apologies, Father!" He spread his arms and demon fire burst from his body. It shot forward, slammed into the Demon Lord, and Maciji tumbled through the air.

I looked askance at Nakada, who ran to the edge of our mist column and jumped. I followed his lead.

"You ungrateful wretch!" Maciji screamed, and he sounded much closer than he should have been.

Fire hit my back just as I leapt. It pushed me into the yawning mouth of green-lit passage and I careened into Nakada. We went down, both cursing as we toppled onto the floor.

"You slithering worm!" Maciji's voice reverberated off the walls, sending tremors through the air around us.

We jumped to our feet.

"Run!" Nakada shoved me forward. "Run, run, run!"

As though I needed further encouragement.

We ran. And I prayed. *Actually* prayed to my Father, Ubangiji, Creator God, Lord of Jangare, that I would escape this place in one piece.

"Left! Left!" Nakada shouted.

I swung into the left passage with Nakada on my heels. Orange light cut through the dim green, and I saw the doorway in the distance.

"Move!" he said behind me.

I urged myself forward but was still powerless and could only move as quickly as my legs would carry me. Ahead, the door started to close.

Nakada made a sound of frustration that echoed my own. I heard his loud intake of air but did not hear him exhale before fire engulfed me. It lifted me off my feet and sent me hurtling down the passage. I collided with the closing door, daylight flooding my eyes, and crashed onto the ground outside. I looked up in time to see the doorway seal itself back into rock.

"No!" My powers had returned, and I pounded at the rock but left not even a crack. I took in a deep breath and felt the demon fire tickle my fingers before I let it loose. To no avail. The rock did not even smolder. My manipulation of fire was weak in comparison to Nakada's displays.

"Dafaru!"

I turned to see Salima running toward me. Her wounds were no more. No blood, no filth on the naked body that was, undeniably, that of a young woman. Gone was the grey hair, replaced by thick, lustrous brown. She had been pretty in middle age and was much younger now than I had known her to be in life. *Pretty* was too dull a word to describe the woman scrambling over the rocky terrain. In her mind, I saw my own nakedness and clothed myself. She reached me and flew into my arms, as I clothed her, too—though I did not cover much. It was good to be in control of my powers again.

Rendered temporarily vapid by her drastically changed appearance, I managed only "You are healed."

The old man, content in his demon skin, stood apart but nearby.

Salima said, "You're also healed."

I nodded, disengaging from her, and turned back to the rock. "Nakada is trapped."

"Oh." The sorrow in her thoughts melded with mine. Then panic obliterated all other emotions, and she said, "Dafaru, don't go back!"

"I cannot." My fingers traced a path where the doorway had been. "I cannot open it."

I turned away from the door, brow furrowed in consternation. Salima gasped and raised a hand to her mouth. I whirled back around and saw a crack appear in the rock. It spread outward.

"No." Salima grabbed my arm with both hands. "You can't go in!"

"Nor do you have to," Nakada said from the other side of the opening door. He stepped out, and the rock slid back into place. "I am exempt from that pact between my father and yours." He flashed a smile. "And I knew you cared, Brother."

A retort formed on my lips, but I swallowed it. Nakada was the child of whom Maciji had spoken. Though it pained me to admit, we were, in *essence*, brothers. Of the four brothers I already had, I truly cared for only one while I tolerated the others. So it surprised me to find myself glad that Nakada was unharmed.

He glanced at Salima's hands on my bracer and gestured between she and I. "You must tell me more about this soon."

It was unclear whether he was speaking to me or to her, but he regarded her intensely now and, still, it seemed had not looked into her mind. In many ways, he was not the god I remembered despising before my exile. She, however, was the same woman I had known in that dark time, and she met his gaze unwavering.

"So, he is your father," I said, dispelling the palpable magic growing between them. We started away from the entrance to the underworld. "It explains much."

J.S. Emuakpor was born and raised in Nigeria, West Africa. While she is not the widow of some Nigerian prince with millions of dollars in an American bank that she needs you to access, she does insist that royal blood flows through her veins. She is a married mother of four, a scientist, and co-owner of Afrocentric Books. Most of her writing draws upon the spiritual beliefs of the ancestors who frequently whisper in her ear as well as the superstitions that she refuses to relinquish.

www.jsemuakpor.com

CLIVE TERN

The Black Birds of White Oaks

STEAM CLEARED from the platform like a Boston mist disappearing in the summer sun. A crow sat in the rafters and cawed as Margaret Winthrop looked left and right. A young porter approached, pushing a trolley cart containing her traveling cases.

"Miss Winthrop?"

"Yes."

"Mr. Spaight has sent a carriage. Please follow me."

The porter turned toward the station exit. Outside, Main Street was a packed earth track. Dry and dusty in the September heat, it was bordered on each side by buildings of clapboard or red brick. There did not appear to be a saloon. She nodded approvingly.

The porter and a liveried carriage driver lifted her cases onto the carriage. When they finished, the porter bobbed his head. Margaret thanked him and gave him a quarter. She looked at the dark-skinned man dressed in a warm yellow jacket and trousers who stood holding the horses' reins.

"Hello, I'm Margaret," she said.

"Hello, Miss Winthrop. I'm Thomas. It's an hour's journey to White Oaks. Is there anything you need to do in town?"

"Well, Thomas, I have a letter to send to my fiancé. Could you direct me to the post office?"

He smiled, white teeth in a mahogany face. "Yes, Miss Winthrop. Right there." He pointed behind her, a small doorway that was part of the station building.

She posted her letter, and Thomas helped her into the carriage. They rode into the countryside; streets gave way to fields. Scarecrows stood in some; hordes of workers worked in others.

Beyond the edge of town, Thomas spoke over his shoulder. "Mr. Spaight sends apologies he's not here himself, but he had to go to Raleigh, and he took his daughter, Miss Millicent, with him. But he left introductions for you to make start on your work."

"Oh, thank you, Thomas." A thought struck her. "Thomas, my project is to record history from ex-slaves. Would you be willing to tell me about your family and history?"

"Best not, Miss Winthrop. It doesn't sound like something Masser Spaight would approve of."

"Oh."

"I reckon you could speak to Miss Demeter, Miss Winthrop."

"Miss Demeter? Will she help? Who is she?"

"She's Mama, Miss Winthrop. She knows all the stories."

❋

The next morning, Thomas took Margaret to a simple, single-story house with a small verandah. Similar properties stretched along the road.

The steps creaked as she walked up them. Before Margaret could knock, the door was opened by a tall woman. She was clad in a brown cotton dress several shades darker than her skin. Margaret had expected someone the same mahogany hues as Thomas after his comment about her being "Mama." Now she guessed he meant she was a wise woman among the ex-slaves.

"Miss Winthrop?"

"Miss Demeter. Thank you for seeing me."

"Call me Athena. Come in, come in."

"Thank you. Please, call me Margaret."

She followed Athena into the house. A single upholstered chair and a small, but full, bookcase stood in the corner on the left, near the window. Farther along the gable wall was a small potbellied stove, logs stacked neatly beyond it. Straight ahead, an opening led into a kitchen area. On the right were an internal door and a bench table. On this, there was a tray with an earthenware pitcher and two glazed beakers.

"I thought we could sit at the table. As you see, I don't have much in the way of fine furniture," said Athena.

Margaret was unsure whether the woman was being deprecating or making sly commentary on the difference in their social condition.

"That's fine," said Margaret.

They sat. Athena leaned back, her elbow on the table, resting comfortably. Margaret remained straight-backed, placing her small bag by her feet.

"So, Margaret, Thomas tells me you want to record the history of slaves, sorry, ex-slaves. Why would you want to do that?"

"There has been a similar project with the Indian tribes. I suggested we do it for the peoples brought from Africa. My professor spoke to someone in the Department of American Culture. They liked the idea."

Athena watched Margaret. Her face was impassive.

"The history of African slaves. People will be interested in this, you think?" she asked.

"Yes. I think they will. Without recording history, it is lost. Why, if no one had written such things down, then we would not know that your names are—"

Athena interrupted. "Greek goddesses of wisdom and earthly fertility." She watched Margaret's surprise. "Yes, I know the derivation of my names." She waved a hand toward the bookcase. "I knew it before I could read it in those books, before I could read any book. Writing things down is not the only way to remember things. Thousands of years of knowledge existed before anyone thought to scratch a line in damp clay."

"Well, yes, but now we can record it and share it with people who would never have had the chance to learn oral history. Including future generations."

"And what do you hope these future children of ours would learn? How it is efficient to enslave people to work for you? That ripping men, women, and children away from their homes and whipping the survivors until they are cowed and fearful is how to build an empire?"

Athena's words were aggressive, but Margaret could detect nothing malicious in her tone. "No," she responded, "I would have them learn of our inhumanity and know it was wrong. I would have them learn that in the short history of this great nation there are things we should be ashamed of."

"Ashamed? The slave peoples have nothing to be ashamed of. Only you white people should feel shame."

Margaret's face flushed. Try as she might to empathize, she had never experienced the callous deprivation this woman and her kin had. She stopped and thought for a moment. "Not quite, Athena. What about the slaves purchased from other blacks? The history of African slavery predates the age of white empires. Black man has sold black man for longer than white man has been buying." She took a deep breath and prepared to collect her bag. The argument she used was one that she'd heard in defense of slavery. She did not agree with the reasoning, but it had stuck with her. Today was obviously going to be a waste of time, she'd find someone else to speak with.

Athena's face creased into a smile, and she leaned forward, patted Margaret on the arm, and chuckled.

"You're right of course. Now, have some lemonade, and we'll talk."

She poured from the pitcher.

Relief coursed through Margaret. She took the lemonade and drank gratefully.

Athena sipped, waiting for Margaret to finish drinking. "So, what would you like to know, Margaret Winthrop?"

Margaret put her beaker down. She looked at her host. Since arriving, she had been trying to gauge how old Athena was. Initially, she'd thought them to be similar ages, within a few years at most. But now she looked at a woman who could easily be as old as her mother. It was unclear where the upper and lower boundaries of a guess should lie.

"Why don't we start with basics. Tell me about yourself."

Athena nodded. Was it approval? Margaret still couldn't read her expressions but chose to interpret it as such.

"How old are you, Athena?"

"How old do you think I am?"

A deflecting question, and now Margaret was forced to make a guess. "Midthirties?"

Athena chuckled again. "A little older, let's leave it at that. Now I'm pretty sure that life as a plantation slave ain't what you're looking to record."

Margaret shook her head.

Athena continued, "My people were in North Africa. The Anti-Atlas Mountains." She stopped and smiled for a long pause. "Where the heavens are held up from the earth itself. Our name, I-Mazigh-en, means 'the free.' I suppose we lost the right to call ourselves that when slavers fell upon our village, killed the old and the sick, and chained us together to begin the long walk to the coast, and from there on a blackbird—a slave ship—to these shores."

Margaret intended to take notes, but Athena began her tale before she could ask. So she listened to oral history at its most primal. Athena did not recount dry, dead history, remote knowledge bound to the page and recited by rote to earn a teacher's praise. She told the story like a personal tale, an account of experience and empathy that was compelling. She told of families ripped apart, of casual killings on the path down the mountains, of cadavers tossed to sharks that trailed the ship across the Atlantic, of the slavers' mart where people were sold as chattel.

Eventually Athena stopped talking and poured more lemonade. Margaret was shocked to see how far the shadows had shifted. Late morning had passed to late afternoon with the swiftness of memory.

"I'll get a child to run for Thomas. By the time he gets here, we'll have had time to eat," Athena said.

"Can I help with anything? Set the table or . . ." Margaret trailed off.

Athena laughed, shook her head, and stood up. "You sit and write in the notebook I'm sure you have in that bag."

Margaret laughed and reached down, drawing out her notebook and a pencil. Athena went out front and called for a willing messenger. Margaret started jotting down what she remembered.

She was taking a moment to think when Athena walked past the window. A panel of small colored-glass pieces hung before it, rotating, scattering light in unusual ways. When Athena passed in front of the shifting light, she looked almost like a bird, pecking outside the window. Margaret blinked and shook her head.

Athena came back inside and walked through to the kitchen. A couple of youths barreled up to the door, calling loudly for Miss Demeter—the accent mangling it to MissD'm't'r. She told them to go fetch Thomas for Miss Winthrop, and for them to stop staring at the lady. Like magic, she produced a small sticky bun in each hand. They departed with the same noisy exuberance, catcalling each other as they ran in the direction of White Oaks.

"They seem like good kids," said Margaret.

"They are. Now, shall we eat?"

❋

The next few days followed a similar pattern. Thomas dropped Margaret at Athena's. Athena told stories or had neighbors come and recount their families' tales. When they finished, a child was dispatched to fetch Thomas, and the women ate lunch together.

But when Thomas came to collect her on Friday, she could tell something was different.

As Margaret got out of the carriage, Thomas turned and said, "Master says he'll meet you in the library."

"Oh. Right. I'll put my bag away and freshen up," Margaret replied.

Thomas's eyes widened, and he shook his head. "No, best go in now. He's expecting to see you when you get back."

Margaret was surprised but began to have an inkling of what had caused the change in atmosphere.

She went to the library and knocked.

"Enter."

She opened the door.

"Come in, come in. Don't huddle at the door," said Malcolm Spaight.

Margaret had seen the picture of him, young and in Confederate uniform, which hung on the landing. In the painting, his hair was chestnut brown; he wore a wide mustache and sat on a piebald roan. The man facing her still had the mustache, but his face was lined, with a deep leathery hue. His hair was a yellowed white, and he wore a cream linen suit. He looked to be taller than Margaret by a couple of inches.

Deep blue-gray smoke curled from a thick cigar held between his fingers. He looked at Margaret and took a puff.

"It's good to meet you at last, Mr. Spaight," said Margaret. "It is very kind of you to be so hospitable."

"Always a pleasure to assist old friends in the Department of American Culture," he replied. "I asked in town what history you're recording and got some nonsense about slave stories. Couldn't make sense of the jabbering. Then I'm told you spend your days with that pale negro woman with Greek names. I must say I find it a strange thing." He took a deep draw on his cigar, sending a spiral of smoke into the room.

"Athena Demeter has been most helpful. Your friends in town were quite right. I am recording the oral histories of ex-slaves," Margaret said.

Her host stared, unblinking. The silence went on, and Margaret began to wonder if everything was okay. Eventually he responded. First with a harrumph and a shrug of his shoulders.

"A strange waste of time, if you ask me. Better recording the people who achieved something, made this land the fine country it is. But I'm sure you've some highfalutin reason why this is the way to do it." He shook his head.

Margaret stayed silent; he hadn't actually asked a question, and she was tired and uninterested in arguing.

"Well, I suppose you'll want to get washed before dinner. It's good to meet you," he said.

He turned and walked over to a bookcase. Margaret watched, not realizing at first that she had been summarily dismissed. She resolved to have as little to do with Malcolm Spaight as possible. As she reached the door, he spoke again.

"Just one thing. This Athena woman, pale for a negress, but that's what she is. A child of slavery with no love for those who saved her forebears from heathen savagery. And wont to lie for fun. I'd prefer you discontinue meeting with her. There are some good upstanding negroes who work hard. I'll arrange for you to meet them."

Margaret froze. Eventually she found a voice she could use and turned.

"That would be most kind. I finished meeting with Miss Demeter today. She has been most helpful. Of course, I'll need to spend more time with her when I start collating my notes. But that won't be something you need to concern yourself with."

His face flushed dark. Margaret guessed he was unused to being defied. She left the room before he could respond.

※

Margaret spent a week interviewing other ex-slaves. The majority remained slaves in all but name. Eking out a living, tied to a single plantation and reliant upon it for all their work—paid a pittance from the plantation owner and often still living in what had been, until recently, slave quarters.

Sitting in the small coffee-shop in town, she pondered the difference between her two weeks of research. Nothing from this week carried the same vibrancy as her meetings with Athena Demeter and those she had introduced Margaret to. She pondered the determined action by Athena to maintain the oral histories of her people.

Athena had welded those around her into a people. Their commonality might only extend to the condition of having been property, but now they were something else. By encouraging them to remember and share histories, she was restoring identities that had been stolen.

Margaret looked at the clock. The train with the mailbag from Boston would arrive in ten minutes. George's letter should be in it. She had posted hers yesterday. Six pages describing her week, excitement at the project, and the desire to see him soon.

Looking along the street, she saw Athena waving. Margaret paid her bill, and the two women met outside the haberdashery.

"How are you, Athena?"

"I am well, and you? I thought I may see you this week."

"I've been meeting with others. But I'd like to talk with you again. Though it seems my host disapproves."

Athena raised an eyebrow. "He does. Oh my!" She laughed, then said, "Why don't we make sure he has something to disapprove of. Come round Sunday evening, a few of us ladies go to a bend on the river to bathe. We'll talk and gossip together."

Margaret nodded and was about to ask for more details when a train's whistle reverberated along the street. She turned.

"Are you expecting someone?" asked Athena.

"My fiancé's letter is due with the mail."

"Well, you should collect it. I need to finish my shopping, and I'll see you Sunday evening."

Athena smiled, turned, and crossed the street. Margaret watched her go. A young man was watering baskets that hung from the corners of the general store's canopy. The sprinkling water scattered sunlight into a small, sparkling rainbow. Athena passed behind the coruscation, and again Margaret saw Athena as a bird. She blinked, enough time for Athena to have moved beyond the miniature rainbow. Margaret watched her enter the store and pondered exactly what she may have seen. The train whistle blew again. She shook away her fanciful notion and started toward the station.

The postmaster grinned when she came in. "Here you are, Miss Winthrop," he said.

There were two letters, one from George, the other from her father. She hadn't expected the second.

Thanking him, she left. Thomas was due to pick her up at half-past three, and she had intended to read on the journey. But the letter from her father worried her. She sat on a bench and broke the wax seal.

Dearest Margaret,

Your mother and I are as perturbed by George's actions as we are sure you are. I have spoken with George Sr. He stands with his son's despicable course, in fact I have suspicions that he is behind the whole distasteful episode.

Your mother wanted to travel straight to you, but her health does not permit. And I hope you may be returning to Boston.

Darling daughter, we know that you will display your customary fortitude and resilience in this difficult time. Our hearts are with you.

Your ever loving Father xxx

Margaret stared at the letter, confused. She reread it, and her heart skipped. She looked at the other letter, George's letter. When they had been apart previously their letters were five, six, seven pages long. The envelopes were always full. This one felt light.

She didn't open it. The sun beat down, but that wasn't the reason her mouth was dry. She looked at her father's letter again, holding it in her right hand while her left clamped George's missive.

❄

By Sunday morning, Margaret felt strong enough to leave her room. She went to church with the Spaights. Reverend Davison was a fine preacher, but Margaret's mind drifted. She imagined her parents and George and his family, all members of the same congregation. She wondered what sermon Pastor Burriman was delivering.

Tears threatened to flow again, and she was relieved to hear the minister call a hymn. Singing drove back the tide.

On the ride back to the plantation, conversation was limited to small gossips that young Millicent Spaight had garnered. Her father ignored her, staring intently at the fields. Margaret did her best to feign interest.

Suddenly Malcolm Spaight spoke. "Dinner will be later this evening. I may not be back until seven or eight."

"Oh! I didn't know you were going out, Daddy."

"Now you do."

"That reminds me," Margaret said, "I will be out this evening." She had forgotten about the invite from Athena until Malcolm's announcement.

Malcolm turned and stared at her. "I was not aware you had an engagement."

"I had forgotten. I've had other things on my mind. I'm sorry if it causes an inconvenience."

Malcolm harrumphed. Margaret had noticed he used this vocal tic to indicate a range of thoughts, feelings, and emotions.

"I'll ride myself then, and leave Thomas to transport you. You hear, Thomas?" he called forward.

"Yes suh, Masser Spaight. I'll drive Miss Winthrop."

"Please, don't inconvenience—"

"No inconvenience," Malcolm interrupted.

❋

Malcolm left without any announcement. Margaret was unaware he had gone until Thomas knocked on her door just after six.

"Carriage is ready, Miss Winthrop," he said.

"I'm sorry if I've had you waiting, Thomas," Margaret said.

"No problem, Miss Winthrop. I've been enjoying the fine sunshine. Now, where are we going this evening?"

"Could you take me to Miss Demeter? And, Thomas, I keep saying you can call me Margaret when it's just us."

"I know, miss. Best not get too casual. Masser Spaight wouldn't appreciate that."

He flicked the reins.

"Is that why you talk differently when you are with him?"

"What do you mean, Miss Winthrop?"

"You know what I mean." She mimicked his accent, "Yes suh, Masser Spaight. Uh, uh Masser Spaight."

Thomas laughed, then said, "I ain't admitting it."

"You're not denying it either," Margaret said.

He laughed more.

Soon they were on the long stretch of road where Athena's house was.

"Is that a pony and trap outside Miss Demeter's house?" Margaret asked.

"It is, Miss Winthrop."

"I wonder whose it is. I know she said there would be others. But I didn't expect ladies from town."

"Uh, that ain't who it belongs to Miss Winthrop."

"Who's is it?"

"That's Masser Spaight's trap."

Margaret leaned forward. "I wonder why he's here?"

Thomas said nothing.

Athena's door opened, and Malcolm stepped out. Seeing the approaching carriage he paused, then turned and said something through the door. He climbed into his carriage and pulled away. As they passed, Thomas touched a white-gloved hand to his forelock, Margaret lifted a hand to wave. Malcolm Spaight stared forward and hurried the horse pulling him up to a swift trot.

Athena came out as they pulled to a halt.

"Good evening, Thomas."

"Evening, Miss Demeter."

"Good evening, Margaret."

"Is it still convenient to visit?"

"Of course. Thomas, we'll be finished by eleven."

"Yes, Miss Demeter. I'll be back at eleven."

"Thank you, Thomas," Margaret said.

"Come in, Margaret. I'm not quite ready." Athena disappeared inside.

There were beakers on the table, used. The other door in the room was open, showing an unmade bed. The room had an air of recent use, an unsettled dishevelment. Athena moved about out of view, and Margaret heard splashing water and the rustle of clothing.

Margaret waited, uncomfortable at the suggestion of carnality between the unlikely pair. It was clear Malcolm had been embarrassed, and while Athena displayed no such emotion, the evidence of the bedroom seemed obvious. Or did it? Maybe Margaret's recent disappointment made her overly conscious of intimacy between others. That she was seeing such between a woman she felt warmly toward and her host—whom she disliked—pointed to her making the unlikeliest of assumptions.

She stared out the window. The colored panel reflected shafts of light around the room, and Margaret remembered seeing Athena as a bird. She laughed at the ridiculousness.

Athena came into the room. "You sound happier than I expected," she said.

"Were you having relations with Mr. Spaight?"

"Would it matter if I was?"

"No, it's none of my business. I don't know why I asked. But . . ."

"Since he was fifteen."

Margaret bit her lip.

"I've shocked you," Athena said.

"No. Yes. You choose to do this?"

"Not always. Sometimes I have no choice. But it's generally easier to go along."

Margaret said nothing.

"Come, let's walk," Athena said. "Did you bring a towel?"

Margaret followed Athena out the door.

She had little time to think more about what Athena had said. But some questions would not go away. How old was she? Did Malcolm Spaight really rape her?

As they walked, more women joined them, and Margaret realized she knew them all. She had heard their stories, met their husbands, seen Athena give their children little treats. The bond between the women indicated long years of association. Yet they accepted Margaret without reserve.

They cut across a wide field to where the river took a loop, creating a patch of quiet water with a small beach of dry soil. Margaret gasped as the women casually disrobed. She turned, blushing.

Athena laughed. "Margaret, you'll find it difficult to bathe with your clothes on," she said.

"She looks like a frightened dove," called someone.

There was a ripple of laughter.

Athena walked over; her skin glistened with sweat, and Margaret was conscious of how the woman's breasts hung against her chest, of the sparse thatch of hair between her legs.

Athena stood in front of Margaret, putting a hand on her arm. "It's no different to bathing at home," she said. "We just don't have a fancy bathhouse so have to use what nature provides." She waved her arm to indicate the river.

"I've never seen another person naked."

"What? You poor smothered child."

"What's the matter?" someone called.

"This poor girl's all bound up in her clothes and don't know how to be naked."

Soon Margaret was surrounded.

"It's just flesh." "Skin s'all." "Lose the clothes."

The voices were all encouraging, cajoling. Hands helped her strip. She stood naked, self-conscious. Her skin was pale and flaccid when she compared it to the darker hues and firmer muscles of the women around her. They dragged her into the river, and she sank into the water, covering her nudity.

The women washed with bars of hard soap. They helped each other scrub backs and rinse hair. They swam and talked and laughed. Slowly Margaret relaxed. The evening sun shone along the river, splashes of water sprayed small sparkles of rainbows that flickered in and out of existence. Laughter hung on the gentle breeze.

Athena began to lather her hair. Margaret swam over.

"Let me help," Margaret said.

"Thank you. How are you coping with being naked?"

"It still feels strange."

"There's nothing better than being as nature intended."

Margaret didn't reply, concentrating on her task.

"Here, let me do yours," Athena said afterward.

Margaret turned to let her. "Athena, can I ask you something?"

"Of course."

"How old are you? And why do I keep seeing you and your friends here as birds."

She ducked her head under the water, rubbing soap from her hair. She turned while she was under and came up facing Athena. Water streamed down her face, blurring her eyes, and again she saw the outline of a bird. She blinked, and there was Athena.

"Well," she demanded.

"You wanted to know about history. But I had to be sure you had the eyes to see it. Come, we'll dry on the bank, and you'll hear our real history."

Margaret followed Athena out of the water; the other women also came. They sat naked, some on towels or small blankets, others on their dresses.

"Do you know the story of Prometheus's punishment for stealing fire?" asked Athena.

Margaret frowned. "Yes."

"Tell us."

"Prometheus steals fire for humanity. Zeus is enraged, binds him to a rock, and sets an eagle to peck out his liver. His liver grows back every day, and the eagle pecks it out again. Eventually Hercules kills the eagle and sets Prometheus free." Margaret looked around. "There are different versions, but that's pretty common. What?" She looked around confused.

The women were smiling and chuckling.

"That's part of the story," said Athena. "But there are gaps."

"You have another version? Where does it come from? Will you tell me?"

"So eager, Athena," said one of the women.

Athena turned to her and nodded, her breasts bouncing in delayed unison with the nods. "Yes, she is," she said, and turned back.

"Zeus and Prometheus were firm friends," she said. "The only things they disagreed on were beautiful women and mortals. All beauty is subjective, so their arguments on that matter never went beyond idle teasing. But on mortals, Zeus viewed them as an inferior branch of humanity. Prometheus thought them different but equal in standing to immortals."

Margaret listened attentively, considering how she would use this new version of the myth to illustrate the way ancient stories were used to reflect desires and wishes.

Athena continued, "When Zeus became ruler of the immortals, he determined that lesser humans would forever be vassals, paying tribute to those lucky enough to be born forever. Prometheus disagreed. He helped mortals in ways no longer understood, the greatest of these was *pramantha*, by which they made great fire. The mortals grew strong and rivaled the immortals. War followed. Around the earth, the immortals all lived together in a few large communities. A surprise attack, using the power of *pramantha*, killed most immortals. Enough remained to retaliate. They struck back, reducing mortals to a few scattered outposts, scrabbling for survival in a world that they no longer recognized. So began the last ten or twelve thousand years of history."

"Afterward, few immortals remained. But Zeus did, and Prometheus. They fought and Zeus prevailed. He bound Prometheus high in the mountains and set a manifestation of himself, an eagle, to torment his old friend. Daily the eagle tore the prisoner's flesh, consuming it, scattering it. As the sun set each evening, in a final act of vengeance, it pecked out Prometheus's eyes."

"But vengeance becomes tedious, even for an immortal—and who of us ever knew a man to maintain focus on a job?" There were chuckles from the other women. "Eventually Zeus's avatar tired of its daily task and looked around. A murder of crows had taken to gathering nearby, feeding on flesh the eagle scattered around the mountain. A pact was made. The eagle would fulfill its desire to soar the heavens, to roam the winds. The crows would feed on Prometheus."

"So it carried on for years uncounted. But as they fed on the flesh of an immortal, their nature was changed. They became less crow and more human. Over time, their torment of Prometheus dwindled. Eventually they agreed they could not torture the man. But Zeus's eagle returned, savaging Prometheus as had not been done in many a year. His screams shook the mountains, causing rocks to slide and mountains to split."

"The crows swiftly agreed that they would resume the torment, if only the eagle would stop destroying their home. Distrustful, it stayed to ensure the crows kept their word. Prometheus whispered words of forgiveness as they pecked at him. When eventually the eagle was satisfied and left, the crows and Prometheus discussed how to end the cycle of torture and what could be done until it was."

"After so many generations consuming immortal flesh, the crows had developed the ability to take human form. In vain, we sought to undo the bindings Zeus had laid upon Prometheus. When it became apparent we could not, Prometheus bade us peck out his liver. We wanted to refuse, but he assured us it was a pain more bearable than the torture the eagle's return would lead to. So while some of us kept up this daily torment, others departed, seeking a way to free him."

"Eventually they returned with Hercules, the son of a mortal father and immortal woman. Taught by his mother, knowledge that was already fading into fragments, he reckoned a way to loose the bindings and at last Prometheus was free. A short while after, our stories split. We made our home in the Anti-Atlas Mountains, calling ourselves I-Mazigh-en in honor of freeing Prometheus. And now, Margaret Winthrop, you know our real history."

A warm breeze rustled the leaves of the trees on the bank. The sun was dipping into the hills and light was fading.

"You tell the tale as if you are the birds, the crows," she said.
There was a collection of nods.

"I don't understand."

"Let us show you."

The women started to shift about, small sinuous movements.
With a shimmer of air, they transformed, first one, then another,
and finally all. No longer eleven women, but eleven crows.

Margaret froze.

Ten of the birds took flight, rising in gentle swirls above the
river. The one that remained shimmered again, and Athena was
there once more. She stood, naked and dark in the gloom. "Do
you understand now, Margaret?"

Margaret looked up. "Why?"

Athena lowered herself onto her towel. "Because you asked,
and you saw the bird, and you are right. There are tales that
should be written down before they fade from the minds of
mortal man."

"No one will believe this. I don't believe it, and I have seen
it." She stopped, looked imploringly at Athena, and shivered.
Suddenly she was conscious of her nakedness. She started drawing on her undergarments.

Athena slipped her shift dress over her head, rolled her towel,
and helped Margaret. When Margaret was dressed, Athena took
her by the shoulders and looked her in the eye.

"This has been much for you to hear and see. We will talk
more. You will decide how to tell our story. We will try and
answer your questions. But now, it is time to return."

Behind Athena, the other crows were landing and changing
form, returning to women. The journey back was slower in the

starlight. The women talked and laughed and joked. Margaret walked with them, thinking.

"If you can fly away, why did you allow yourselves to become slaves?" she asked.

The group halted on the road. The smell of ripe tobacco plants hung thick in the cool night air.

"Not all of us could change. Some of us were married to ordinary men and women. Some of our offspring can't change, even if both parents can. We couldn't abandon our family."

Margaret nodded, and her heart burned with the pain she could only dimly imagine. They carried on walking.

Back at White Oaks, Margaret wrote down everything she could remember from the evening. By the time she finished, Sunday had become the early hours of Monday. She slid into bed and dreamed of crows descending on Boston and carrying her away to far mountaintops where George lay bound to an altar of burning tobacco bails.

She awoke to bright sunlight sliding through a gap in the thick curtains.

The house had a relaxed stillness that she couldn't identify at first. Someone was singing a familiar Baptist hymn but with an unfamiliar cadence. It changed the mood of the hymn to something deep, yet joyous and uplifting. When she heard a whistle that she recognized as Thomas's, she knew what was different. Malcolm Spaight must be away and not expected to return imminently.

Coming down the stairs, she saw Thomas, he was swinging a carpenter's pail jauntily and still whistling.

"Good morning, Thomas."

"Heh. Good afternoon, miss. We wondered if you was going to sleep the whole day through. But then, you was up late."

"I had things to finish. Where is Mr. Spaight?"

"Him and the young mistress went to Raleigh on the first train this morning, miss."

"Raleigh?"

"Yes, miss."

"But no one mentioned anything about going to Raleigh."

"My impression was, it wasn't a long-planned trip," he said.

The following three days revolved around her work. She met with Athena, the other women, and their partners and children. She worked hard to write their stories and not to try and resolve them with her own understanding of world history. At night, by paraffin light, she went over her drafts. She started writing down question after question, some she found answers to, others remained in her notebook, underlined, circled, repeated, starred. Constant nagging questions that made her doubt what she knew was certain, that demanded answers she believed impossible.

When she finished writing, she lay in bed and still questions assailed her. She had seen the transformation herself, and not just once. Some had arrived at Athena's in their bird form. Hopping into the bedroom and robing in dress or dungarees before sitting with Margaret. It was no sleight of hand, no elaborate trick to gull the Northern woman.

Eventually she would succumb to sleep, and strange dreams.

❋

On Friday, Malcolm Spaight returned. Margaret was in the library. She stood as he came in.

"Good evening," she said.

"Miss Winthrop."

"Would you like me to leave?"

He harrumphed; she interpreted it as no and continued reading.

Malcolm opened a cabinet and poured from a decanter, which he placed on a small table. He sat in a leather wingback chair and emptied his glass in two large gulps. He poured another glass, and it followed the first as swiftly.

Margaret kept her head down.

"You do not approve of me drinking bourbon, Miss Winthrop?"

"What I approve or disapprove of is irrelevant, Mr. Spaight. I am a guest in your house and would not impose my views."

He harrumphed and poured a third drink. Finishing that, he stood and walked over to where Margaret sat.

"A shame to hear about your engagement being broken," he said.

Margaret looked up. "Thank you, Mr. Spaight. It's been a difficult week."

"Yes, a shame. You aren't unattractive. Quite comely in your own way." He stroked her cheek with the back of his hand.

Margaret jerked back. "I think I'll go and get ready for dinner."

She scraped the chair back and stood up. Malcolm gripped her wrist and spun her around. He slid his arm around her back, crushed her toward him, and pressed his lips onto hers. The hand on her back slid down until it cupped her backside; he squeezed roughly.

Margaret shoved as hard as she could, anger fueling the movement. Malcolm stumbled back. As he did, she struck his face with her palm, snapping his head sideways. He collapsed against the shelving.

"You bitch!" He spat the words out while rubbing his cheek.

Margaret stood with her back to the table. Her breath was short, adrenaline roiled through her system. The suddenness of the attack bewildered her. "How dare you—"

"How dare I? A woman who forsakes her betrothed, a woman who consorts naked with negro women. Oh, don't look so shocked. Everyone knows of their deviations. You're nothing but a Northern strumpet."

"I think it would be better if I stayed elsewhere, if you have such a low opinion of me. As wrong as your information is."

Malcolm had recovered from his slumped position and walked back to his decanter and glass. He poured another drink and harrumphed. He waved a hand, bourbon slopped onto the carpet.

"Oh, stay here. I have little desire to remain myself. I'll have Thomas take me . . ." he trailed off and stomped from the room.

The door slammed, a thunk that reverberated around the room.

Margaret heard Malcolm shout for Thomas. Then another door slammed. With that, a dam burst inside Margaret, and she wept. To be attacked, humiliated again, after George's callous rejection, was almost overwhelming.

After a few minutes, the door opened again and the cook came in. Margaret did her best to wipe tears away, but there were too many.

"It's okay, miss. He's away. Won't be back tonight definitely, and I heard him tell Thomas to have mail delivered to the town house. That generally means he won't be here at all."

Margaret nodded, trying to stem the flow.

"I'll put some soup in the dining room for you, miss, and there's some chops if you feel like it."

The cook left, allowing Margaret to compose herself.

After another restless night, Margaret again woke to early afternoon sunshine. A breakfast tray of fruit, yogurt, and juice sat on her dresser.

After eating and dressing, she went downstairs. Speaking with the cook, she discovered that Malcolm was definitely staying in town for the immediate future. Thomas was unavailable but had prepared a trap and horse if Margaret wished to go out. She did. She wanted to see Athena. She needed to discuss the previous evening with someone.

She was near halfway when, in the distance, she saw a flock of birds circling. As Margaret drew closer, the flock resolved into crows. She couldn't help wonder if they were actually birds or I-Mazigh-en.

Nearer still, she could hear the birds call out, coarse caws which echoed in the still air. More crows fluttered around something on the ground. Slowing the trap she stood to get a better view. She saw a boot and halted the horse before jumping down.

Running forward she called and waved her hands, trying to scare the crows away.

Most of them scattered. Two remained. One was clearly injured, but the other wasn't. A big crow with lustrous feathers standing on the chest of Malcolm Spaight. Margaret recognized the suit and hair, despite the bloody carnage of the body.

With certainty, Margaret knew that the crows were I-Mazigh-en. But who? She looked back at the one on Malcolm's chest. It watched her with deep black eyes. Blood glistened on its beak. Malcolm groaned.

Margaret gasped but was galvanized. She moved forward again. The crows above flapped about her head, never touching her but driving her back. The big black crow let out a huge cry. It pecked forward, and Malcolm screamed. It pecked forward again. In its beak were two eyeballs. It flapped twice and lifted into the air.

Unseen by Margaret, the injured crow had crawled away from the body. The other crows drew upward, cawing to each other and gradually flying off in different directions.

Approaching the body, Margaret was unsure what to do. A whimper to the left caught her attention. Another body, Athena.

Margaret knelt beside her, then recoiled. She was badly injured, though not from bird beaks. Her face was a bruised, bloody mess. The bright eyes were shut inside a puffy mass. Her left arm hung limply by her side.

"Oh! Athena, what happened to you? Who did this?"

"Sometimes, I'm not given a choice," Athena said, her voice drawn and thin.

Margaret looked at Malcolm. His body was still, with no signs of life.

"But why? And . . ." Margaret couldn't formulate questions properly.

"He was mighty angry about something. I tried to soothe him. But he wasn't interested." Athena coughed. "It's happened before. He always was a man of violent passions."

Margaret cradled her friend, who winced wherever she was touched. Even after last night, she would not have imagined Malcolm capable of this, but the evidence was undeniable. She understood the rage that led to him being attacked. Though still there was a question.

"Athena, who was the other crow?"

"You've met my son before. He was just looking out for his mama." She coughed again. There was frothy blood on her lips.

"Your son?"

Athena nodded.

No one had been introduced to Margaret as Athena's son. She wondered if it was delirium from the pain. Then she thought about the crow, the deep luster of its feathers, the bold stare.

"Thomas?" she guessed.

Athena nodded faintly, coughing again. There was more blood. Margaret wiped it with her dress.

"We need to get you help."

Athena shook her head. "Just hold me. I'm too cold for help now. But with him and me both gone, my boy should be safe." She pointed a finger at Malcolm's body, then reached up and took Margaret's hand. "I trust you to tell our story."

"But, you're immortal."

Athena shook her head slowly, "No, just very long-lived."

Margaret squeezed her hand, unable to speak. They sat in the dirt. Athena's breathing shallowed, and she faded out of consciousness. Margaret held her friend and wept for the senselessness of it. Athena coughed and stiffened, her grip on Margaret's hand loosened, sliding away.

In the distance, voices could be heard calling. The crows had flown home, now they were returning on foot. Too late.

"Miss Winthrop?"

"Thomas."

Thomas knelt down. "She's gone?" he asked.

Margaret nodded.

❋

Steam swirled around the platform. Thomas opened the carriage door and helped the porter lift Margaret's cases in.

"Thank you, Thomas."

"You're welcome."

"What will you do now?"

He smiled sadly, "Only thing keeping me here was looking out for Miss Dem—Mama. It's time I found my father."

"He's I-Mazigh-en as well?"

"Not quite. But he's known us from the start."

Margaret frowned, unsure what he meant.

"You'd best get aboard, Miss Winthrop. Conductor wants to be leaving."

Thomas helped Margaret climb the step and closed the door behind her. The whistle blew and the train lurched forward. She pitched into her seat, and it was like the jolt knocked pieces together. Thomas was already walking toward the station exit. Margaret silently wished him well in his search for Prometheus.

Clive Tern is a writer of short fiction and poetry from South-West England. Apart from writing he enjoys open water swimming, cooking, and a well made martini.

www.clivetern.com

MALLORY ST. CLOUD

Starfall

Starrise,
Starfall,
Grant me this wish,
The one I desire most of all . . .

CAELESTIS HUNG IN DARKNESS, awash in wishes as he was every night. Some were petty, others banal, most hollow. These were the ones he'd learned to ignore, letting them blend and fade with the static of space. His siblings twinkled around him, and he wondered if they, too, were restless. The space between them was vast and lonely. If there were air in the interminable void, he would have sighed. It had been so long since he'd been pulled to the little blue planet below to serve his duty.

Then, as if his own had come true, a wish came. The star leaned forward, trained on the sound. The purest wishes rang like bells—some deep and resonate, others high and silvery. These were always accompanied by a shift that felt at once familiar and terrifying—the way it feels when the world unexpectedly falls away from you.

Unbalanced.

He had learned that word on Earth, as balance wasn't a concern in the weightless nothing of space. And that's how this wish, with its crystalline tinkle, made him feel as it reverberated through him and burrowed to his core. There it tightened into a fist, and he lurched forward, the desperate plea pulling him from his home in the heavens and toward the ground far away.

Without further warning, Caelestis fell.

Shooting through the sky, his wake rent a silvery gash in the darkness. He howled against the familiar rip and burn of atmosphere, squinted against the blinding light of descent. In a grating skid, he landed, having hurtled his way through tree and earth. When he opened his eyes, he no longer looked down at the tiny planet but up at the twinkling sky.

He sat up, stretching and twisting in an effort to work out the rude kinks set into his bones by the suddenness of gravity. How long had it been since he'd last fallen? He hadn't remembered it hurting this much, but it had never been easy.

Opening and closing his newly formed fingers, he marveled at the novelty of his broad palms, the weight of his hands. Pale skin stretched smoothly over bone and tendon, the thick pads at his fingertips sensitive to every touch. So real, so firm.

Different from the formless glow of his astral body, his corporeal form always amazed. He stood slowly, adjusting to the precarious fight to gain balance between weight and gravity, and turned his gaze toward the sky. His brothers and sisters hung above him, not much farther than usual but more distant than ever. With a bit of effort, he found the void that marked his place in the sky—a blackness beyond blackness—and he felt the fleeting pang of homesickness.

Behind him, marred trees cut a long scar well into the distance. He breathed deeply, respiration a newly burning necessity. The air carried the scent of charred wood and friction-heated soil. Scent was one of the things he liked best about Earth because space had no odor.

Scrabbling from the crater, he stumbled onto a bed of sweet-smelling summer grass and lay down on his stomach. The earthen scent of life filled his head. Plucking a single blade between his forefinger and thumb, he rolled it back and forth until it hung, pinched and limp. *Touch.*

He put his fingers to his nose. *Smell.*

And then to his tongue. *Taste.*

The wind rustled the leaves in the trees above, dark shadows against the clear night sky. Sound was one thing he had in space, but not like this. Not the whispering song of leaves, nor the creak of wood. At home, his ears only filled with the endless stream of wishes before they passed into nothing.

With that, he remembered the wish that had brought him down. Closing his eyes, he strained his ears, searching for and then turning to the sound. That helpless cry, which had pulled him from the heavens, called again. Rising to his feet, he cracked his neck and moved his shoulders as if shrugging into a heavy coat, although a midnight robe light as a moonbeam was all he wore.

He began walking. Moving in slow, deliberate steps, he used the muffled cry and the undeniable tug in his chest to guide him. The person that had brought him hurtling to Earth was near, somewhere beyond the woods. He walked a fair distance until the sound grew louder. At last, he came to a Moon Pool. These small reservoirs were scattered across the earth and collected the tears of Mother Moon. On Earth, the vitreous black liquid, which reflected no light, had no real magic. But the pools were held as sacred and believed to amplify the wishes of those in need.

He stood in the shadows of the tree line and observed the clearing. The pool was of modest size and surrounded by boulders and the remnants of gifts brought by pilgrims and wish makers. A gray-cloaked figure sat on the edge just across from him.

The trees around Caelestis whispered, causing the figure to raise its head. He could not make out any features under the darkness of the hood, but the person beneath drew back in shock, fear, or both. These were common emotions, one for which he could not blame the humans. After all, each of his footfalls left a glowing trail of stardust in his wake, and his skin gave off a faint, silvery light. Caelestis had learned that humans responded well to smiling, so he let his face lift into an easy, practiced one. To his satisfaction, the figure's shoulders relaxed ever so slightly.

"Are you all right?" His voice, now having a substrate on which to travel, came in warm, vibratory tones. He extended his hand.

The huddled figure tilted its head. Two hands emerged from the folds of the cloak. Small, delicate fingers with skin like rich mahogany pushed back the hood of the cloak, revealing the tear-streaked face of a young woman.

Caelestis blinked at her and swallowed. Her almond-shaped eyes sat wide on a face framed by profuse curly black hair, parted down the middle. Her strong face was careful yet curious, handsome but decidedly not beautiful.

Even so, he found himself unable to look away from the swell of her high cheekbones or the moonlit darkness of her skin. There was something haunting about the way she watched him with irises—the color and depth of the Moon Pool—gravid from desperation.

"Who are you?" she asked, not breaking her gaze.

"I am the star, Caelestis. You may call me Cael if you wish."

The young woman's eyebrows rose.

"You called me here," he prompted.

The woman pulled her cloak close to her as if it might quell the subtle trembling of her body. "You—you heard me?"

"I did." He smiled again, marveling at the way the muscles stretched over his face. It was a good feeling; stars didn't get to smile. "What is your name?"

"A—Anush. My name is Anush."

"That's a pretty name. *Anush.*" He tested the word, liking the soft whispering of it as it passed between the hardness of his teeth.

"Is it true then?" Anush's eyes glittered. "You'll grant me a wish? Anything at all?"

"Yes. One wish, anything your heart desires."

The young woman's eager face broke, her eyes filling with tears. She put her face in her hands, her shoulders shaking. Cael frowned. He did not like it when they cried. It was not an emotion to which he could relate.

With a certain amount of effort, the woman regained her composure. "I'm sorry." She sniffed. "It—it's my sister, she has fallen ill and desperately needs your help."

Cael cocked his head to one side. "The wish isn't for you?"

The woman shook her head, her dark eyes now full of worry. "Will you still help me?"

"Of course. I didn't travel all the way from the heavens to leave without fulfilling your wish."

Relief passed over her face, pulling the corners of her mouth into a small smile. Just that tiny change filled her features with warm radiance. But that warmth was quickly gone as the lingering shadows of sadness settled back over her, the smile frozen on her lips. She began to weep once more. Caelestis did not understand sadness, but the odd combination of crying while smiling was an even greater mystery.

Anush led him down a well-worn path that wound through a pine forest. Clouds drifted overhead, covering and uncovering the moon, plunging them into dark and light. The sun would rise soon. In fact, Caelestis could just detect the faint glow at the edge of the sky. According to Anush, they'd make it to her village by daybreak. He guessed it wouldn't be much longer now.

They walked in silence for a time, Anush glancing at him sideways as if she expected him to vanish at any moment. The attention didn't make him uncomfortable. Humans, he'd found, were prone to staring. He supposed they couldn't help it. It seemed a reasonable reaction. Even so, he felt different under her eyes. Unlike most of the humans he'd met, there was no ambition or pretense, only genuine curiosity and gratitude.

"Cael." She cleared her throat. "Can I ask you a question?"

He nodded.

"Why did you come to me?"

He looked at her curiously. "You called me, didn't you?"

Anush nodded. "Is that all it takes? To just ask?"

He chuckled. "If asking were all it took, I'd never go home again." He looked down at her. "But you, your voice rose above all others and pulled me to you. It is a rare thing that happens, perhaps only once in a generation."

The smile returned to her face, this one wider than the last. Once again, the shadows lifted from her countenance and revealed an even brighter radiance. She turned her face to the ground, but not before he started to consider that she might be prettier than he initially thought.

"Is there anything else you'd like to know?" he asked.

She turned back to him and bit her lip.

"It's silver. Your hair, I mean." The words came quickly as if too much thought would otherwise hold them back. "Just like starlight."

Her fingers reached out as if to touch it, but she made a fist instead and lowered her eyes back to the ground. "It's beautiful."

He regarded the young woman, her head down in an effort to hide the embarrassment he had briefly seen in her eyes. Hers had been a statement, simple and without appeal—unlike most others who had fawned, poked, or made demands for locks to carry as talismans.

"Will it make me stand out in your village?"

She shook her head without looking at him. "It's a trading post. There are many unusual strangers who come to our town." She glanced behind him and gestured at his stardust trail, its glow much softer but still impossible to miss. "But that will."

"It diminishes as I walk," he said with a quiet laugh. "You needn't worry. It should fade entirely by the time we reach your village."

She nodded, and another layer of shadow fell away.

They both went silent for a long while. Birds sang to one another in the thicket of trees—greetings to each other and to the day.

"Does it hurt?" she said.

"Does what hurt?"

"I saw a shooting star. It seemed so close, but then it flashed in the sky and was gone." She gave him a shy, furtive glance. "Was that you?"

"Yes."

"Does it hurt when you fall from the sky?"

"Yes." He looked down at her, watched the way she tucked an itinerant strand of hair behind her ear and, for the first time, felt the urge to touch someone else's hair. He ignored the nagging feeling. "The air against your skin burns like fire. Landing feels as if your bones have been crushed into dust. You break a lot of things—trees, boulders." He inhaled deeply just to feel his lungs expand. "Then you stop. Eventually."

"But you aren't broken."

A broad grin spread across his face. "No, because I do not break."

She touched his face then. Her fingers were soft against his skin and burned in a way no less intense but wholly different from the sensation of falling.

"What?" he asked.

She pulled her hand away and shook her head. The plume of dark curls moved too, a beat behind. "I just can't believe you're really here." Dark eyes penetrated his.

His skin still burned where she had touched him, and he suddenly found it hard to meet her gaze. He cleared his throat as though it would clear the strange emotions rising in him. "Why don't you tell me about your wish? What is it that you want?"

"It's my sister, Sani." Her gaze broke from his and dropped to her feet. "She's my twin." One edge of her mouth pulled up as if remembering a happy memory. "We don't really look alike. She's beautiful and I—well, I'm just me. But she is sweet and kind with a smile brighter than the sun." Her mouth turned sharply down. "And . . . she's sick." The last word came out as a bitter, choking sound.

There it was. She would ask him to heal her sister. *Selfless*, he thought. Most asked him to grant them love or wealth or sex—or all three.

They arrived at the edge of the wood and the thatched roofs of the village could be seen past the rolling hills, in the valley below. Tender columns of smoke twisted toward the sky. Beyond, the horizon brightened with the coming day. Anush stopped and turned to him. Tears now streaming down her face.

"Sani isn't just sick." Her breath caught. "She's dying. No one can save her." She lifted her dark eyes to his.

His chest clenched, the depth of her despair physically painful to him. His insides twisted at the sight of her sadness, a sensation new and completely unpleasant. Yet he had the fleeting thought that if he could take her pain into himself, he would without hesitation. He reached out to wipe a tear from her stricken face, but thought better of it and placed his hand on her shoulder instead. He touched his other hand to the vial of dark liquid that hung by a cord around his neck.

"I can," he said.

❄

The sun hung well above the horizon by the time they reached the valley floor. Caelestis guessed it was midmorning when they entered the tall wooden gate set into the stone and mud wall. It was a market day, and the village pressed against them from all sides, overwhelming his unaccustomed senses: riots of color from the farmers' stands, the call and answer of the fishmonger and the butcher, the taste of dust and blood and spice on the air, the press of strange bodies against his.

Anush had been right: no one so much as batted an eye at his towering stature or silver hair. The villagers bustled about, haggling, squeezing, and sniffing wares in a kind of communal intimacy. A dog ran down the market street chased by a handful of laughing children. Lower now, the moon still hung in the sky. He sent a silent prayer of thanks to his mother; it was a lovely day to be on Earth.

As they walked through the market, the commotion around them began to lessen until it stopped. They turned down the nearest side street and followed its winding path. The buildings became shabbier and more run down until the huts gave way to hovels in various states of disrepair.

Anush came to a stop in front of the worn wooden door of a small shack. Checking that Caelestis was still behind her, she pushed the door open and gestured for him to follow her inside.

It took a moment for his eyes to adjust to the feeble light filtering through the single, grime-stained window. When his vision had adapted, he saw that the house was made of only a single sparsely-furnished room with a worn table set in the center. The hearth was on one side, two beds sat on the other. The only privacy a set of moth-eaten curtains.

"Mama!" Anush rushed toward a woman who sat with her back to them, hunched in a chair by the meager fire.

Startled, the woman looked up, her mouth framed with worry lines. "Anush! Where have you been? I've been worried sick."

A small, round head popped up over the mother's shoulder. "Nush!" cried the boy. Two dimples sank into grinning cheeks.

"Hi, Lor," she said to the child before he dipped his head back to his mother's breast. "I'm fine, Mama. I went to find help for Sani, and I did. I found . . . someone." She gestured toward Caelestis, and he stepped farther into the gloom of the hut.

Anush's mother looked up at him, her eyes growing wide just as her daughter's had done. He attempted the reassuring smile, but his senses were still muddled by his walk through the marketplace. He hoped he had managed something that would at least ease her worry about the presence of a strange man in her home.

"He's all right. His name is Cael and he's here to help us." Anush gestured for him to step forward. "Cael, this is my mother, Emese."

He bowed his head. Emese's eyes slid from him to her daughter, and she shook her head. "I don't understand. How can he help us? We've asked every shaman and every priestess known to walk this valley for help."

Emese cast a glance toward the beds behind her. For the first time, he noticed that one was lumpy with a figure huddled under a mass of quilts.

Anush spoke next, her voice barely a whisper. "How is she?"

Emese's eyes cut to his before dropping to the boy at her breast. She shook her head.

Cael walked silently to the bedside. He expected the girls' mother to stop him, but she didn't. Her face hung slack, the expression empty, gone with her hope. A girl with the same build as Anush lay in the bed, draped in heavy quilts. Her black hair spilled over the pillow, her skin greyed and sunken. He placed the back of his hand against her cheek. It was cool to the touch. Anush appeared at his elbow.

"What's wrong with her?" he asked.

"Stone's Plague." She carefully brushed a wisp of hair from her sister's face.

He shook his head, not understanding.

"She's"—her voice hitched—"hardening. Turning into stone. It's getting worse. Some days she can barely move. Other days are better, but these last few have been very bad. She won't eat and insists we take her portions, that we need them more than she does. So she grows weaker. There's no cure, and even if there were"—Anush glanced toward the hunched figure of her mother—"we couldn't pay for it."

He watched a tear slip down her cheek. As if aware of his gaze, she brushed it away with the back of her hand.

She turned to him, her deep eyes begging, the familiar tug at his core. "Can you help her?"

This time when he smiled, his focus was clear. "I told you, I can do anything. Are you sure this is how you want to use your wish?"

Anush nodded vehemently. "Yes."

"The wish is yours and can't be forced on another. She will have to agree. Can you rouse her enough that I may speak to her?"

"I think so."

"Good, then all will be well."

Anush spoke softly to Sani, her hands gently shaking her sister's shoulders as her mother watched from the chair. The little boy, Lor, had climbed off his mother's lap and now played on the floor with a ragged doll by the hearth.

Caelestis, having lifted the vial from around his neck, studied the crystalline container. Vertically divided into two, the dark liquid sloshed inside, a small glass stopper atop each portion.

A loud rap at the door startled everyone in the room. Anush froze, her eyes clouding with trepidation. Emese jumped to her feet and headed toward the door to peek through the cracks. With her hand to her mouth, she stepped back, her face showing the first sign of emotion Cael had seen in her.

"It's Kamen," she whispered as another loud rapping came against the door.

Anush scrambled to her feet, hands shaking.

"Who is Kamen?" he asked.

Anush frantically grabbed each of the tattered curtains and pulled them closed, concealing the beds behind them. "Sani's betrothed. He can't see her like this."

Lor, sensing the tension, toddled to his mother's worn skirt and clung to it. "Mama, Mama," he cried as Emese opened the door.

The vacant expression vanished, and her face cracked into welcoming smile as she greeted the young man on the other side. "Kamen, what a treat. We weren't expecting you."

A stocky young man with thick brown hair walked into the small home without further invitation. His nose wrinkled at the deficiencies of the hut.

"To what do we owe this pleasure?" Emese asked. Her calm voice was betrayed only by the tremble of her hands. She wound them into her gown.

"Nothing. Only the desire of a man in love to see his betrothed." His cold tone belied the warmth of his words.

"She's gone for a walk," Anush offered, staging herself just in front of the curtain. "You know how she is."

Kamen turned to her sharply. "No, I don't think I do. For whenever I come to call, she is never here. Now tell me, how is a man supposed to get to know his bride if she's never home?" The words hissed between clenched teeth.

Caelestis stood quietly at Kamen's back, as yet unnoticed. He'd had too many encounters with humans of this type, and Kamen wasn't making him feel particularly optimistic.

Kamen spun away from Anush, his eyes falling on the other man. "And who is this?"

Anush exchanged a nervous glance with her mother. "A cousin, Kamen. Come to celebrate the wedding of course."

Kamen stepped toward Caelestis, squinting at him in the dusky light. "Not much of a family resemblance."

"He comes from my husband's side. A distant relation." Emese spoke through tight lips. "He's traveled a long way and is unfamiliar with the language."

Caelestis, taking the cue, nodded politely to Kamen. Kamen turned back to Emese and Anush. "I will return tomorrow—with my father. I expect her to be home."

"Of course," Anush placated. "I'll be sure to relay your request when she returns. I'm sure she'll be most happy to comply."

Kamen opened the door to step out but hesitated and turned back. "I'd like to remind you that there is still plenty of time to cancel the arrangement." He slammed the rickety door behind him.

Legs trembling, Emese sank into a chair and laid her head on her arms. Poor little Lor stood clutching her skirts looking bewildered.

"Cael." Anush, pulling the curtain back, waved him over. "We must hurry. She *has* to be better by tomorrow." She turned back to her twin's motionless figure and shook her. "Sani! Please, wake up."

Caelestis could only watch as Anush tried to rouse her sister to no effect. Placing a gentle hand on Anush's shoulder, he motioned for her to stop.

"What if it's too late?" She choked down a sob.

He looked at her perplexed. If Anush loved her sister so much, how could she so eagerly hand her over to a man like Kamen? He could see the tender affection in her eyes but did not understand the complexities behind those human emotions.

He moved toward the bedside and knelt, placing his hand over Sani's heart. Closing his eyes, he focused that part of him that could hear even the faintest plea in the void of space. Sani's heart beat with quiet regularity, and her breath came easily, if shallow.

"She is not too far gone," he concluded. Then, in anticipation of Anush's impatience he added, "But in order for the magic to work, she must consent. We should let her be."

Anush's black eyes relayed the pain caused by the delay. After a long moment, she nodded reluctantly, then tucked the quilts warmly around her sister's still body.

Anush took him by the hand and drew him from the closeness of the hut. He squinted against the noon sun and pulled out the vial once more. Anush had begun walking at an anxious pace. He followed behind as she took the path along the village wall.

She led him through a small door in the rear of the wall and toward a copse. Once inside the cool shelter of the trees, she stopped abruptly, her whole body shaking. He raised a hand to touch her shoulder when she turned and pressed her face against the midnight of his robes.

He hesitated, unsure of what to do. Then he wrapped his arms around the bereft woman. Holding her close, he found himself stroking the dark mass of her hair, his fingers lost in the soft, springy curls.

She cried against him for a while. Sobs racked her body and vibrated through his chest until they quieted into shallow, hitching breaths. Humans had such a marvelous breadth and depth of emotions. It never ceased to amaze him, and now he wanted nothing more than to take away this woman's pain.

At last, Anush pulled back. "I—I'm sorry, I shouldn't have—"

"It will be all right. I'm going to help you. Just as soon as your sister—"

Anush pulled away, and he frowned, wondering if he'd done something wrong.

"I hate him," she said, her voice low. "He's horrible!"

"When she's well, she doesn't have to marry him. The man said it himself, that it's not too late to break the contract."

"She will never break her marriage contract." Her voice was thick with bitterness. "*Never.*"

"Why not?"

She strode forward several more steps before plopping down on the weathered remnants of a low stone wall. "We weren't always so poor you know."

He took a seat beside her.

"My father, when he was alive, was much respected, an honorable man. We weren't wealthy by any means, but his position under Magistrate Berk was more than enough to keep us well fed, clothed, and in a bright, dry hut with stone floors. He was a scribe for the magistrate." Her eyes filled with a sudden pain. "Magistrate Berk is Kamen's father."

Anush recounted her family's fall into poverty, and Caelestis listened with quiet intent. It had started when her father discovered the magistrate's corruption. Anush had overheard her parents talking about it. Her father had confronted the magistrate. He had wanted to give the man the opportunity for honor by giving him a chance to confess to the king. Anush's father had made it very clear that if the magistrate didn't do it himself, he'd do it for him.

But her father had never carried out the threat; he had died soon after, murdered by a band of robbers. Everyone said it was just bad luck, the danger of the road, but Anush and her family knew better.

With her husband gone, Emese had looked for work. But no one would hire an enemy of the magistrate. The only value left to the family was Sani's uncommon beauty, which quickly caught Kamen's eye.

"He's never shied away from showing his desire for her. But he cares not for love. It's her beauty he wants to possess." Anush's voice turned icy. "She's no more than an ornament for his arm, a prize to feed his conceit."

But Kamen had been persistent, and the family had fallen deeper into poverty. Without even consulting their mother, Sani had come home one day to announce her marriage. She had been shrewd in her marriage negotiations. In exchange for her hand, Kamen would take care of her family and give them the same respect and honor as his own.

"She knew she was ill," Anush said, shaking her head sadly. "She made him guarantee our place in his house even after her death." Her voice faltered over the last word. "And if she dies before the wedding, then the contract will be revoked."

Caelestis contemplated the dichotomy of humans, unable to process how they could be so horrible to one another and yet so capable of such selfless love. A millennium of watching Earth and he still couldn't understand it.

Anush seemed deflated. She massaged one hand with the other, slowly flexing her fingers. "We're on the verge of being cast into the street. If Sani dies, then we die too."

He took her trembling hands in his. "Sani will live."

※

While they walked slowly toward her home, Anush told him stories of happier times. The radiance brightening her face as she recounted past joys filled him with an unfamiliar warmth. He remembered the heat of her fingers on his face, her slender shoulders as he wrapped his arms around her, her thick curls sliding between his fingers.

They turned down her crooked street, and before they reached the house, her mother poked her head from the door.

Eyes glassy and excited, she shouted, "Anush!" She looked nervously between their two faces. "Come quick, she's awake!"

They rushed into the house. Again, he struggled to see in the low light of the hut. Eventually, he made out the figure in the bed. Sani sat upright, and Anush rushed to her bedside. She clasped her sister's stiff hands between her own, their heads bowed together in silent greeting.

Cael approached slowly, not wanting to intrude. He watched them with interest. Their movements mirrored one another, a hush of whispers flowing between the two. Anush stroked her sister's hair. Sani mirrored her, but her pain was obvious in her labored movements. They broke apart, and Anush waved him over, her eyes bright with hope.

"Sani, this is Cael. He is going to make you better."

He knelt by the bed, his hand on the vial at his neck. He lifted the cord over his head.

Sani's voice came as a struggle. "What is it?"

He held the vial up between his thumb and forefinger. The dark liquid sloshed inside. "They are tears of my mother, the moon," he said. A pang of longing shot through him, the end of his time on Earth was nearing. He looked at Anush. "With this, I can grant you a single wish, anything you desire at all."

"I wish for Sani to be well, to live a long and happy life." Anush spoke quickly, her voice thick with emotion.

He nodded in understanding and cast a glance toward her sister, his eyes questioning.

"What about the other vial?" Sani blurted. Her eyes moved from his hand to her sister's face. The small, hopeful squeeze she gave Anush's hand didn't go unnoticed.

He pursed his lips. "I can only grant one wish. The other vial is for my return."

Anush shook her head at Sani almost imperceptibly and smiled sadly. "I want Sani to have my wish." Her voice was firm. "Sani, say you'll take it."

"Will you?" Cael asked.

"Please," Anush begged at her sister's hesitation.

Sani's weak smile was enough to break his heart. "For you. Yes."

"Your wish shall be granted." He solemnly removed the stopper on one half of the vial and held it to Anush's lips.

"But," Sani began.

Before her sister could change her mind, Anush snatched the vial, tilted the liquid into her mouth, and swallowed.

"Do you feel anything?" Anush's eyes glistened.

Sani began to nod, but she didn't have to. Her skin plumped before their eyes. Incredulous, she raised her hands with ease, watching the fluidity of her wiggling fingers. She sat up and swung her legs from the bed to a chorus of cries from her mother and sister. Caught up in the excitement, the little boy squealed as well, clapping his hands in delight as his sister stood up.

Sani rushed to Caelestis and took his hand in hers. She looked up at him with eyes as dark and fathomless as her sister's. "Thank you."

"Marry Kamen and all will be well," Anush said. "He will take care of the family."

The expression on her face confused him. She seemed relieved yet unbelievably sad. The sisters fell into each other's embrace, joined by their mother and brother.

Caelestis quietly stepped outside, leaving them to their joy.

❋

The sun now hung low. Like the sun, his time on Earth was nearing an end. He lifted the vial to the sky and watched the liquid shiver with the promise of return. The thought made him uneasy.

He had been drawn to Anush by a fervent wish, but the hook that had sunk into his core hadn't released at the completion of his duty. Instead, over the course of his time with her, it had transformed into something hot and compelling. Something he didn't want to lose. Cael didn't belong on Earth. It was a strange place. Full of love and joy that could be dashed in a moment.

The complexities of human nature confounded. Their cruelty was beyond compare.

A cold dread settled in him at the thought of the family living under Kamen's rule. Kamen was not marrying Sani for love, and surely he would give her none. The thought left Cael feeling sour—a new lesson in human emotion.

The hut's dilapidated door creaked behind him, and Anush gingerly stepped out of the house. She pulled her cloak around her, despite the lingering warmth of the setting sun. Together they watched it dip toward the horizon.

It was a long while before she spoke. "I'm glad you waited. I need to thank you." She turned to him and placed a cool hand on his arm. Her dark, bottomless eyes locked on his. "You've saved my sister from death and my family from starvation. I don't know how to—"

He silenced her with a shake of his head and took her hand between his own. "There is no need."

She looked away, back to the horizon. "I suppose it's time for you to return home?"

"Yes." The word cut him.

"Do you have to go?"

He regarded the setting sun. "I must take my share of the vial before the sun sets, or I risk being trapped here forever."

She turned to him now. "Then you must return home." She took the vial and lifted it from his neck. Uncorking it, she held it to him. "Take it. Please."

He reached for it and hesitated. "Do you not want me to stay?"

Tears welled in her eyes. "You will not be happy here. You are better off in the sky where humans can only look at you, not hurt you."

Bitterness rose in him. Human hearts and emotions were volatile, unstable things. He didn't understand what he was feeling. His emotions were a mess of confusion. But he knew it was because of Anush and didn't want it to stop, which only confused him more.

"Please, go," Anush said, her voice heavy with regret.

It was time, and once he was back in the sky, his feelings would sort themselves out, Caelestis reasoned, even as he imagined the unending loneliness of space. Anush would be happy now with her sister in good health; her family would be taken care of. If Kamen did not love Sani, her family did, and that was all that truly mattered, wasn't it?

Only the edge of the sun peeked above the horizon now. He tilted the vial to his lips and swallowed the dark liquid. Silent, Anush leaned her head against his chest. His heartbeat quickened at her closeness. A soft wetness bloomed on his robes where she cried against him. Cupping her chin between his hands, he lifted her face to his.

"Why do you cry? Have I not given you what you desire?"

She shook her head and clenched her eyes closed, squeezing out a stream of tears.

It hurt his heart to see her like this. "What can I do? I have no more wishes left to give."

Her eyes opened and met his. "I have one more. I wish to be kissed."

Again, he remembered the heat of her palm on his face. It spread into his chest and burned like fire in his heart. A taste of human love, perhaps. He leaned his head down to hers, slipping closer as the sun slipped beyond the horizon. His lips turned to starlight.

Anush stood alone and cold, her face upturned for a kiss that would never come.

❋

Mother Moon was neither uncaring nor unkind. But as mother of the stars and goddess of the night sky, she had no time to waste with mundane matters. So it was with trepidation that Caelestis called out to her. With a voice that rent the vastness of space, he appealed to her, begged to be human. To *stay* human.

"Child, are you not happy in the heavens with your brothers and sisters?" Her voice rang in the darkness.

"Mother." Caelestis could hardly keep the pleading sound from his voice. "I am happy in your home. But I'm enamored with Earth, with the humanity you so graciously grant me."

Her bodiless voice hummed. "But humans are cruel. Surely you've learned that."

"Yes, they are. And I've witnessed it with my own eyes, been cut by their words in my heart—the heart you gave me. But I've also come to experience love and happiness with that same heart. It is the greatest experience I've known."

Mother Moon was silent, but at last she spoke. "Is this your final wish, my child?"

Caelestis looked to the blue speck hanging in the darkness. A terrible, frightening place full of love and joy. The juxtaposition confused him. Intrigued him. Called to him.

"It is," he replied.

"Then I will grant you one wish and command you to go and be happy with the understanding that you may never return here. But if you do not use your wish by sundown, you will forever return to your place among the stars."

At once, he tilted toward the Earth in that strange, jolting way. *Unbalanced*, he thought. Consumed by heat and flame, he made his descent.

※

Caelestis knocked upon Anush's door, excited to see her radiant face. Instead, he was greeted by the solemn faces of her mother and sister.

"We don't know where she's gone." Emese's red-rimmed eyes darted about. "She said she was going into the village, but she never returned." The last word came out in a stuttering sob.

"It's been three days." Even with her health returned, Sani was pale. "We've searched everywhere."

Cael felt as if he'd been hit in the gut.

"She's sick. She needs to be at home." Emese sobbed into the back of her hand.

A cold lump wedged in Cael's throat, startling him with its choking pain. His mind spun as he tried to digest Emese's words. *Sick.*

Dark eyes, so much like her sister's, bored into his. "Do you know where she might be?"

"No, I—" A slow realization took hold. *The Moon Pool.*

Without so much as a goodbye, he dashed from the hut and ran through the streets toward the city gate.

✳

Following the path to the pool, Cael was acutely aware of the sun's position in the sky. It was already too low for comfort. He replayed every moment as he ran, remembering every touch and word. He'd been so blinded by her goodness that he hadn't seen what had been right in front of him. For the first time, he felt anger. At his own thoughtlessness, at the unfairness of the fleeting human life.

At last, he reached the clearing where the Moon Pool lay. A solitary figure sat hunched by its edge, just as he'd first found her. He knelt by her side.

Anush turned toward him, her movements slow, the pain written clearly on her face. "You came back."

His heart burned in the friction between joy and abject loss. *Bittersweet.* The humans had a word for everything.

"Of course I did." He took her hands, held them to his lips, and kissed her cold fingers.

Anush's brows knitted together. "But why?"

He reeled at the question. Did she not know what he felt for her?

"I came back for you. I love you, don't you see?"

"You do?" She shook her head in disbelief.

He pressed his forehead to hers. "I asked my mother to grant me a wish. And she did, so that I may be with you."

She drew back, pulling her hands from his. "But I am dying, Cael." Her voice broke.

Tears stung at his eyes, but he blinked them back. He took the vial and lifted the cord from around his neck. "No, I can save . . ."

The words died on his tongue as he stared at the last wish he would ever grant. The crystalline vial on his palm contained only one dose of the black liquid. This time he could not stop his tears, and they burned bitter silvery streaks down his cheeks.

"You take it," he said, holding out the vial.

She shook her head. "But what about your wish?"

His eyes went to the sky. The sun would set soon. "I will return home to my mother where I will forever stay. But you will live and that is enough. Besides, what would my life be on Earth without you?"

Anush started to speak, but a wrenching tremor shuddered through her body. She cried out, toppling. He caught her and held her close.

She placed a chilled hand against his cheek and tilted her lips toward his. He bent to her, his lips warm against the cold creeping in her veins. Time stilled, silence falling around them as heat blossomed through his chest.

Love, he thought.

In a moment that stretched into eternity, there was only the feeling of her lips against his, her smell, her taste. The sound of her breath and of her heart.

Until there was not.

Cael broke away, but Anush did not move. She sat perfectly still, a fine-grained statue of jet, lips permanently upturned in the joy of her lover's kiss. A single crystal tear streaked down her cheek.

Caelestis stared with sightless eyes at the vial in his hand. The light in the woods had a dusky quality now. He knew that he could not navigate the curious twists and turns of this human world without Anush by his side, nor soothe the tearing pain in his heart without her.

In an instant, he made his decision. Uncorking the vial, he swallowed the liquid down, then kissed his love for the last time.

❋

Sani awoke early the next morning and arose as easily as a feather lifts on the wind. The feeling of lightness was short lived at the sight of her sister's empty bed. Her thoughts turned heavy and gray like the rain clouds in the valley. When she considered that the strange young man hadn't returned, they threatened to burst in a torrent of despair. Her stomach sank as she recalled him standing in the doorway, his starlight hair catching the late afternoon sun. It made her think of the Moon Pool, and she smiled to herself sadly.

Anush had never believed in magic, not even when they were children. She had always said the pool and its mysterious black waters were "for crones and lost souls who had nowhere else to turn."

And now Sani had nowhere else to turn.

Through the gate, she followed the winding path out of the valley and into the woods until she stood in the clearing, the Moon Pool as fathomless and black as she remembered. Across the pool stood an unfamiliar sight—a statue. She took in the shape of it, her heart stopping in a painful moment of familiarity. Before she knew it, she had burst into a sprint, stumbling forward on unsteady legs. Upon reaching the other side, she fell to her knees before the jet figure and stared at a face so much like her own: her twin frozen in a silent monument to selfless love.

With tears in her eyes, she stroked her sister's cold cheek and choked back a heaving sob. She would have squeezed into the circle of her sister's arms if it hadn't already been occupied by a second figure, one of the brightest moonstone. For here in the space between Anush's hands and her heart, which had always seemed so infinitely large, sat the stranger with the starlight hair. His arms encircled her waist, hers his neck. With smiling lip to smiling lip, Anush pressed into Cael's eternal kiss.

Sani sat for a bitter moment. The strange man had gone with Anush to a place where Sani could not follow. Beside her, the pond rippled. Her breath caught in her throat; she'd never seen so much as breeze disturb the surface of the depthless pool, nor any glimmer of light reflect from its surface. But for a brief moment, she saw the moon looking up at her. Sani lifted her eyes to the sky where the silvery orb hung, full and strangely melancholy.

At last she understood. She turned back to the statue of Cael and placed a hand on his shoulder. Head bowed, she sent up a prayer of thanksgiving for the sister who died so that she and her family might live and the man who gave up the heavens, the Earth, and all the stars to follow her into the unknown.

Mallory St. Cloud lives in a castle on a mountain made of cloud-stuff. She is an illustrator and photographer and the mother of two children who share her cloud castle but not her last name. She writes under many pseudonyms, and she'll never tell you what they are.

BRITTNEY SANKOFA

Intangible Evidence

"BROCK CHAPMAN IZ A UNKLE TOM ASS NIGGA"

This time the words are written in mustard, which won't be too difficult to clean, thank God. He had designated time this morning to accommodate for any possible slander needing immediate attention. A bag of hot feces bubbling on his doorstep. Or razor blades kicked into his tire (that was a horrible day). But today is the first occurrence in over three weeks—PROGRESS—and mustard on the windshield isn't too bad. An improvement, maybe? He grabs a squeegee and a spray bottle of all-purpose cleaner from the trunk of his SUV. Eight minutes tops. Still time to grab a coffee.

The Wednesday newsroom meeting is its usual grade of bubbly. The anchors—calm, docile, and tenured—offer minor quips as the producers and reporters fight over assignments like Olympic journalists. Criticisms fly out of powdered-sugar-dusted lips as the two fluorescent ceiling lights flicker rapidly from

192

water damage. Brock sips his latte and hums Yolanda Adams in his head.

"So you're saying I can't do homicide?" Liz, the network's new blonde bombshell, argues with Bill, the news director. He's been here longer than anyone.

"I'm not saying that."

"Well, then what's the problem?"

"You just got to Mobile."

"So?"

"You've never been to Prichard."

"Oh come on, I'm going during the day. It can't be that bad. Right, Brock?"

Brock looks up from his latte as the milk curdles in his stomach.

"I've never been to Prichard."

Liz blinks as Bill runs his fingers through his hair. Wanda, the black news anchor, lowers her eyes immediately. She wants absolutely nothing to do with this situation.

Finally, Liz chuckles. "Well at least pair me up with a big camera guy like Jimbo or Paul. Not one of those scrawny interns."

The meeting continues and Brock goes back to Yolanda Adams, imagining her pronounced cheekbones and whether she might be a complete bitch beneath that radiant smile. He really doesn't have to be here. This Friday makes four months since his News Package Fiasco where he congratulated Officer O'Brien on his acquittal after shooting an innocent black teenager, or, as Brock controversially stated, "a likely criminal." Two nights later, as a mob of protestors picketed in the lobby, Franz, the executive producer, met with Brock in a dimly lit back office.

"It's not that we're upset with your story, but we're losing your demographic. Diversity is *very* important and *necessary* to us."

Instead of firing him—they had, after all, encouraged his news pitch—the producers agreed to place him under "content supervision" which, in network speak, meant he would be spoon-fed all of his material in order to win back Negro viewers. He would cover Black History Month specials, drive-by shootings, church drives, and black kids with heartwarming stories who could sing and/or dance. A steady rotation of tragic, comedic, and sentimental stories to show how much their beloved Brock Chapman *frum right he-uh in Mo'Beel ain't forgot who he is!*

The dusty blinking light in the newsroom reminds him who he is: a college graduate with lowered expectations.

After the meeting, Brock and Franz ease into a press room and shut the door. Everyone knows about Brock's stipulation, but the two have agreed to maintain a level of discretion.

Brock's watch goes off, reminding him to take his blood thinners, and Franz reads a sheet printed from the wire feed. He paces wildly about the room, jerking his neck like Quentin Tarantino and constantly stroking his greasy graying hair. *Former coke addict*, Brock is convinced.

"Okay, so we got a tip here that's pretty fucking bananas."

Brock dispenses a cup of water from the machine and sits down. "What you got for me, Franz?"

Franz stops pacing and slides the paper, facedown, across the table.

Brock reads, and the pills make their way back up his throat. "Leprechaun?" This can't be serious.

Franz throws his head back and laughs. "Isn't that great?"

Brock continues, "Three sightings of a leprechaun . . . living in a *tree* . . . in Crichton Court?"

"And the town's going nuts!" Franz exclaims. "I mean everybody's convinced there's a pot of gold under that tree. And St. Patrick's Day is coming up. Now *this* is going to be a fun story."

Brock tries not to sigh, but his face muscles can't seem to relax. His jaw clenches; his eyebrows stretch toward his hairline. *This can't be good.*

Franz takes notice. "Now, Brock. I know you have some apprehension. But, trust me, *I* get it."

"You *get* it?"

"You think I like being a Jewish TV producer? So typical, right? Shit, I should be a break dancing legend right now, but my parents threatened my trust fund."

Brock offers a weak smile.

"Look," says Franz, "every time we do a story in Crichton, it's a homicide, or a robbery, or a drug bust. You remember that last one you did?"

"It was my best one."

"And it sure was! But, how about taking a chance and showing this community in a . . . well . . . *softer* light. Something friendly . . . and fun!"

Brock moves his head in a circle, unsure whether to shake his head "no" or nod "yes."

"Besides." Franz sits on the arm of Brock's chair and speaks in a hushed voice. "Pull this off and I'm sure the network will take you off supervision."

Outside, the morning sunlight bounces off the building's steel window frames and hits Brock's watch, a vintage Ferragamo. It was his first expensive gift to himself after working at News 12 for six months.

When his mother saw the watch last Christmas, she gushed to her big sisters, "I've always told my baby to mind his time, and look what the Lord done blessed him with." Having been a retail associate for over thirty years, she knew quality beyond her means. She carefully examined the bezel and laughed. "But you know, for the life of me, I caint figure out why niggas got to get everything in gold."

The day is equal parts amusing, annoying, and absurd, with Brock clumsily floating around Crichton like Josephine Baker on a return trip home. He grew up nearby under the watchful eye of his mother and five aunties, so walking the streets in a Brooks Brothers suit is a bit unsettling. On the other hand, Jimbo—the fat redneck camera guy who fucks highway prostitutes in the station van during off hours—is fully enjoying himself. These are his kind of people, only a few shades darker and with different tastes in music and beer.

They meet a bevy of characters, including Montae, a local club promoter, who doesn't believe there is a leprechaun but rallies a mob of believers within ten minutes of spotting the news truck parked near his unit.

Ernestine Jenkins, a nurse's aide with two grown children, is convinced that the leprechaun is just a drug addict "hooked on the wrong stuff."

And then Fife, a former drug dealer, more concerned with the treasure than the leprechaun, states his plans to uproot the tree after everyone leaves.

But the most interesting character of the day is Bill Spragley, better known as "Sarg" for his tendency to take charge of any activity coming through Crichton. Rumor has it that he was, in fact, a sergeant in the US Army for many years but was later discharged for exposure to a deadly herbicide. Donned in an army fatigue shirt and brown heavy-duty coveralls, Sarg has appointed himself "tree traffic guard," guiding passersby and assuring them that there is nothing to fear.

Every story needs an expert, Brock thinks upon first meeting Sarg. This is his man.

Though he doesn't allow them to record footage, Sarg invites Brock and Jimbo into his two-bedroom shotgun house. They are immediately greeted by the strong smell of roasted meat. The walls are crawling with rustic artifacts—black-and-white family photos in dusty frames, newspaper clippings, fishhooks, horseshoes, and animal skins. Sarg shares the house with his father, Bruce, who wheels around in a wheelchair as embellished as the house's walls.

"Just cooking a little something for us later," says Sarg, trying to mask his deep southern accent with northern eloquence. At the fireplace, some charred, unrecognizable cuts of meat lie on top of a grill rack.

"Well, Mr. Sarg," says Brock, "it seems you have a bit of experience in this sort of . . . field."

"Yes, indeed I do, Mr. Chapman," says Sarg, poking out his muscular chest. "I toured Ireland while serving in the army. Lot of leprechauns out there."

"You don't say?"

"And they liked to mess with me because they could tell my great-great-grandfather was Irish."

Brock glances over at Bruce for some reassurance. Bruce remains silent.

"It was on my mother's side," Sarg says defensively.

"In fact." Sarg grabs a small box sitting on the mantle. "He left me this Irish flute when he passed away."

The flute is so old and worn, Brock can't tell if it's made of silver or tin. He tries to get a closer look, but Sarg holds the flute like a mother protecting her newborn from a stranger's germs.

"Whoa now. Be careful. This here is a leprechaun flute. You play and it wards off bad spells. Those leprechauns are a tricky bunch, and they don't really like us black folk, specially mixed breeds like me. They get by around us colored folk because nobody would believe a nigger that seent a leprechaun, anyway." *So much for northern eloquence.*

The room grows tense and silent for a few seconds. Brock feels his heart pounding against his pocket square and remembers he left his blood thinners at work. From down below, Bruce lets out a tiny, encouraging grunt, and Sarg sighs heavily before he speaks.

"Mr. Chapman, this ain't the first creature been running through Crichton. This whole area been they testin' ground for years now. Now I trust we in good company, correct?"

Brock looks over to Jimbo who is stuck in a staring contest with a stuffed squirrel mounted on the wall.

"We good, man. I promise," says Brock. "I'm curious though: what makes you so sure this thing is a leprechaun?"

"Like I said, we get all kinds of things that run through here. Aliens. Gnomes. Mole people. You name it," says Sarg. He begins rummaging through a trunk on the floor next to the fireplace.

"But, see, leprechauns are night creatures. That's why they hide their gold under rainbows, so the other night creatures won't get to it."

Sarg hands Brock a handheld radio and a pair of stretched-out headphones. He turns the dial. "You know about AM radio and FM radio right?"

Brock shakes his head. No.

Sarg continues, "Well they put talk radio on AM because it's an outdated system. FM radio, the waves move a special kinda way where the earth don't interfere. You can play all day and night, and it still sounds clear. Good for music. But AM radio, the waves move different. They go up and the sun helps them go back down where they supposed to go. But what you think happens at night?"

"Ooh!" cries Jimbo, taking interest. "They don't go back down where they should?"

"Right!" Sarg exclaims, stretching his large hands. "They bounce around to different towns and make that static sound that'll drive you crazy." He crosses the room to a vintage stereo topped with a messy pile of CDs and cassettes. He puts in a tape labeled "Bruce." "Now every day around this time, I record Miss Aggie's Bible Study on 87.1."

"She still got that radio show?" asks Brock.

"Yep. It's Pops's favorite. Now take a listen to the show from Monday." He plays the tape and there is Miss Aggie's singsong voice, still preaching the New Testament.

"Now take a listen to what the station sounds like right now." Sarg switches the stereo's controller to "radio" and tunes it to 87.1. Nothing but static. "See there! It's been like that since that thing landed here. That shouldn't be happening. It's still plenty daylight outside."

Bruce smirks slightly while Brock and Jimbo look to each other for answers.

"Maybe something's wrong down at the tower," Brock suggests.

"Okay, now. Mr. Chapman, that radio you got in your lap has been DX'd—or programmed—to the stations in Tuscaloosa. That's two hundred miles, roughly. Now I want you to stand on that metal square on the floor next to Pops and face that wooden clock."

It takes everything in his power not to roll his eyes, but Brock obliges. This is some Toys"R"Us, My First Ouija Board type shit, and Franz definitely owes him a pay raise. He plants his feet and turns on the radio . . .

"But Paul lists it all clear as day in Corinthians! Everybody wanna inherit God's kingdom but don't wanna . . ."

Brock's eyes widen. *Well, I'll be damned.*

"You see! Pops, you see that? And y'all know they got all kinda missiles in Tuscaloosa."

Bruce gives a testimonial nod, and Brock chuckles. "You might be onto something there, Sarg. We'll see."

"But wait," Sarg pleads. "One last thing before you go. You got to hear this."

Sarg grabs Brock's elbow and drags him back to the stereo. Brock is surprised, yes, and having a little fun, but the station switch doesn't prove anything. Radio towers always mess up when the seasons change, and Sarg clearly isn't hip to XM radio. Sarg plugs Brock's headphones in the stereo's jack and whispers sharply, "I'm gonna turn this up, and I want you to listen reeeaaalll careful."

Brock closes his eyes as static buzzes in his ears. Lo and behold, beneath the grainy sound is a faint modulated rhythm like a wah guitar. *Wah-wah-wah-wah-wah . . . wah-wah . . . wah . . .* Then nothing. Brock takes his headphones off and looks at Sarg.

Jimbo clambers over. "I wanna take a listen!"

"I dunno, Sarg," Brock says hesitantly. "Maybe that's the feed just flickering back in?"

"But you heard it though, right? That 'wah-wah' sound? Sound like Sugarfoot from the Ohio Players."

"I did."

Jimbo pouts. "Aw, I don't hear anything."

Sarg pierces a piece of meat on the grill rack with a large grill fork. He chews the meat and picks the charred black bits from his teeth, never taking his eyes off Brock. "Mr. Chapman, if you really wanna help us out, then try and get the president and them over here and explain what's going on."

Brock smiles and gives Sarg a pitying pat on the shoulder. Sarge grabs Brock's wrist and smiles. "Hey, you're all right, Mr. Chapman. Even after that shit from back in April."

When they exit the small house, Brock is awash with relief. They manage to get an on-camera interview outside the house during which Sarg makes no mention of Crichton's other creatures and his theories, declaring that he "don't wanna end up like Denzel in *Manchurian Candidate*." Brock can't help but wonder if he would have been better off leaving his momma and joining the army like Sarg. And losing his sanity like a man.

✳

It's dark by the time Brock finishes shooting. Six hours of listening to the most improbable stories told by witnesses with questionable credibility. Six hours with Jimbo. By now, the two are starving. Jimbo tracks the closest pancake house on the navigation system while Brock drafts his voiceover on his iPad. He contemplates switching up the story's angle into a broader conspiracy on government-issued tests in black communities. Dropping in some Five Percenter shit just to spite Franz and those stuffed shirts from the network.

"Hey Jim, what do you think about this leprechaun?"

"Oh, I believe it, man," says Jimbo, more enthusiastic than usual. "Not sure if it's a leprechaun, but there's definitely something there."

"How do you know this ain't just some Salem Witch Trials type of shit? Like one person sees something then the whole town claims to have seen it too, you know what I mean?"

"I see your point. But that doesn't answer the question—what the hell is it?"

"Like that lady said: a midget crackhead."

They laugh.

Suddenly, there's a loud rapping on Brock's window. He sees two bucktoothed black boys, both under the age of ten and happily sucking on popsicles. One is waving a piece of paper. An autograph? How sweet. Brock flashes his news reporter smile and rolls down the window. "Good evening, young men—"

"Here," the taller boy interrupts. "This what the leprechaun look like."

Brock unfolds it and finds an elementary sketch of the leprechaun drawn on yellow lined paper. No shading or details whatsoever.

"You drew this."

"Yuh," says the boy, fidgeting uncontrollably like most boys his age when eating frozen sweets.

"Aye," says the shorter of the two. "The leprechaun almost kilt that man right thur." He points to a gentleman standing near an ice cream truck, helping younger kids with their change and opening their ice creams. He's a much taller man, visibly in poor health. His feet look clownish in diabetic shoes sticking out from underneath a pair of linty sweatpants. Plastic tubes run from his nose to a wheeled air tank resting behind him.

"Mista James!" the older boy yells, then motions him to come forward.

"Tell him 'bout what happened!"

"Yeah, tell him, Mista James."

Mista James walks over, clutching his chest anxiously.

"Y'all leave that man alone. He been out here all *day*, Jesus."

Brock starts to roll up the window, but Jimbo leans over his seat.

"These young men say the leprechaun tried to kill you?"

"Look," said Mista James. "All I'm saying is I ain't going nowhere near that tree till that *thing* is outta there."

Brock and Jimbo look at each other.

"Hey," Brock says, "would you mind telling us what happened?"

"I don't do no cameras. Sorry."

"We don't have to record. You can just talk to me."

Mista James looks back at the kids, who all seem to be satisfied and are now eating their ice creams. He sighs. "Aight. I *guess* so."

Brock gets out of the car and mouths to Jimbo, "Keep the car running."

As they walk around the corner, Mista James describes the events surrounding his ordeal.

"I live in that house *right* there. Yesterday I was walking over to see what all the fuss was about after everybody left cuz Mista James don't *do* no large crowds. So, I'm walking, right, and I get 'bout to where that Chevy is parked *right* there and I start hearing this high-pitch sound in my ears. Like a dog whistle or something."

Brock jots notes on his notepad.

"Then all of a sudden, I get this cold feeling right here in my chest. And it just *spread* all through my body. Felt like all my bones turned to iron."

"And it happened out of nowhere?"

"Out of nowhere! Next thing I know, I'm *laid* out on the ground. See, I had that happen to me once befo' when I was training down at the city dump. I got too close to that machine with the big battery attached. You know, the one that picks up all the metal pieces. It upset my pacemaker. The *same* thing happened yesterday, and if it weren't for my grandbaby—"

Brock stops jotting notes and takes a sudden interest.

"Wait, you said you have a pacemaker?"

"Yeah, I got all kinda health problems. The warning on those cigarette packs *ain't* lying to you."

Brock looks up into the night sky, and his thoughts travel back to 1997 and the high school track meet.

❁

He had been training for weeks. A pain had developed in his chest, and he hadn't told Momma. Coach assured him that he was finally gaining that muscle mass he prayed for every night. Running builds testosterone which builds muscles. Plus it was too close to the tournament to give up now. *Pain is just something you run off, young man. Pain is just something you run off.* The words echoed through his head and over the stadium's uproar as his body crashed against the rubber track with a stiff thud.

His pacemaker was now his best-kept secret, the handicap to his collegiate all-American dreams. While his mother had chided herself for passing along her heart condition, his aunties had gathered like crows around his hospital bed.

"His grades ain't the best, but he talk real proper—"

"And he's a looker too, just like his daddy."

"Once them braces come off, he gonna have the prettiest smile."

"He kinda favor that man on channel four."

"That could be something he could do. Work for the news!"

"Yeah, and they make good money."

"And he's smart enough to do it."

"He struggle with math and science, but he writes real good. Real good."

"Yeah, he's too smart to be running around some track."

❇

And now here he is, back in his hometown slums. Living out his aunties' dreams with his Ferragamo watch. Listening to tales of aliens and magic flutes and cursing the inkling creeping up the side of his neck that this leprechaun is anything but pure nonsense.

He shakes his head. "With all due respect, that's just . . . Look, I have a pacemaker. We've been past here several times, and I haven't felt anything."

Mista James gives him a sideways look. "Okay, but you the one asking me—"

"Here." Brock pulls on Mista James's hand. "Show me exactly where it happened."

Mista James yanks his hand back. "Oh naw! I ain't going back over *there*! All these medical bills *I* done got, I can't *afford* to take on no more."

Brock stares angrily at the tree looming over an abandoned patch of nothing in the distance. He tries to discern which is more ridiculous, the idea of the "thing" in the tree or his burning desire to go over there and disprove the myth.

"You can go over there if ya want to," Mista James says, heading back toward his house. "That's a trek *you* gon be taking *alone*."

Brock rolls his eyes. He marches, or, rather, stomps toward the tree, mumbling, "This trifling bullshit. Niggas don't got nothing else better to do than make shit up. Probably somebody sprinkled angel dust in his blunt and he don't know how to act!"

Brock's face loosens once he realizes he's past the point where Mista James almost died. He walks closer, quickening his pace and laughing. "Ridiculous!"

But then *pop*. That deafening dog whistle, stinging a nerve in the back of his head. An icy sensation bursts in his chest and spreads throughout his body. Once it reaches his fingertips and toes, he collapses like a felled tree with his eyes and hands open to the heavens.

His body is completely numb except for the space around his heart, beating strong but moderate. He can feel the cold asphalt underneath and the evening wind tugging at his pocket square. But nothing more. Strange. Surprisingly, his senses are still intact. Laundry wafts to his nose from a nearby vent, letting him know he's still in Crichton. He sees that the air around him has adopted a gray, digitized fog, as if submerged into a pool of translucent TV static. To his right, a busy rustling can be heard from the base of the supposed-leprechaun's tree. The rustling turns to footsteps. Then suddenly . . .

Thud.

A tiny golden shoe plants itself next to Brock's ear. He directs his vision from the shoe and up the body, a tiny frame clad in an emerald-encrusted suit of armor. Beneath the golden helmet, however, is a face of complete darkness aside from a pair of glowing lime-green eyes. The eyes are neither aggressive nor menacing but alert and a bit nervous, like those of a small child.

Who are you? Brock tries to say, but he's lost his voice along with all feeling in his neck. He has no choice but to surrender to this small warrior, who is now on its knees and moving its hands in circles inches above Brock's chest. With each rotation, the cold ground beneath grows warmer and warmer until it's about a hair below unbearably hot. His pacemaker doesn't skip a beat as a huge vortex of green light shoots up from his chest and into the heavens. The TV static buzzing around him slows its rhythm. The figure leaps to its feet and tilts its head way back. Green gauntlets cup the dark space where its mouth would be, and it lets out three earsplitting modulated screeches from the back of its throat.

Wah-wah-wah-wah . . . *Wah-wah-wah-wah-wah* . . . *Wah-wah-wah* . . . *wah* . . . *wah* . . .

The piercing vibrations slice through the hot asphalt and send sharp daggers of light up the vortex.

The warrior tries a few more times but to no avail. For what seems like an eternity, all is silent. The laundry smell has grown faint, and Brock can hear the small warrior's heavy breathing. Its shoulders hunch, and its head hangs heavy.

As Brock lies there, paralyzed and vulnerable, he realizes that the figure hasn't yet harmed him. If it had any intention of doing so, it surely wouldn't be standing just a few yards away looking so dejected and pathetic. *He must be some sort of child*, thinks Brock. *Cartoonish, in fact. Like Marvin the Martian.* His inside joke quickly dissolves into a pool of new questions and realizations. Who or what is this little guy calling out to?

A small shape forms in the sky. Brock assumes it's an airplane at first, but as it gets closer, he sees that it's a large and colorful serpent with opal eyes and an iridescent tongue. Straddling its neck is a woman as black as the warrior and swaddled in emerald-green silk. The warrior, still dejected, doesn't take notice until the woman's golden bracelets and anklets beam light in its direction. It immediately hops up and down in excitement, its gold shoes clanging hard against the ground.

As the serpent hovers a few feet above the ground, it lowers its tongue to pick up the warrior. The woman stretches her slender arms and welcomes it into a long embrace. If Brock could shed a tear, he would, but instead he lets his mind wander from the now into the next. What if he never recovers? If his body remains paralyzed forever? How will he explain what he saw tonight? And what will become of this news story?

The thoughts flood his mind so quickly that he doesn't see the snake's head inches from his own, nor the bare black feet that have stepped down onto the asphalt and are now on either side of him. The figure crouches down and rests her palms in the middle of his forehead. Instantly, feeling returns to his body—toes, knees, shoulders, and, finally, his head. The black face, cloaked in green, is void of emotion, but Brock is certain she is smiling. Once he finds the nerve to smile back, the TV static fog speeds up to its normal rhythm then slowly disappears. The woman crawls back onto the serpent's back, and as they make their way up into the sky through the green vortex, Brock is engulfed in a blinding white light.

※

Brock finally opens his eyes, and all he can see is saturated color for at least fifteen seconds. The sounds are muffled but familiar. Heart monitor. Nurse's chatter. Intercom. The colors slowly bleed into objects. A silver curtain rod. Art deco wallpaper. A baby-blue hospital robe. Clear plastic tubes sticking out from his wrists. Everything smells sterile and unfriendly. Brock feels exhausted as he feebly pushes a red button on the control panel attached to his bed.

A frumpy nurse with stubble on her upper lip rushes in.

"Oh you're awake, are ya?"

She has a thick Long Island accent. Brock wants to respond, but a rubbery mask covers his mouth and nose.

"I'm gonna ask ya some questions, okay? Raise one finger for yes, raise two for no. Can you do that?'

Brock raises one finger.

"Is your name Brock Theolonius Chapman?"

One finger.

"Are you from Wichita, Kansas?"

Two fingers.

"Are you from Mobile, Alabama?"

One.

"Thirty-three years of age?"

One.

"Born October 21, 1979?"

Two fingers. *I'm definitely a Capricorn*

"Good. Looks like your memory is intact. Here, let's take this thing off." She removes the mask, and the inside of his mouth feels like sandpaper. A few minutes later, Dr. Bethea, an attractive woman in her late thirties, comes to his bedside.

"Mr. Chapman, the batteries in your pacemaker were completely drained. We don't understand why. The unit itself seems to be functioning perfectly. You usually only see this sort of thing when the patient has been in the vicinity of a large magnet or high-voltage power lines. But you don't have a history of that." She flips through his chart, like she's already read it front to back and front again. "This is very odd." She looks up from the chart and smiles absently. "These things do happen, though. It's uncommon, but not unheard of."

She places a cold hand on Brock's as he does his best to avoid eye contact. He's not foreign to these prescribed forms of affection, but it's a little embarrassing to be in this condition before a woman he wouldn't mind taking out to dinner.

"We contacted your mother, but she's on a cruise and won't be back until the end of the week. Her sisters, however, have been here. Twice."

Brock raises an eyebrow. Dr. Bethea seems a bit amused.

"They were here for most of the night and briefly this afternoon, but I assured them you'd be fine so they'll be back in the morning."

Brock's throat is parched. The words come out sharp and crackly. "Time . . . What time—"

"It's eight p.m. The nurse can bring you some water. Your friend Jimbo is floating around here somewhere. I'll send him in if I can find him."

Brock nods. Half an hour later, Jimbo enters, concerned and munching on a honey bun.

"Dude, I thought I lost you! I was soooo worried. I came over, and you were like . . ."

He mimes a dead man, limp with his eyes closed and tongue hanging out of his mouth.

Brock clears his throat and faintly whispers. "Wha . . . What happened? I—"

"Sounds like you had a heart attack or something. Dude, I didn't know you had a heart condition. I mean you're kind of young but that's pretty cool, I guess."

The nurse returns with a disposable cup of lukewarm water.

"I rode in the ambulance and then I realized, 'Shit! The van!' Had to take a cab back."

"Oh shit," says Brock, in a much clearer voice. "Did they take anything?"

"Yeah. A couple mics and cables. They probably won't notice so I'm not going to say anything." He grabs the remote from the side of Brock's bed and begins to flip channels. As if reading Brock's mind, Jimbo adds nervously, "So, about that story . . ."

"What's going on, Jim?"

"It's supposed to air tonight. I sent over the footage. Heard they turned it into a VOSOT."

"A *voice-over?*" Brock almost bellows, sitting up in his bed. "How in the hell could they have done a voice-over if I wasn't even there?"

"Apparently, they used that dude who works in the cafeteria. You know the one that's always singing? Pretty funny, right?"

Brock falls back onto the bed and groans. "No. That's not right. They can't do that."

"C'mon Brock, they do what they want. We both know that."

Jimbo grabs the remote and scans through the channels. He finally lands on channel twelve where Wine Addict Claire delivers the evening weather with perfect diction despite her flushed face. Jimbo quips and wisecracks as they watch, but Brock's mind is elsewhere, trying to traverse the fuzzy line between this reality and the one he witnessed earlier. Yesterday, rather. He can clearly recall that numb, cognizant feeling, the warmth in his chest, and the hard clanking sound of metal on concrete. But everything else is wispy, faint. Green jewels and flowing fabrics. A rainbow, or perhaps a snake? Dull gray dust or fog, floating and spinning. The blackest black he'd ever seen and, now, pining for his mother in ways he hadn't since childhood. All these wisps have purpose, he decides *But what is the actual story?*

Jimbo taps Brock on the leg. "Oh shit, man. Here it is!"

The evening anchors, Carl and Wanda, are clearly tickled as they present the story. Wanda's smile looks more painted on than usual. The story that follows is a slapstick tale, one better suited for World Star Hip Hop or Tosh.0. Gold-toothed Bamas so intoxicated by their own poverty that they've started hallucinating.

"Everybody seen the leprechaun say *yeeeeeeeee!*"

And Sarg, intelligent despite his eccentricities, is painted as a maladroit bumbling idiot.

Could I have done him better justice? Brock wonders.

Silence looms over Jimbo and Brock once the segment is over. The loudest noise in the room is Brock's heart monitor, which has miraculously maintained a steady rhythm. Even Jimbo, just two generations removed from his grandpa's "Whites Only" general store, seems to fathom Brock's humiliation. He breaks the sullen mood.

"Hey, that Liz is a cutie, right?"

"She's cool. Not my type."

"Yeah, she's got a nice mug, but I need mine thick. Like Wanda."

"Okay, Jim."

"I'm for real. Me and Wanda used to go out for a little bit."

"You're lying."

"I'm serious, man. I really dug her. But she had to chose between a camera guy and a lead producer so . . ."

"Wait, don't tell me."

"Oh come on, man. Everybody knows that. That's old news."

"Wow. I guess it all makes sense."

He scratches a space underneath the IV sticking out of his right wrist.

Damn, he thinks. *I hope nobody took my watch.*

Brittney Sankofa is a filmmaker, writer, and theater artist based in the Washington DC Metro area. She has been writing since 3rd grade when a teacher allowed her to daydream in class because she knew she was thinking up a good story. An alumnus of New York and Virginia Commonwealth University, she attributes much of her interest in black mysticism and science fiction to all the characters and spirits she encountered while living in Richmond VA. She thanks them for giving her the voice and ear to carry on the storytelling tradition.

www.brittsankofa.weebly.com

GARY PRIEST

The Cradle and the Scribe

"THE WORLD WILL END WHERE IT BEGAN."

Grandma Nini's voice sang soft in his head as Abdalla sat atop the hill in the light of a new moon and looked down on her freshly dug grave.

The world had shrunk in a series of ecological disasters that were often referred to as "the hand of God" or "the unmaking." Nini had always said that the planet would not always succumb to the will of men, that she would one day turn on him like a beaten dog and so she did.

All those bright places he had only read about were gone now. America, Europe, Asia were all swallowed by the saltwater or burned black by holes in the sky.

Africa had been the last, but now it too was dead. Everything had drawn to a close, and as he sat there, he knew that he was the last person left, not just in Kenya, not just in Africa, but in the whole world.

"Everything connects. We were the first humans, sitting at the feet of God, and we shall be the last, sitting in the shadow of his sorrow and desolation," said Nini as she cooked the daily meal of *Gĩtheri*. A simple dish of maize and beans, and yet the thought of it now brought Abdalla close to tears.

Nini had been the last to die. She knew of the vital forces of things. Long after everyone else had given up on God, had buried their hearts in circuitry and sin, Nini had still kept to the ways of the first people, the ones who sat just below God.

When he was younger and his parents had left him alone with Nini while they worked, she had told him her tales of vital forces and swore him to silence, lest his parents, long since lost to the modern world, think her a witch.

"How old are you, Nini?" he had asked, not realizing the impudence of such questions.

She had let out her rattling laugh that bounced off walls and escaped through windows and filled up all the spaces in the sky. "I am as old as I wish to be" was always her answer.

Her skin was creased with age. Her thin frame a little stooped, yet her back was strong and her wide brown eyes yielded no signs of fatigue or that bitterness he had seen in the eyes of his parents and so many other adults.

Of course, simple mathematics told Abdalla that she must be in her seventieth decade, this based on his mother's age and the fertile years of a woman, but when she said those words, when she fixed him with her dazzling brown eyes and told him she was whatever age she wanted to be, he never doubted her.

Back then, he never doubted her beliefs either. He believed in the vital forces, and she taught him how to identify that specific point in every manifestation where that force was at its most potent.

"An unwise person can use this knowledge to invoke the higher forces and be rich or desired. They can pluck the apple from the highest tree. But these people are often lazy, they do not adhere to the rules. They try to invoke the higher forces directly, without a sacrifice of an animal or plant. This is *thahu*. A crime against God that will be punished."

He loved Nini more than anyone, more than his parents, whom he loved and respected as all children must but not in the way that he loved Nini, in that breathless way, that way that made his heart leap when he heard her laugh or she took him up in her arms.

He also feared her. She saw inside him. Knew when he had been bad. Knew when he had been lazy or arrogant and punished him. Not with beatings or curses, but with silence. She would not speak to him until he righted his wrongs, until he learned to be a better man.

His parents died in the first of the heat swarms in 2167. It was a heat like no other before. Swept from the heart of the sun and laid across the earth. It killed hundreds of millions and then was gone, another unexplained phenomenon from a planet sick of humanity and its exploitation of its skin.

"God is taking us back to the cradle," said Nini as they stood by the mass grave that he believed contained his parents as well as most of their village.

"God is sending us to hell," he said, tears, fat and relentless, streaming down his face. It was not just his parents; it was the sheer brutality of this world, and the absolute failure of science and technology to do anything except melt into oblivion under the thumb of the vengeful creator.

"No, no, child. He loves us. He is giving us a second chance."

"But there is no us, Nini. The maker is wiping the planet clean," he said. Abdalla was angry and scared, standing by a hole in the ground filled with the dead, unable to believe in Nini's old stories of God and the vital forces. There was no control here. There was only desolation.

"God is collecting the life force of all his children. Taking it back into his heart so that he can start anew. He does this because he loves us. When the last life but one is gone, then the work will begin again. From the grave will come a new cradle. That is the way of life. Everything connects. There is no end."

She pulled Abdalla against her thin body, and he sobbed into her chest. Her fingers were tender against his arm. "I have protected us both until now, for there must always be one to bear witness. To write the word of God. That is you, Abdalla. Servant of God. Scribe of the creator."

For three years after that day, Nini had taught him all she knew, and as she did, he saw her age. It was as if she was ceding control of her powers to him and with them her life. At first, he had been reluctant. His faith had been shaken by the death of his parents, by the further disasters that flattened Nairobi in a single day and boiled the Rift Valley lakes into deserts of salt. But Nini had been persistent. She had been stern, and she had been loving, and slowly, even as the death toll rose, he began to believe again.

They abandoned the villages and towns and cities and found a peaceful hillside. Nini insisted they relinquish all modernity. "Such things are dust to God. They do not belong here."

So Abdalla built a cabin from scratch instead of growing one from a kit. He grew vegetables and hunted the few animals that still roamed instead of eating the synthesized proteins of the bankrupt world.

As time went on, Nini spoke less and watched more as he went about the business of living. He began writing each evening before the light went, and the following morning, he read what he had written to her. He wrote of the end of the world and his wait for the beginning of a new one.

"Yes," she said. Her voice thin and tired. "You write well, my boy. Yours will be the tale they tell for centuries to come."

"When will it come, Nini?" he asked. "When will God start again?"

"When all that is left is the cradle and the scribe," she said. "Then the Lord will relinquish those vital forces, and the seas will rise again, and the sun will no longer be broken, and his children shall be reborn to know him and love him again. Now hush with your questions and read me some more."

Abdalla read on, and when he was done, the silence was absolute, and he knew that Nini was dead, as was the world.

He buried her at the foot of the hill. He sang and prayed and wept. He cursed and laughed and roared at the expired planet.

Finally, he walked up the hill as the moon rose above him.

It seemed a little brighter than the night before.

Gary Priest writes short fiction and poetry. He has over twenty publications online and in print. Recent or upcoming publications can be found in *Vox Poetica*, the *Eunoia Review*, and *Literary Orphans*. He lives in the UK at the end of a dead-end road, which may explain everything.

www.facebook.com/garypriestwriter

LELA E. BUIS

Death in Nairobi

I'M INVESTIGATING luggage theft for Lufthansa this week, playing bait, and in a brief swing through Europe and the Mediterranean my luggage has been stolen twenty-seven times. In eleven cases, the thieves were airline employees. Eight of the other bandits were professional types—doctors, lawyers, businessmen. Somehow I'm not surprised by the stats.

The luggage tour has veered south, worked its way through Egypt and Tanzania, and now we're going to wind it up in Nairobi. For the fourth time, I'm standing in line at Jomo Kenyatta International Airport for a visa stamp. My dark skin blends in with the crowd, even if my face doesn't quite fit—I'm a Black Seminole. I shift from one foot to the other, search visibly through my purse. I jiggle the lure, set it down and move a few steps away. The lure is an expensive-looking piece of luggage I've been towing behind me, and I'm much better dressed than I normally would be on my pittance of a salary—courtesy of Lufthansa—like maybe I'd have high-priced jewelry in the bag. Within seconds, a man excuses himself through the line, headed for the restrooms on the other side of the terminal. As he goes by me, he snaps at the hook. Security nets him within a few yards, and he leaps and thrashes like any fish, tries to run. The waiting line flinches, startled and ready to duck, but nobody gives up their spot. The immigration guy hardly looks up.

The commotion dies down, and I step out of the queue like I'm headed to get my bag back. Actually, we're going to call it a wrap, and I'm set up for a meeting with the Lufthansa agent in his office. He's tall and polite and offers to help me with local arrangements, but I've already got things set up with my friend Sylvia. Before I fly back to Miami, I'm going take a few days off to see some of the countryside here.

I head back to the claim area for my real bag then, a duffel that's quite a bit scruffier than the decoy and completely unlikely to get stolen. On the other side of the gates, I run smack into Sylvia.

"Anna!" she shrieks and grabs me in a hug, duffel and all. "Did you bring Paul?"

I manage to get my breath.

"God. No," I croak.

"But I thought . . ." Then she catches my expression. "Oh, Anna, what . . . ?"

I don't really want to talk about it. He's been drifting even farther away from me since our recent job in Mexico—like something happened inside him when he was almost killed. I'd wondered if the dangers of the job were suddenly getting to him, but instead it almost seemed to be me. Did he think he owed me his life, maybe? Was that what suddenly made him uncomfortable around me?

"Somebody's got to watch the shop." I shrug and dredge up a crooked grin.

It's glossed over the awkwardness, and Sylvia gallops ahead. "Well, is this all your luggage? God, Anna," she says, "but you look great. It's been such a long time . . ."

Jomo Kenyatta International Airport is eleven minutes from downtown, per the travel guide. My impression of the city is bright flashes: mosques, bazaars, and curio shops flashing by the car windows, a tangle of streets, all brash with noise and color. A few years ago, people were still killed by lions in the streets of Nairobi, but now the old colonial core is surrounded by high-rise office blocks and modern apartment towers. I get a glimpse of slums around the outskirts, tin-roofed shanty towns that house the migrant unemployed. Still, overall, my impression is that the place is thriving.

Sylvia is, too. She's a golden blonde, seared by the tropics and noticeably ripened since Miami Dade Junior College—how many years ago, now? She went on for a master's degree and now she's in love with an older man, from her letters, a wildlife researcher that she's anxious for me to meet.

"Wendall's going to wait for us at Abdul-al's," she says. I've got no idea where that is, but it's okay with me. She accelerates like a NASCAR driver, then slams her foot down on the brake. We lurch to a stop, cut off by a mass of cyclists. "I'd hoped he could take you out to the research camp," she says, frowning pensively and biting her lip, "but now . . ."

Whatever that thought is, she's forgotten it in a second and accelerates into traffic again. She chatters on about local sights as I nod and smile, clutching the car seat in terror.

I briefly relax as we stop at her apartment to ditch the duffel. But then we're off to see Abdul-al's and her darling sweetie, Wendall.

Abdul-al's appears to be a restaurant and bar jammed in behind an old market. There's a flight of steps down, beaded curtains, an impression of alcoves for dining, and a mahogany bar. It's dark and cool inside, quiet as a sigh after the garish-bright glare of equatorial streets. The waiters slip by on sound-less feet, and someone who must be Abdul-al himself greets us, a pale shade in white Muslim robes and a cap.

"Ah, Ms. Westlake." He has a soft voice, a welcoming smile in a dark, bristly beard. "The gentlemen are waiting."

Gentlemen?

Sylvia is fast. She's had to arrange this little addendum while I was making my pit stop at her apartment.

"Shut up," she says, catching my eye. I decide to take it in the spirit it's offered.

Wendall doesn't look like a handsome, darling sweetie to me—but of course that's all a matter of taste. He's a smallish man with a sunburnt dome and tufts of hair like pampas grass sprouting above both ears. He smiles at me distantly and forgets completely to shake hands.

The other guy does better. He's movie star-ish and maybe thirty-five: light-brown hair, wire-rimmed glasses, and heavy, muscular arms. He reminds me of Paul—but then, that's my taste showing. Sylvia would know what type I go for.

"I'm Carson Stern," he says, standing and extending a friendly hand. "I work with Dr. Wendall Holmes Harriman, and I'm"—he glances at Wendall, apparently to see if he's noticed the "Holmes" part—"extremely flattered to be associated with someone who is so noted at the famous Serengeti Research Institute."

"Huh?" I say. "I mean, what for?"

"In his research on lions, of course."

"Oh. Uh . . ."

We sit down. Wendall stares into the middle distance. Stern is teasing both of us, but his grin quickly dies. He's distracted, too. Actually, when I notice it, they all look pretty grim.

They order Bloody Marys, Nile perch, and fried bread. It sounds good to me, so I follow suit. Then I plan to relax and follow the conversation as the first round of drinks starts to have its effect. There isn't any conversation.

"What's wrong?" I ask, finally.

They've forgotten I'm along. Sylvia actually starts. It's Carson who explains.

"Someone was killed last night out in the bush," he says, "apparently by a lion."

That's why, I assume, my trip out to Wendall's camp may be off.

"Oh?" It seems a safe comment.

"This is disgraceful," fumes Wendall. He flaps his napkin, repositions it in his lap. "I have been barred from all activities until the problem is solved."

"Oh," I say again. "Ah. That's too bad." I'm wondering if somehow I could get another drink. "How is a problem like that usually solved?"

"Well," says Sylvia. Her eyes skate sideways at Wendall. "If it is a lion, they'll probably find it and shoot it eventually."

It's my turn to blink, just as the waiter arrives with the dinner tray. He's obviously responded to my wish.

"Shoot it?" I say. "Is that politically correct?" I shove my glass at the waiter, who nods curtly as he drops off my plate. He swivels and disappears into the bead-laced dimness.

"It may not be a lion," says Carson.

"Oh?" Now I am curious, and I study their expressions, looking for a clue.

"The victim wasn't exactly politically correct," he goes on. "He was a safari guide, in the old sense of the term. Snows of Kilimanjaro. Stuff like that."

"I must be jet-lagged," I admit. "I thought all safaris were photo ops these days. Endangered species and such?"

Sylvia snorts. At first I think she's choked on the perch, but it's just a comment.

"You can still buy a white rhino," she says, "if you're rich enough. Lions go a dime a dozen."

"Oh." I feel naive, but I've caught the general drift. "So the guy was an asshole, and it's likely he was murdered?"

"The police are looking for an old native from one of the farms," says Carson, "who's supposed to have threatened the man earlier in the week . . ."

The waiter arrives with my second Bloody Mary, and Sylvia's fork clanks suddenly against her plate.

"Anna!" she exclaims, throwing up her hands. "What an idea!"

"Huh?" At first I think she's talking about the Bloody Mary.

"I'd totally forgotten you're a PI!"

Wendall blinks, coming back a bit from the distance. Carson falls back in his chair, looking shocked. "Not Ms. Agatha Christie?"

I give him a withering glance. There are times and places for a sense of humor.

"I'm on vacation," I say. "I just want to see a little scenery."

"Ha," says Sylvia. She subsides, finds her fork. "Visits to the research camp will be strictly limited until this is over." She gives me a seductive smile, spears her fish. "Unless someone can solve the crime, of course."

I try the withering glance on her, but it bounces off.

"It's a ridiculous idea," I say. "I don't speak the language. I don't know my way around."

"Wendall can get you an escort from the staff."

"The police will throw me out of the country."

"Joseph Gatora is just the man," says Sylvia. "Don't you think so, Carson? He's a smooth operator, knows the countryside . . ."

I frown at her. I can see she's got it all planned. It's blackmail to get her darling sweetie back to work, and there goes my holiday out the door.

But maybe I can just stir around a little and pretend to investigate. I could see the countryside just as well that way and keep the peace with Sylvia, too.

"Okay." I sigh. "I'll think about it. Just tell me a few of the details."

Over the Turkish coffee, I've got the rest of it, and I don't like the facts. I'm reminded that this is a foreign country. Outside of this circle of faces is a different world—a native culture—and what I said about the police is likely dead on.

The deceased was Bryant Garr, a definite Hemingway type, heavy drinker—arrogant, racist, misogynist—you name it. He must have annoyed everyone in Nairobi at one time or another, blacks and whites alike, and his affronts didn't stop at the city limits, either.

He committed regular scandals with bored socialites from the local estates, and the squabble that was supposed to have killed him was with an elderly man from somewhere north of the city. Something over killing the wildlife, or messing with the man's grandson, or both. Sylvia's not completely sure.

Garr was found in the hills, clawed to ribbons, disemboweled, and what looked like lion tracks were easily visible around the body, overlaid by other prints. So why didn't the authorities think it was really a lion?

Africa, the "Dark Continent," was a hotbed of cults not that many years ago. The British colonials made a sincere effort to stamp out the various quasi-religious rites because they promoted organization in the native societies—and not only that, but disrespect for white claims on the best farmland. One of the most stubborn cults used forged-iron claws and carved-wooden sandals to obscure the evidence of their terrorism. The "lion-man" cult disappeared without leaving any trace of what its other functions might have been, but the police thought the old man might have had the requisite implements hidden away somewhere. They couldn't ask him about it in person because the old guy had hobbled off into the bush, taking his grandson with him.

"It's tantamount to admitting guilt," says Carson, waiting while the waiter fills his coffee cup. The pot is Arab-style, brass and long-handled, and it glitters darkly in the room's obscurity.

"No, it's not." Sylvia's hair stirs against her shoulders, dark gold as the brass. "Of course he'd be scared to death," she says. "He threatened Garr right out in front of a whole crowd of people, and those claws aren't so hard to come by. Even the Serengeti Institute has a set. I've seen them in the display case."

"Oh really," says Carson, noncommittal.

"Don't they, Wendall?" she asks, turning to him.

"Eh?" says Wendall, looking up from his coffee.

The evening flickers out, and morning comes too soon for me. Sylvia routs me out of a warm bed in her apartment at seven.

"Joseph's going to be here at nine," she says. "Do you want something to eat?"

"God," I say, burrowing under the pillow. I've never exactly been a morning type. "Can't we just forget all this?" I ask.

"I thought you wanted to see Kenya," she says.

"Maybe we could do some shopping later."

"You can't disappoint Joseph. I told him you'd offered to pay him."

"What?" I lurch upright. "Pay?"

"Ha, ha," she says. "That got you up, didn't it?"

It turns out that Wendall is going to pay, for Joseph's time and mine, too. Sylvia's a great operator. Fortified by two cups of coffee and a fat sweet roll, I follow Sylvia down to meet Joseph at nine and to start the investigation, whatever it's going to be.

Surprisingly, Carson is there too, turned out in a smart white hunter outfit. "Hello," he says, with an engaging smile. "I hope you don't mind if I come along."

Joseph is sturdy and athletic looking, attractive but old enough to seem grizzled, which probably means he's a grandfather, at least. He's wearing a loose chambray shirt and dark shorts and shakes hands with a definite reserve.

The truck is a Jeep Cherokee painted with vivid stripes, and I wonder if that's for visibility, maybe to keep errant safaris from shooting at us by mistake. Joseph takes the driver's seat, and we head off through the warren of streets, encounter farmland quite suddenly.

Carson goes into a canned tour guide routine, and when I ask a few questions, he starts to tell me about the people and the countryside. It's interesting. To this point, I have had nil education on African history.

"These are mostly Kikuyu who live in this area," he says, "and they're farmers. The Masai and some other herders live to the south and west, over near the Serengeti."

He points out that we're headed into the Great Rift Valley where hominid hunters constitute the fastest growing population segment.

"They're looking for the Gumba," Joseph says, "the little people who were here in the earliest times. They disappeared underground and never came out."

Carson frowns at the interruption. I give Joseph a sidelong glance and find his face is completely deadpan. The man's sharp. He's got Carson's number already—and likely mine, as well.

The farm plots march up the hills, some with new tin-roofed buildings and wire fencing, and others with round thatched roofs and stick fences that look more traditional and picturesque. Beyond the hills, the mountains of the Rift walls loom sheer and distant through the morning haze.

The Kikuyu were always a progressive people, Carson explains, generally interested in new methods and advantages, and after the first colonial contacts, they quickly adapted to British ways. The Europeans actually held them in contempt for their friendly attitudes—which was a mistake. The result was the Mau Mau wars of the 1950s when that cult conducted a bloody campaign of assassination and sabotage from camps hidden out in the local mountains. The British responded with executions and torture, and most of the Kikuyu people were imprisoned.

Thirty-two white settlers and thirteen thousand Kikuyu died before the rebellion finally broke the British rule and Kenya found its way to independence. Then the Kikuyu got their land back. Lately, they've made the leap to professional positions: doctors, lawyers, financiers . . .

. . . and under their administration, Kenya is doing just fine now, thank you.

Joseph doesn't come right out and say that, but I've got a handle on his attitudes now; I can feel what's behind his stoic reserve. The wars left hard feelings that still haven't gone away, and the natives might just as soon be free of Westerners, except they need the investment capital.

The tension between the men leaves me pissed off. I'm supposed to be on vacation here, and I don't like being in this cross fire. I appreciate the history, but Carson has been an asshole in the way he has related it. Whatever, it's a relief when the tea plantation finally heaves into view.

We're about fifty miles from Nairobi now, on the southern fringe of Aberdare National Park, where Garr was found dead. Carson has reverted to tour guide mode and left off with the history. Apparently, it's served his purpose for now.

The fields are green and waist high to workers with baskets strapped to their backs. Beyond a screen of trees, I can see the plantation housing, neat rows of whitewashed huts facing the road. We stop at one of the fields. Joseph calls out a question and gets an answer, after which we drive on. We're looking for the old man's daughter.

"Dede Njere is at least ninety," Joseph comments, pulling into the access road. "He would make a very mangy lion."

The daughter's gone to visit relatives in a village somewhere off in the hills, but we find a neighbor who's willing to talk. She doesn't look so young herself and neither does her husband. He's toothless, dressed in shorts and a faded shirt, and she's outfitted in a Grateful Dead T-shirt and a native wrap. The visit takes a while, as I gather Joseph has to go through formalities before we can ask any questions: inquiries as to their health and that of their families, etc., at great length.

Finally, he turns to me and asks, "What would you like to know, Ms. Detroyer?"

"Um," I say, trying to get together a train of thought. "Where was Mr. Njere the night of Mr. Garr's death?"

He asks and they answer.

"Out prowling the bush, they think. The old man comes and goes as he wants, and his daughter has no control of him. They are pleased that Garr is dead."

"No alibi," says Carson.

"Shut up," I tell him, without even looking. "Do they know where the old man is now?"

The woman shrugs.

"Dorobo," Joseph interprets. "By this, they mean 'wild,' that he has gone to the bush to stay and taken the boy with him."

They've answered these questions before, and it's the same answers I've been told, but now the difference is, I get to watch their faces as they talk.

"Why did he take the boy?" I ask.

"Because the boy is like him."

"Oh?" It's not what I'd expected to hear. "And how is that?"

"Of the old way," they say, and with that I catch the mismatch of assumptions, the sham of their ragtag Western clothes. I have my granddad's talents as a spirit talker, and I see realities other people don't see.

I take a breath. "Ask them about the iron claws and carved sandals," I tell Joseph, and they laugh.

Damn.

"Does Njere have relatives anywhere else?" I ask.

The woman thinks. "In the village where his daughter has gone. A cousin in Nairobi."

"What's the boy like?"

"A good boy, but like his grandfather."

"Would Njere have killed the safari guide?"

"If he wanted to," they say.

I'm grappling with ephemera. The two of them look simple and solid, but they're elusive, slipping out of my grasp like a fog. Joseph sees it, but Carson only looks sullen and miffed.

"Can we find the daughter?" I ask, turning to Joseph.

"Perhaps," he says. "We have to go to Limuru anyway. It's near the park, and the men who found the body are from there, too."

We head into terrain that's volcanic and rough, north of the prime farmland and so relatively unpopulated. The truck raises a wake of ochre dust that settles on the forested veldt behind us. I'm glued to the window now, watching for wildlife in the scrub—it's mostly birds and antelope in the daytime, but still exotic to me. Once, I see a pack of hyenas. The vista looks almost familiar now, thorn trees and yellowed grass right out of *National Geographic*.

"Like it?" Carson asks. He's apparently recovered from his snit.

"Sure," I say. And then the track runs out, like we'll have to walk the rest of the way. I wonder if hyenas will bite. I'm afraid the answer is yes.

It's a rough climb up an animal trail to the first trace of civilization, which is a partially harvested field. The village is just beyond, a dirt track through a clutter of family compounds, and we immediately attract a crowd. It turns out no one's here that we've come to see. Njere's daughter is already headed home, and the men are all gone hunting. Everyone's excited but polite, and Joseph cuts a deal for us. I'll stay and rest in the village while he and Carson go out to see if the hunters are headed back this way.

I'm not sure that it's fine with me, especially as the plan seems to irritate Carson. Still, it seems to please our hosts, so I gather I've been placed in the traditional female role. What the hell? I don't mind—it would be about the same thing in a Seminole village.

As soon as the guys are gone, I'm offered lunch. The women and kids are shy and curious. Soon they're asking questions in broken English. Lunch seems to be mush and greens, bland but not inedible. I have no instructions about what's safe from Joseph, so I go ahead and eat.

Questions eventually get to my love life, and when they find I'm unmarried, I'm shuffled off to someone who can help. It's a middle-aged man sitting in a hut that smells ancient as the land. When my eyes adjust, I see that there's a grass mat on the ground, a couple of cartons against the wall and hay-scented herbs in the rafters. One of the girls has come to interpret, and she tells me to leave my shoes at the door. At the old man's invitation, I sit on one of the mats.

"Daughter," he says, "do you want a love charm?"

"Will it really change the man?" I ask.

He smiles faintly. "No," he says. He's thin, dressed in a knit polo and skirt, and his earlobes are stretched and bound into knots with thick silver rings.

"Then I'll pass," I say.

"You are wise," he says. "What is it you want then?"

"I want to know who killed Bryant Garr."

"The hyenas feasted on his entrails," he says, and looks pleased with the fact. By now I'm not surprised.

"Well, yes," I say. "But do you know who did it?"

He reaches behind him for implements, shakes cowrie shells out of a gourd and studies the patterns they make in the dirt.

"It was not Njere," he says.

"Then who?"

"The shells point to Nairobi," he says. "You will find the killer there."

"Can you tell me how?"

"Wait and he will come," he says. "His fear will bring him to you."

That's all he has to say on the matter.

"Is Njere a lion-man?" I ask.

The girl looks immediately spooked at that, but she translates it for me anyway.

The old man studies my face. "It was said that he is," he answers.

I sort through the grammar, and then I want a second opinion on the definition.

"If that were true," I say, "what would it mean?"

"That he could command lions, and perhaps to become one."

I've got a shiver now. The veil of rationalism seems very thin in this hut, out in this wilderness, just now.

"Do you think he could command lions now?" I ask.

"Oh, no," he says, waving a hand. "His lions are all dead. The Christians killed them many years ago."

Well, damn.

The crime scene is anticlimactic. The grass is torn up, but the remains are gone. The Nairobi police have already searched the area and found nothing at all.

Joseph and Carson seem to have declared a cease-fire on the way back home, and for that I'm thankful. We retrace our way through the green farms beneath mountains floating on the blue clouds of sunset. Nairobi glows ahead of us like a pocket of stars, resolves finally into last night's maze. I've traveled too far, too fast, and now all I want to do is sleep. We climb down from the truck and dust off our clothes.

"Would you like to go out to dinner?" asks Carson.

I study his face, the pale hair and blue eyes, the set of his shoulders. Suddenly, I'm very much aware of Joseph standing behind me.

"No thanks," I say. "I'm really tired tonight."

Tossing in bed later on, I wonder if I was wrong in my choices throughout the day. Maybe I should have taken that love charm after all. Paul seems to have no use for me at all these days, and I can't even think about another man, regardless of the movie star looks.

Sylvia wakes me at six thirty in the morning. If I remember correctly, it's Saturday. The woman must jump up at the crack of dawn every day.

"Well," she says brightly, once I'm upright, "how did it go?"

"It didn't," I grumble. And then, after a cup of coffee, I add, "But it was interesting anyway."

I have to take some gifts home for my cousins' kids, so Sylvia has shopping planned for today. About midmorning, we plunge on foot into the maze near Abdul-al's. It's a bright swirl of carved figurines and patterned fabrics, crude baskets and brown pottery jars. The air is heavy with spice and food scents and boisterous with shouted price reductions, just for us.

We eat dinner at Abdul-al's again and head for home as the city dims, puts on evening like a mask.

There's a shadow waiting by the apartment door.

Sylvia starts. "My God," she says, "Joseph, what are you doing here?"

"I have found the cousin," he says.

I thought I'd finished with all that yesterday.

Joseph's brought his own truck this time, and Sylvia swears she'd come along except that she's got to meet Wendall at eight for some lecture. I climb into the Jeep beside Joseph all by myself. After a while, I don't like the look of the streets.

"Where are we going?" I ask.

"Kibera," he says.

The word is a challenge. I study him sideways, see he's waiting for a reply.

"Fine with me," I say. "But you're in charge of safety. Okay?"

His chuckle cuts through the dusk like a growl.

Kibera is a slum, and it stinks. Open sewers, I think, testing the wind—or maybe it's none at all. The roads are dirt and too narrow for a truck; we have to abandon it early on. A yelling tribe of kids offers to watch it for us, but Joseph hires a scar-faced thug instead.

The whores that work the backstreets are blatantly sexual. One of them tries to pull Joseph in through a doorway. There's a shouting match, and I wonder if I should act possessive, but Joseph seems to do all right by himself. We make another turn into red dirt alleyways lined with shacks built of piled debris. Mostly naked children play in the dirt.

Finally, we arrive at something that looks like legitimate apartments, a building five spalling stories high, decorated with dank strings of hanging laundry. The stairs smell like piss, and cockroach bodies crunch underfoot. In the gloom of the fourth-floor hallway, something larger darts by us—a rat, I figure. Joseph pounds on a rickety door.

The man who answers is short and ugly, dressed in dirty shorts. Behind him, three women are sitting in a circle, cooking over a brazier. Half a dozen children stare at us with curious eyes.

The cousin seems evasive, producing a monologue that's truly amazing, even though I can't understand a word of it. The women stare and scowl.

"Now what?" I ask, as the door slams behind us.

"The neighbors," says Joseph. He's got a good head for de-tective work. He gives the woman who answers the first knock a coin, and she opens the door up wide as her gap-toothed smile. She doesn't like her neighbors much.

Musa has too many wives and can't support any of them, she says. Yes, he's had visitors from the country, just this week, an old man and a boy, but they didn't stay for very long. Maybe Muthoni downstairs could tell us where they went. She knows everybody's business, whatever you want to know.

Muthoni isn't home. She's gone to the bar to find her husband, who usually spends his whole week's pay on beer. She wants some money herself this week. Her oldest daughter says we can come back later on.

"Now what?" I ask Joseph. It's full dusk now, shadows closing down on us. Music drifts in the air, the sounds of distant carousing. The smell of cook fires wafts through the alleyways.

"We should try again tomorrow," says Joseph. "It's too dangerous to be here now."

We start the trek back to the car. There are no streetlights here, only the distant music, and stark, moonlit shadows flare on the walls. Soon I have icy fingers on my neck. I turn, staring behind us through the gloom. I start as a rat squeaks, reach out to catch Joseph by the arm.

He gasps as my nails dig into his wrist.

Suddenly, the world has changed. I don't know what it is, maybe a sixth sense developed from years of experience—or maybe the insights of a spirit talker. It's the sharpening of my ears that catches the faint shift of a heavy body behind me, the faintest rasp of breath from the shadows. Now I've caught the glimmer of something that looks like eyes. Likely it's the rat—but maybe not. Who else? The scar-faced thug? Friends of the rejected whore?

I'm pumped with adrenalin, and now I think Joseph feels something, too. I motion for a split, head off noisily down the alleyway. He stays behind, hidden in an alcove. When I hear a commotion, I wheel and dash to help, but there's no need.

The boy's wearing traditional African garb, which is to say, nothing much—only a beaded G-string and a blanket. He's like an animal, twisting under Joseph's weight, lithe and sleek, with delicate features, hollow cheekbones, and a mouth that looks bee stung.

Joseph plants a knee on the kid's back and twists his hands up to loop them together with a leather thong. But before he does that, he pries off a silver bracelet. The boy says something in a peremptory tone, and Joseph comes right back at him. He sticks the bracelet in his shirt pocket, but somehow he doesn't look comfortable with what he's done.

"What is it?" I ask.

"A *bolniga*. I have pulled the cub's teeth," he says, showing his own. "At least as much as I can."

I let out my breath, decide not to ask what the hell he's talking about.

The boy looks to be about sixteen. The sleekness comes from the good jobs his parents have at the tea farm.

"Kamau," says Joseph, "where is your grandfather?"

The kid hisses something, likely curses. Joseph shakes him.

"Don't," I say.

Maybe it's good I do; the old man is standing there now, slid out of the shadows behind us like a phantom. He motions. Joseph tugs the thong loose, and the boy twists to his feet, fades into an alleyway. Somehow I don't think he's gone very far.

"What is it you want of me?" asks Njere in a voice as old as the valley walls.

"Just to talk," I say.

Joseph must be right about his age. The old man is shriveled as a dried plum and snowy-haired, nearly blind. Propped on a carved wooden stick, he looks completely incapable of killing anyone as young and strong as Garr was supposed to be—still there are ways, I suppose.

"You are not the police?" he asks.

"No," I say.

He shifts his weight on the stick. "Then why do you want to talk to me?" he asks.

"The . . . uh, investigation is stopping people who want to work," I say.

He considers, likely wondering if I'm for real.

Joseph puts in his two cents worth then—dialect I can't follow, and the old guy looks at me again and nods like it could make sense after all.

"I did not kill Bryant Garr," he says. "But of course I had thought of it. I was tracking him, and I saw the man who did it . . ." He has his mouth open to go on, but then his milky eyes blink, fasten behind me.

I jerk sideways. I'm half expecting this will be the boy, but somehow I know it's not. There's a thump and a grunt to my right, and Joseph falls. Light flares, blinding, into my face.

If Njere were any younger, he'd probably have run, but instead he's maintaining his dignity. He grips his stick, peers into the glare with narrowed eyes—the same as me.

"Well, sweetheart," says a voice I recognize. "Somehow I thought you'd find him for me."

"Carson?" I gasp, trying to block the light with one hand so I can see him. "What the hell are you doing here?" Like it's not obvious. His hazy shadow has a gun in its hand.

"I'll have to kill you all," he says, "so no one else will know. The setting's perfect—the slum, the riffraff. Thank you, dear . . ." It's that damn sense of humor again—an appreciation for irony.

"You killed Garr?" I ask. I'm stalling, trying to decide what the hell to do about this. Dive for the alley mouth? Then he'll get the old man—and Joseph too, lying unconscious at his feet.

I want my gun, but I've left it at home. I could never carry it here.

"I had to," Carson explains. "Garr killed my lions, half the pride I was studying. My research was ruined."

"You got the claws out of the case at the Institute?"

"Of course," he says, "I . . ."

The old man dodges suddenly sideways. Stern jerks, lines up to fire at him. Too late. A heavy shadow leaps, and he goes down, screaming. The gun slides. I grab for it and roll, come up behind Joseph with the pistol aimed and ready.

For a second, I freeze. It's a lion, and a young one. The body is supple and taut. A fine, wispy mane clothes the shoulders in a halo of light. The animal crouches over the body, eyeing me balefully, its tail twitching. It's watchful, green-eyed and ghostly in the wash of the fallen torch.

I blink, gasping for breath. This is a modern city. There are no lions in the streets of Nairobi. Still my brain is working. Slowly it processes, decides, and then I know who I'm dealing with. I raise the gun and click on the safety.

The moonlight flickers briefly. A cloud crosses the moon's face, and then it's gone. The alley's empty, except for me, a definite corpse, and a man's dark, stocky body stretched on the ground beside me.

"Ouch," says Joseph, stirring faintly. "What happened?" He sits up, feels along the back of his head. "Are you okay, Ms. Detroyer?"

"Yeah," I say. I stand and shove the gun in my pants, lean to help him up. My hands are shaking.

He looks at Carson's body. "What happened?" he asks.

"Don't ask," I say. "Joseph, get us the hell out of here. I think we've earned our pay."

Lela E. Buis is an artist, author and poet. She grew up in East Tennessee and lived for a long time in Florida, working in engineering at Kennedy Space Center and as a teacher of various subjects and levels. She began writing as a child and leans toward genre fiction in the writing, having published mainly science fiction and fantasy stories and poetry. When she's not painting or writing, she looks after four barn cats and a part-time dog.

www.lelaebuis.wordpress.com

MARIJA SMITS

The Eyes of the Goddess Herself

N'GAI HAD BEEN BLESSED with a rare gift. She could see things that others could not. While the rest of the girls and boys played in the shade of the great goddess tree, N'gai would simply look at the world around her: the sky, the landscape, the huts in her village. And marveling at the beauty of it all, she would draw what she'd seen by carving lines into the dry red soil with a stick.

"It's the tree!' said B'golo, pausing beside her. "What about me? Could you make a picture of me as well?"

N'gai nodded. "I can try. But I would need you to stay very still so that I can look you all over."

But B'golo could not stay still, and after only a few cycles of the *timbala* cicada's song, he rushed off to return to his games.

"I'll stay still for you," said N'giri, N'gai's younger sister.

So N'gai looked at her sister, really looked at her, and before long she'd created a true likeness of N'giri in the soil.

When she saw the finished picture, N'giri laughed and clapped her hands. She then rushed off to find their mother, who came running, a worried look on her face.

"What is it N'gai?" called her mother. "Are you all right? Your sister says there is something I must see."

N'gai looked down at the picture, and as her mother came close, her expression softened.

"N'gai!" she exclaimed, suddenly grinning. "You have eyes as keen as that of the mother-goddess herself." And she took her daughter into her arms.

Later, when the sun had set and the three moons—N'luna, N'lina, and N'lon—shone bright in the night sky, rain fell. As N'gai and her family slept, her pictures became mud and were lost forever.

※

The next day, N'gai's father, who had been told of his daughter's gift, instructed her to accompany him to the mark-makers who worked in a large hut at the south of their village, close to the river. These men and women, gifted with the hands and eyes of the mother-goddess, asked N'gai to show them what she could do. So she studied the features of one of the female mark-makers and with a pointed stick drew the woman's face in the soil. It was a good likeness, and the woman was pleased. This woman nodded to N'gai's father.

"After her work, your daughter can come to us and use our tools. We will teach her how to paint and carve and sculpt. If she is hardworking, she will learn much, and if she yokes determination to her gift, she has the chance to become extraordinary."

N'gai and her father, both round-eyed, thanked the woman and promised to return later that day.

❋

So while the rest of the children played in the shade of the great goddess tree, N'gai was busy with the mark-makers. She helped them to gather the plants and berries that they made their paints and dyes from, and she watched them create pictures with their dip pens, their brushes, and their charcoal holders. She learned how to create bark paintings and how to make paper from plant fibers. She shaped clay and carved wood. And always she watched, and copied, and practiced until, one day, she understood that she was no longer a girl apprentice but a skilled mark-maker on the cusp of womanhood.

❋

One day, N'gai's mother asked her for a favor.

"N'gai, my sister still grieves for her youngest, B'geno. She confided in me that she can no longer remember exactly what he looked like, and this is what hurts her the most. N'gai, do you remember your cousin, B'geno? Could you conjure him up with your brush? I think it would ease your aunt's pain."

N'gai closed her eyes and again saw B'geno's face.

"Yes, Mother," she said, on opening her eyes. "I can do that."

And so it was that N'gai painted a picture of B'geno for her aunt. N'gai was pleased with her efforts, and yet when she went with her mother to give it to her aunt, the bark painting seemed to offer no solace. On seeing the picture, B'geno's grieving mother wept like the goddess herself, and N'gai's heart was pierced with sorrow.

"What have I done?" whispered N'gai to her mother. "It must be all wrong."

"Wait," her mother replied.

Just then N'gai's aunt gripped her arm. "Thank you," she said through her tears. "Thank you."

*

Life continued. The seasons were born, they grew, they died, and the next season was birthed with the death of the old. N'gai's family said it was time she found a husband.

So when five wandering plainsmen came from the southwest and settled around the fire to eat with the villagers, she looked at each of them shyly. Which one of them would make for a good husband? The two handsome ones she instantly rejected. She saw only ambition and pride in their eyes. The ugly ones she dismissed too, for there was a torpor about them that she did not like. Yet she warmed to the fifth man, who was neither handsome nor ugly. There was a confusion about him, as though even he himself didn't know what kind of man he was. Yes, she could see some pettiness in his eyes, but a love of beauty was there also. So when his gaze fell on N'gai, she smiled and then bowed her head.

*

"You like that man?" said N'gai's mother, later.

"I *think* so," said N'gai. "Anyway, he is the best of them all, don't you think?"

Her mother sighed and patted her growing belly. "I don't see that you have much choice, N'gai. You will have another brother or sister soon, and as the goddess did not favor us with her tears this season, we could do with a hunter to add to the little food we have."

N'gai nodded. She then placed a hand on her mother's belly and closed her eyes. "I see a boy. With huge eyes and an even bigger heart."

N'gai's mother smiled. "Goddess willing, he will journey to us safely."

So N'gai pledged herself to the man who loved beauty—B'goro was his name—although, on becoming joined with N'gai in the eyes of the goddess, B'goro made the unusual pronouncement that they would not remain in the village. His gift to his bride would be a quest for beauty. He would take his wife to the northeast where, he had heard, there were shimmering salt waters that sparkled with so much radiance that they made the goddess herself weep at such beauty. Also, they were full of fish, and so they would never starve.

N'gai could do nothing but acquiesce. She would be sorry to say goodbye to her family and the mark-makers, but she was also excited by the prospect of seeing this mysterious blue "ocean" that her husband spoke of. So one morning they set off, following the almost dry river to the northeast, their few possessions and some food on their heads.

❋

They walked for thirteen days, the mother-goddess, Solla, impressing on them her divine power: Solla's heat was fierce and their progress was slow. Yet the goddess trees, whose roots burrowed deep into the earth, provided them with water; B'goro would tap the tree for its sweet liquor, and he and his wife would drink and be sated. At each tree, N'gai left a token of their gratitude. She molded clay, taken from the sludge of the riverbank, and shaped it into a bulbous human form. It was Solla, fat with fertility. She whispered "thank you" as she placed the figure against the trunk of the tree and thought of how her husband had held her in the night, his naked body against hers. Soon, perhaps, *she* would be fat with child.

❋

On the fourteenth day, two wonderful sights came into view: a thin band of blue at the horizon and a village in front of it. When they finally arrived at the village, the dark blue band growing ever larger, N'gai was entranced by the sight and sound and smell of it.

"How wonderful!" she exclaimed. "B'goro, what you said is true. This ocean is a beautiful sight indeed."

B'goro smiled.

The villagers welcomed them and gave them food and water. And when night came, they sat around the fire and listened to what N'gai and B'goro had to tell them: about their journey, and of N'gai's village and her mark-making skills, and of B'goro's gift to his wife.

The sea villagers told them about their lives. They spoke to them of the ocean, Seeana, Solla's twin sister, and how she was a generous but sometimes cruel mistress. She provided them with food in the manner of fish, crustaceans, and seaweed; she also gave them brine, which gave them the twin gifts of drinking water and salt. When the freshwater from the river had all but disappeared, the brine was a blessing indeed. But Seeana also took from the villagers. Many fishermen had lost their lives in her embrace, no matter how many tokens of gratitude they left at her feet.

"Tomorrow, though," said one of the elders, "we will introduce you to Seeana. B'goro, we can teach you how to fish, and N'gai you will work with our mark-makers. No doubt you will wish to learn from each other."

❋

So N'gai and B'goro settled into a new life beside the beautiful, if daunting, Seeana. However, life as a fisherman did not suit B'goro. The rocking motion of the boats made him sick to his stomach. N'gai could not help laughing when he returned from a day at sea.

"You look like my younger sister, N'giri, when she first had to wring the neck of a *pullum* bird."

B'goro did not laugh and N'gai fell silent as she saw her husband's eyes cloud with ill temper.

❋

N'gai was learning much from the Seeana mark-makers. They had a particularly intriguing use for sand, which they would melt in a furnace fuelled by the anger of the fire-god himself. The sand turned into a transparent slime that they would twist and turn and add minerals to. They produced many things from this substance, which they named glass: colored vessels, tiles, and spheres that sparkled in the rays of the mother-goddess. When N'gai watched the glass mark-makers at work, she felt awe; it was as though she was witnessing the birth of Solla herself.

❋

One day, B'goro had had enough.

"It is time we left," he told N'gai.

"But why?" she asked, her heart racing.

"I have no wish to become like some of the fishermen who secretly hate to fish and instead drink themselves sick with fire-water when they think no one is watching. No. I am a hunter of creatures that roam the earth. Not the sea. We shall head north, along the coast and to the mountainous regions. We shall settle at a village where my skills can be put to good use."

"But why can't we go back to my home? You were appreciated there. My mother said . . ."

"I don't care about what your mother said. We go north."

N'gai looked into her husband's eyes, and seeing the hurt and confusion in them, she nodded and said no more.

❋

When hearing that N'gai was to leave, the mark-makers presented her with a gift. It was a transparent orb, curved and smooth.

"It is for capturing the power of Solla to make fire. It will help you and B'goro to light a fire without having to rely on the mischievous fire-god."

N'gai took the orb and looked at it. She could immediately see its power; it distorted the world and made things larger than they truly were.

"Thank you, friends, this is a wondrous gift. Goddess willing, we may yet meet again."

❋

So N'gai and B'goro left the village. They traveled north, along the coast, for ten days; the mountains nothing but a dusky haze in the distance. Goddess trees were scarcer here so sometimes B'goro would boil seawater for them so that they'd have enough to drink. N'gai once offered him the mark-makers' orb when he was building a fire, but he waved her away. "Us hunters have no need for such tricksy devices. My flint and knife have so far never let me down." And he continued to call on the fire-god, the flint sparking with mischief.

Occasionally, they would pass fishermen who would be generous and provide them with fish and a little freshwater. At dusk, they ate salted or grilled fish in silence, B'goro's wounded pride still raw, his mood still low.

Yet on the eleventh day of their journey, the mountains became more substantial and a teeming mass of huts and people could be seen in the distance. B'goro grinned.

"That's more like it!" he said, and he hurried N'gai on, although she felt sick and tired.

*

B'goro was right. This community *was* a better fit for him. He immediately fell in with a group of huntsmen who took him into the mountains daily. When he came back to N'gai in the evenings he would boast of their exploits, his eyes full of pride.

N'gai found work with the mark-makers, and for a while she thought they'd be happy here. However, skilled as she was in producing likenesses, word soon got about: a woman with the eyes of the goddess herself was among them. This pleased many of the community who longed to see their own faces in paint on paper, but two people in particular were not pleased with this development: B'goro and the goddess-speaker.

B'goro did not like the way that N'gai was often regaled with gifts and admiring words, for it was he that was doing the hard and brave work. N'gai was just doing what she usually did: making people look better in paint than they looked like in real life. What was valiant about that? And the goddess-speaker, who was full of bitterness, didn't like the way that people no longer looked to her so much. They had N'gai instead. The newcomer could give them pretty reflections of themselves; she could also conjure up pictures of long-dead relatives, merely with a description. Her marks had the power to inspire and enthrall. No, something had to change.

One day, though, it did, when the head huntsman sought out N'gai at dawn and asked her to give his body a mask of paint so that he could go about the mountains unseen. N'gai obliged, and that day the hunter caught the elusive mountain *cugarra*, the beloved cat of the despised fire-god himself. There were celebrations in the village that night, yet B'goro, angry at the praise the head huntsman lavished on N'gai, slipped away from the crowd and went to the ramshackle hut of the goddess-speaker.

"Do something," he said, "about my wife." He puffed out his chest. "I am tired of the way people treat her. She is only a mark-maker, and yet they look on her as though . . . as though she is the goddess herself!"

The goddess-speaker sucked air through her yellow, broken teeth. "That, she is not!" She parted the long, greying locks in front of her face and, turning away from B'goro, surveyed the crammed shelves by the light of her unearthly fire. They were full of pots of potions and withered plants and animal pelts. She muttered to herself as she picked things up and then put them back down again.

"Well?" said B'goro. "Can you do something?"

The goddess-speaker turned her head toward him sharply and looked into his eyes. "You want me to take away her powers?"

"Yes," he said slowly, for a moment considering how bereft N'gai would be without her ability to make marks. He then disregarded the thought. "It is for the best. She has me. And one day, soon, she will give birth to my child. That is enough."

The goddess-speaker grinned. "I can do what you ask. Though I will have to invoke the wrath of the fire-god himself. What will you give me in exchange?"

B'goro laughed. "My, you're a cunning one. I know as well as you that this request can only benefit you. But still . . . I'll bring you enough fresh meat to put some flesh on your bones."

The goddess-speaker laughed horribly. "Come back tomorrow evening."

❋

The morning after B'goro had seen the goddess-speaker again, he unstoppered the jar full of black liquid that she'd given him. He poured a few drops of the evil-looking potion into N'gai's jug of water.

"Drink up," he said as N'gai rose. He offered her a cup of water and some fruit.

N'gai drank. She sensed that something about the water was wrong, but she couldn't pinpoint what. It tasted the same. It had no smell, but it looked . . . a little grey, perhaps? Her eyes seemed to be almost, but not quite, seeing something, but the "something" slithered away from her when she tried to focus on it. So she dismissed her concerns. It was kind of B'goro to think of her, usually he'd already be gone with the other hunters into the mountains. She bit into the yellow fruit, which tasted good. "Thank you," she said with a smile. It was good to see her husband looking happy. Perhaps this *was* the right place for them both. Although, with the new life in her belly, she had to admit that she missed her family. She particularly longed for her mother; she wanted to be in her mother's arms, to be told that everything would be all right.

❋

Day followed day, with B'goro continuing to give his wife the goddess-speaker's potion. And as day followed day, N'gai's sight began to fail her, until one morning she woke to nothingness. She cried out, her arms flailing.

"Where am I? Is it nighttime still? B'goro!"

B'goro woke and, trembling, tried to calm his wife, who was now eyeless—where once her eyeballs had been, there was smooth, spherical rock. And instead of tears, there was sand.

"What has happened to me?" N'gai wailed, putting her hands to her solid eyes. "I cannot see, I cannot see!"

B'goro didn't know what to do. "Be still, I will look after you. I will . . . fetch the goddess-speaker. Yes, that is what I will do. She will know what is to be done."

"Do not leave me!" said N'gai, grasping for her husband. "I am scared!"

B'goro extracted himself from his wife. "I promise I'll be back very soon."

✳

B'goro ran to the goddess-speaker's hut and seeing her asleep on her mat shook her awake. "What have you done, you wicked crone? You have deformed my wife! Her beautiful eyes are now . . . rocks."

The goddess-speaker looked at him disdainfully. "Wasn't that what you wanted? N'gai's power lies in her eyes. So I took away her eyes. Like you asked."

"But I didn't want this!" B'goro said, shaking the goddess-speaker once more. "Undo what you've done!"

"I can't," said the crone. "It cannot be undone."

B'goro, full of the rage of the fire-god himself, began to throttle the old woman. But the next moment, he was holding nothing but air. A snake fell to the ground and slithered away from him.

"Why you wicked old . . ." he began, scanning the hut for a weapon. He picked up a large rock, which was the color and texture of N'gai's new, dead eyes. "If you don't turn back into your real shape and undo what you've done, I swear I'll smash you to pieces."

The snake paused in its retreat and turned to face B'goro, her forked tongue flicking as she considered the man with the rock in his hand.

The snake, quicker than the man, lunged first—she made for B'goro's right foot and sank her fangs into his flesh. B'goro cried out but still managed to bring the rock down on the snake's thick body. The snake writhed under the weight of the rock and, unable to escape, dug her fangs ever deeper. B'goro continued to fell the snake with the rock until he could no longer lift his arms. The snake's poison coursed through his body; it slowed his heart and froze his blood.

The snake, now a bloody pulp, lay at his feet inert, and as the last of B'goro's strength left him, he collapsed. The snake became the goddess-speaker once more, and there they lay on the floor of the hut, together united in death.

❋

N'gai, frightened and in pain, waited for her husband for as long as she could stand to, and then propelled by fear, she stumbled through her hut to the front door and called for her neighbor.

"N'mata! N'mata!" she cried.

N'mata, a babe strapped across her chest, came running. When she saw N'gai, she gasped. "What has happened to you?"

"N'mata, I cannot see. And B'goro has gone for the goddess-speaker. But he's been gone so long. Please, can you find him for me? And hurry him along. I am so frightened."

"Of course. I will come back as soon as I can."

❋

It did not take long for N'mata to discover what had happened to B'goro. A crowd was beginning to form around the goddess-speaker's hut, and the horrible news went about the onlookers: There had been an argument between B'goro and the goddess-speaker. A deal gone wrong. Both were dead.

N'mata took the news back to N'gai, who insisted on being led to B'goro. The crowd parted as they saw N'gai, eyeless, leaning on N'mata's arm. The two women entered the hut, and when they were close to B'goro, N'mata whispered to N'gai that here he was, at her feet. N'gai fell to her knees and placed her hands on the dead body of her husband. She reached for his face, his familiar features smooth and cold under her hands, and then placed a hand on his lifeless chest. So, it was true. She reached for N'mata and then rose. They left the goddess-speaker's home and the whispering crowds, and when N'gai returned to her own hut, she took to her bed and wished for death to come.

❋

N'mata visited N'gai every day, placing fruit and freshwater by her bedside. "You must eat. If only for your baby's sake," she said, stroking N'gai's hair.

The mark-makers came too.

"As the goddess-speaker did not have an apprentice, there will be a time of choosing," began one. "The elders will find another goddess-speaker. In time, she could maybe undo what has been done to you."

"What?" exclaimed N'gai. "Do you think me stupid enough to entrust myself to a novice? Never. No, there is only one goddess-speaker I trust, the one who has known me since childhood, and she lives a long way away from here."

"But N'gai," entreated another, "this is not the end. It is another beginning. Your hands . . . they can still create marks. The images are still within you, behind your eyes, and your hands will do the work for you."

N'gai turned to where the voice was coming from. "The pain . . ." she said, her hand at her eyes. "It is like a thousand knives in my skull. But it is nothing to the pain I feel here," she said, her hand on her chest. "Now I understand all. B'goro's betrayal has killed my spirit. And without my spirit, there is nothing to create."

The mark-makers said no more and left. N'gai was right. Without spirit, there could be no act of creation.

❋

There was one person, though, who disagreed. And that was N'gai's child. She had spirit enough for the both of them, so one day she kicked her mother into action.

N'gai, aware of the internal challenge, spoke to her daughter. "What would you have me do?" she said.

A kick.

"Get up?"

Another kick.

N'gai rose and slowly walked around her hut, her hands her eyes.

"I could go to the mark-makers and sit with them. Sculpt."

No movement.

An image came to N'gai. "Or I could return to my family. Talk to the goddess-speaker."

Two kicks.

N'gai smiled. "Very well," she said. "Home it is. Though the journey will not be easy."

✻

"Do not go," said N'mata. "It will be hard on both you and your baby. Alone and unseeing . . . you are vulnerable."

"But I do not belong here. I must return home. The goddess-speaker may be able to help me, and besides, I want to be with my family. To be with my mother again. You understand what it is like. And I do not want to be a burden to anyone here. You are kind to me. As are the mark-makers, but I will need much help when the baby comes. I cannot ask it of you."

N'mata nodded. "I *do* understand. But promise me this. That you let my eldest go with you for part of the journey."

N'gai began to shake her head.

"I insist!" said N'mata, placing a gentle hand on her friend's cheek. "And there is no point in you continuing to say no. I would just make B'mebo follow at a distance."

N'gai laughed. "I see there is no way to outwit you, so I will accept your kind offer."

＊

So the next day, N'gai and B'mebo journeyed south. N'gai carried a stick in her hand, for testing out the path ahead of her, and she took B'mebo's hand when the ground beneath their feet became rocky. They carried food and vessels of water on their heads, as well as some of N'gai's most prized possessions, and for the most part, they journeyed in companionable silence. After five days, B'mebo said he must return. This was the farthest he had ever traveled, and as loath as he was to leave N'gai, he felt he must.

"Of course you must go," said N'gai. "Please do not worry about me. The mother-goddess will keep me safe. Besides, I have gentle sand beneath my feet and the sea by my side to guide me south to the fishing village I once knew and loved. I have enough food and water for many days. All I need to do is walk. How hard could that be?"

＊

So B'mebo left N'gai to journey alone. The first three days passed by uneventfully. But then the wind rose, prickling N'gai's skin with sand and fear. Dark thoughts entered her mind, and Seeana sent skittish waves across the sand to surprise and unsettle her footing. Solla, too, did not seem keen to make her journey smooth. The mother-goddess argued with the fire-god, their cursing could be heard in the sky above, and it only ended, as it always did, when the tears of the goddess fell from the heavens. It rained so much that the beach was more swamp than sand, and N'gai had to move farther away from the water's edge than she wanted to. She spent much energy in seeking out shelter from the rain, so that she could spend the night in the dry. She woke the next morning, disoriented, to discover that her vessel of freshwater had spilled in the night. Thirsty and dispirited, she went in search of a goddess tree, but there were none. So instead, she refound her path south.

✳

Solla bore down on her. The baby kicked and fussed and made every step across the heavy sand difficult. Thirst tore at her throat. Her head was all pain. N'gai sank to her knees and prayed for a miracle. When none came, she got up once again and walked a few paces. Her sounding stick hit wood instead of sand, and she suddenly thought of the orb that the sea villagers had given her. She would make a fire with it and turn seawater into freshwater. And though she was unskilled in the art of fire making, N'gai understood that this was the miracle that *she* had to make happen.

N'gai found the orb and B'goro's fire-making tools. She recalled the time she'd once asked him to teach her the tricks of the fire-god. *Kindling a fire is man's work*, he'd said. She'd wanted to argue, to say that in her village that was not the case, but the look in his eyes had told her to remain silent.

Careful not to injure herself on B'goro's knife, N'gai felt within her husband's old leather bag and found some tinder and dry sticks. There was enough to get a fire going, and with the several pieces of driftwood she'd come across, she'd be able to sustain a fire for long enough to turn seawater into freshwater. She went to the sea's edge and filled a pan with water. She was so thirsty she considered drinking the pan of liquid, but she knew it would only make her feel worse.

So N'gai set up the fire stack—kindling amongst the smaller twigs, more twigs propped above the kindling, like the poles of a tent, and driftwood beneath—just like B'goro had done. She then held the translucent orb above the dry grass kindling, capturing Solla's rays and focusing them onto the brittle grass. She felt the rising of unnatural heat and suddenly there was a crackle—the kindling had caught alight. The heat increased and grew. N'gai then balanced the pan on the fire, her hands dangerously close to the flames as she placed the curious lid with the downward spout onto the pan. She then put a jar underneath the spout and waited.

Sure enough, Solla rewarded N'gai's efforts; pure water dribbled into the jar, and N'gai was able to drink and be sated.

N'gai stayed by the fire and collected enough water to fill her jar. She ate some of the salted meat and dried fruit N'mata had given her, and then, exhausted, she lay down by the fire and slept.

✳

She woke much later, the cool of dusk on her skin. Still, there in the background was the heat of the fire, although it was much diminished. She sat up, drank some more water, and then chewed on a strip of dried fruit. She thought about the daughters of the mother-goddess, the three moons that would be in the night sky now: N'luna, N'lina, and N'lon. She missed being able to see them.

She suddenly froze as she heard a voice in the distance. A man was singing. And not in a way that was good. N'gai scrabbled about for B'goro's knife, knocking some of her precious pots of ink about the place. The fire! She had to put it out and then hide. She began to throw sand onto the fire.

"Hey!" called the voice. "Don't do that! That's a good fire you've got going."

N'gai stopped what she was doing. She suddenly heard the slap of oars and then splashing. The man, a fisherman she presumed, was pulling his boat ashore.

"N'gai?" said the man, suddenly close by and reeking of firewater. "Is that you?"

N'gai nodded.

"What happened to your eyes? And where's B'goro?"

There was more glugging as the fisherman drank.

"It's a long story," she said, gripping the knife tighter.

The fisherman thrust the pouch of firewater at N'gai. "Have a drink and tell me all about it."

N'gai wanted to push the pouch away, but she sensed it would be the wrong thing to do. With her free hand, she put it to her mouth and took a few sips of the firewater. It tasted foul.

The fisherman took back his pouch and then sat down with a thud. He continued to glug away, emptying the pouch.

N'gai searched her mind for the man's name.

"Well," he said. A belch. "What happened?"

"You're B'somi, aren't you?" she replied. "I once painted a picture of your brother's wife. Such a beautiful—"

"Don't talk to me about that woman! My brother's only been dead for ten days, and she's already chosen her next husband. And it's not me. When it should have been me! She can drown in Seeana's embrace for all I care."

N'gai was silent, her body tense.

B'somi threw down the now-empty pouch. N'gai sensed him move closer.

"Such strange eyes," he said, his hand suddenly on her cheek. "Still, you've got a pretty face." And then his other hand was caressing her hair, his stinking breath on her lips.

N'gai recoiled and then thrust the knife at B'somi. "If you come any closer, I swear I'll use this!"

B'somi backed away, his foul breath receding. But then N'gai felt her head implode with pain as B'somi dealt her a blow; she was reeling backward. Her grip on the knife loosened. Still, she could sense it there, just at her fingertips, unnatural heat behind it.

"Don't you dare threaten me!" said B'somi. "Have you any idea of what I've been through?"

N'gai sensed B'somi coming close again. This time his hands were pulling at her clothes.

N'gai stretched her hand and refound the knife, which was warm from the fire. It was also covered in a slippery liquid she knew well. Ink.

With one swift movement, N'gai plunged the knife into the fire and once more thrust it at B'somi. It plucked at his skin, and he let go of her.

"You're a good man, B'somi, I know you are. Even though I am blind, I can see into your heart. But you're grieving. And poisoned with firewater. And angry with your once sister. And you're not yourself."

N'gai took a deep breath.

"You're stronger than me. And you have the gift of sight. You know I can't do you much harm, but what I can do is mark you forever with ink. And if you choose to defy the goddess and defile me, your skin will forever hold my cry for mercy."

There was a thud as B'somi fell onto the sand. Then the sound of sobbing. And then silence. And when N'gai was sure that B'somi was fast asleep, she packed away her things and walked through the night and most of the morning until the sounds of the people of the sea village came upon her ears. Then she felt the fear that had kept her body moving recede, as she finally realized that she was safe.

❋

When N'gai entered the sea village, the mark-makers took it upon themselves to look after her, and unbeknownst to N'gai, one of them went to fetch their goddess-speaker.

"I see that someone has stolen from you," she said, when she saw N'gai. "And I am sorry for that."

N'gai started when she realized that she was being addressed by their goddess-speaker.

"Who brought you to me? I did not want to be looked over by you!"

The goddess-speaker placed a gentle hand on N'gai's arm. "Forgive me. And forgive the messenger who brought me to you. We did not mean any harm by it."

N'gai's heart softened. "I can hear in your voice that you want to help, but I am sure you cannot."

The goddess-speaker looked at N'gai's sightless eyes. "You are right. I cannot undo what has been done to you, but I can at least give you some relief from the pain. It is a plant that, when chewed, takes away pain. Do you wish for me to bring you this plant?"

A sob caught in N'gai's throat. "Please," she managed to say, willing herself not to cry; experience had taught her that tears of sand were a form of torture almost impossible to bear.

❋

N'gai slept and ate. She told the mark-makers that she did not plan to stay long, that she needed to go home. But the more she chewed on the *kratoma* plant leaves, the less she talked about leaving.

The *kratoma* plant took away her pain, but it also took away her dreams and determination. She kept to her bed, her thoughts folded away, and there she would have stayed for the rest of her life if it weren't for B'somi.

One day, the sound of an argument roused her from her stupor. She could hear the mark-makers telling someone to go away and leave them be. Then she recognized B'somi's voice. Her heart beat like mad and she quickly sat upright.

"I just wanted to tell N'gai something. Please."

She could hear the desire for forgiveness in his voice.

There was a scuffle and then more "go aways." Then noth-ing more.

N'gai's first instinct was to reach for the *kratoma* plant—to blot out the memory of the night she'd met B'somi on the beach—but she found herself trembling and unable to move for shock.

Day passed into night; one of the mark-makers brought N'gai some food and water at dusk. And as the *kratoma* plant took leave of her body, N'gai began to think clearly. What was she doing here still? Why hadn't she left?

A weak kick from within her belly told her to get moving. So, sluggish and slow, N'gai got up and packed her things. And in the middle of the night, when everyone was fast asleep, she clumsily found her way out of the village and to the river, which would lead her back home.

N'gai walked through the night, following the river south-west, her sounding stick her guide. As Solla rose the pain returned to her head, where her hard sandstone eyes met flesh, but the pain, she told herself, was a gift. It would urge her home. To her family, and to the one goddess-speaker who she knew wouldn't fail her.

The recent rain had helped to swell the meager river, and goddess trees were more plentiful here, so N'gai did not thirst for water. One day, stooping at one of the trees, she found a clay statue in the shape of the mother-goddess. It was one that she had made many moons ago, when she had first traveled this way with B'goro. N'gai sighed as she put the statue back. So much had changed since then.

❋

N'gai's progress was slow but uneventful. Then one day, she understood that she was very close to home; she could smell it in the air.

Suddenly there was a shout—"N'gai!"—and the sound of running footsteps. Her siblings. She was being embraced and talked at and then there came the lull . . . Her eyes. What had happened to her eyes? And where was B'goro?

N'gai allowed herself to be carried along to her father and mother and her baby brother, who was fast asleep against his mother's chest. It was only when she found herself being held by her parents that she understood how much she had missed them.

N'gai's mother wept, first with joy, and then with sadness.

"Tell us what happened."

So N'gai told them about what had happened to her eyes. Her father cursed B'goro and the goddess-speaker of the mountain village, and her mother stroked N'gai's hair as she wept her motherly tears.

"You are home now," said her mother. "That is all that matters. We will look after you. And tomorrow we will ask the goddess-speaker for her help."

❋

So the next day the goddess-speaker came to talk to N'gai. She asked to be alone with N'gai, to give counsel with no one else present. N'gai said that she would allow this.

"Your mother has told me what happened to you." She sighed. "Sometimes, for some goddess-speakers, the goddess is not enough. They crave more. They make bargains with unworthy men and the unfathomable fire-god that have cruel outcomes. They end up hurting their sisters. I do not know why these things happen. But they do. However, I also sense that there is more to your story than what you told your family."

N'gai exhaled deeply. "I did not want to add to their sorrow."

"Go on," said the goddess-speaker.

"I almost died of thirst on the journey home. But then the goddess sent me help. I came across driftwood and made a fire with this orb that the mark-makers at the sea village gave me." N'gai took the smooth glass orb from her pouch and showed it to the goddess-speaker. "So I was able to turn seawater into freshwater. But then a fisherman, his blood poisoned with fire-water, saw the fire. He . . . he tried to hurt me. But I managed to escape. I threatened to ink his flesh with B'goro's knife."

"I see." The goddess-speaker took the orb from N'gai and held it up to the light. "Go on," she said, studying it carefully.

"I made it to the sea village. The goddess-speaker there offered me *kratoma* plant leaves for the pain in my head."

The goddess-speaker shook her head. "It was stupid of her to offer it to you. It is like firewater, but more difficult to shake off."

"But I managed to. And now I am here."

The goddess-speaker took N'gai's hands. "You have been through so much, N'gai. And when so many have harmed you, your trust in me has remained intact. If I told you that there might be a way to help you, what would you think?"

N'gai thought for a moment. "I would be glad. It would mean that I was right to return home. But is there a way back? Can you return my sight?"

The goddess-speaker took a deep breath. "No. I cannot return to you your eyes as they once were. But I think I can turn the unnatural eyes you have now into something else. Something better. And the pain should go. But the process will hurt . . . and I cannot guarantee that it will work."

N'gai let go of the goddess-speaker's hands. "Well then, I must think about what you have said."

※

A few days later, and after speaking with her mother and father, N'gai made a decision.

"I do trust you," she told the goddess-speaker, "and I want you to try to help me. But I will only undergo what you suggest after my daughter is born."

"Very well," said the goddess-speaker. "That is a good decision. When you are ready, let me know."

So in the days that followed, the goddess-speaker busied herself with the preparations for N'gai's transformation, and N'gai focused all her energy and determination on birthing her daughter.

※

Weeks passed and as N'gai's baby thrived, so did N'gai. Her spirit had returned in full force with the birth of her daughter, whom she had named N'solla, and with it, the determination to be rid of her stone eyes and the pain and darkness they brought her.

"Do it!" she ordered the goddess-speaker one day. "Before I change my mind." N'gai passed her sleeping daughter, who had just now suckled asleep, to N'solla's grandmother.

"She will be fine with me," said N'gai's mother, putting her arm around her daughter's shoulder.

N'gai sighed and then allowed herself to be led to the goddess-speaker's hut. It was perhaps better that she was not able to see the stone bed at the back of the hut that the goddess-speaker took her to; for with its leather straps on metal hooks, it was not a welcome sight.

The goddess-speaker asked N'gai to lie down on it, which she did. "I must strap your arms down, N'gai, so that you do not try to touch your eyes. And I must also strap down your head." N'gai's heart began to beat fast, but she acquiesced. She felt the straps going over her wrists, a strap tightening over her forehead. "For it is imperative that your head remains perfectly still." N'gai's stomach tightened.

"Now then," began the goddess-speaker. "You must keep your eyelids open so that I can make a fire on your eyes. I will do my best to protect your skin with the ointments I have prepared."

N'gai felt cool, oily cream being placed on her face and the skin around her eyes.

"But you will still feel the heat clawing at you. A great heat. But you must endure it for as long as you can. The longer the better."

N'gai heard the crackle of fire and then the goddess-speaker coming close. She made sure to keep her eyelids wide open. Still, when the first ember touched her solid eyes the heat, dulled though it was, frightened her. She cried out.

"Forgive me," said the goddess-speaker. "There is no other way to perform this transformation."

The goddess-speaker piled on more and more embers. N'gai clenched her fists and bit her tongue and tried to ignore the ghastly smell of smoke.

The goddess-speaker began to chant while stoking the flames. N'gai's whole body tensed, the heat at the skin around her eyes intensifying.

N'gai suddenly felt her head become warm, and the reek of burning hair was at her nose. She screamed and tried to touch her head, but of course her hands were restrained.

The heat at N'gai's head suddenly subsided; the goddess-speaker had poured water on the flames. "Forgive me again! I should have dowsed you earlier. This fire is desperate to escape."

N'gai struggled. "What else is to catch fire? How much longer? The heat is unbearable!"

"Longer!" said the goddess-speaker. "It needs to be as hot as the goddess herself!"

N'gai struggled and writhed as the goddess-speaker continued to pile on fuel and to chant and to add precious minerals to the fire burning on N'gai's sandstone eyes, which were now two glowing orbs.

N'gai cried out again. "I can stand it no longer!"

"Almost there! Just a little longer. Keep perfectly still."

N'gai kicked out and then heard herself scream. She was all pain, nothing but pain, and there was nothing beyond the pain but more pain.

And then there was the whoosh of water and the shock of not-pain.

She heard the labored breathing of the goddess-speaker and then the loosening of her restraints, the scraping of a stool.

Light began to flood into N'gai's eyes. But the images were white and otherworldly, tinged with blue and green, the objects strangely magnified and distorted.

N'gai raised herself and then looked across the smoke-filled hut. The goddess-speaker, exhausted, was on the stool, her body bent double.

N'gai left the bed and helped the goddess-speaker off the stool. "We must get out of here. The air is filthy."

The goddess-speaker allowed N'gai to lead her out of the hut and back to N'gai's home.

"I don't know what you did to me," began N'gai, her voice trembling, "but . . . I can see. Everything looks strange . . . but I can see! What is it that you did to me?"

The goddess-speaker smiled wearily. "It was your orb that gave me the idea. You should look at your reflection one day. For your eyes are beautiful. Like . . . glass."

When N'gai reached her home, her family was astonished by her transformation.

"N'gai . . ." began her younger sister, N'giri. "You have the eyes of the goddess herself! You really do!"

They crowded around N'gai in wonder. They laughed and questioned N'gai and thanked the goddess-speaker over and over.

N'gai's mother, tears streaming down her face, passed N'gai's daughter back to her. "Can you really see? Then what do you think of your daughter?" she asked. "And the pain, is it gone?"

N'gai looked down at her daughter's face and began to cry soft, salty tears. "Yes, Mother," she said, "I can see my daughter." She smiled. "She is beautiful. And, yes, the pain has gone. And all that there is, is light."

※

Later, when the sun had set and the three moons, the children of the mother-goddess, shone bright in the night sky, rain fell. While the rest of her family slept, N'gai fed her baby, stroking her fuzzy black hair as she suckled away. She looked out at the three moons. How she had missed seeing them! As her new glass eyes focused on the moons, she saw what no one else had ever seen before. The faces of three women: N'luna, N'lina, and N'lon. And they were smiling at her.

Marija Smits is the pen name of Dr Teika Bellamy, a UK-based mother-of-two, ex-scientist and editor whose writing and art has appeared in various publications, including *Mslexia, Brittle Star, Strix, Literary Mama, JUNO, LabLit, The Poetry Shed, Picaroon Poetry* and *LossLit.* When she's not busy with her children, or writing or drawing, she's running the indie press, Mother's Milk Books. She is continually delighted by the fact that Teika means 'fairy tale' in Latvian.

www.marijasmits.wordpress.com

Made in the USA
Columbia, SC
17 August 2018